GRADUAL DESCENT

Viktor
A way to escape
from your bees, seduko
and your other responsibilities
Love Pat 6/6/12

PATRICIA MORRISSEY

outskirtspress

DENVER, COLORADO

Outskirts Press, Inc.
http://www.outskirtspress.com

ISBN: 978-1-4327-9344-9

Outskirts Press and the "OP" logo are trademarks belonging to Outskirts Press, Inc.

PRINTED IN THE UNITED STATES OF AMERICA

Dedication

To Drew, my nephew, who inspired me to keep writing
and who suggested how to bring the action alive.

Also published by Patricia Morrissey
at Smashwords.com and available as an e-book from
Amazon.com and other distribitors of digital books.

Digital book ISBN number: 978-1-4581-4309-9

Prologue

Our lives are shaped by anticipated and unanticipated events.

When Margaret Sampson was born, her mother died.

Margaret's father was a pastor—a very handsome pastor named Thomas, who was tall, naturally muscular, with fine features. The ladies of the congregation went out of their way to help him raise his beautiful little girl—fixing her hair, making her pretty cotton dresses, taking her to buy shoes, watching her when he had to write his sermons. Yet he resisted them all. His love for his first wife was so deep that it was almost sacred.

Those ladies implanted in Margaret the functional nature of relationships. None gave her love. Margaret also learned from these ladies, especially one named Eloise, how to manipulate her father and other people.

Margaret had a brother, David, five years older than she. Like his father, David was very handsome. Like his father, he was a good soul. Unlike his father, he had a driving curiosity about how things worked. He was very serious. At seven, having decided he wanted to be a doctor, he practiced on his little sister. He cut off the ends of her pinky fingers with every intention of sewing them back on. Things didn't work out. He did have the good sense to tape the end of each finger when his stitching didn't work. Margaret didn't object throughout the whole ordeal because, before he began, he had given her part of a pint of apricot brandy very slowly.

It was early July, a Saturday, his father was at the church, and Ms. Eloise Robinson, their neighbor, had volunteered to keep an eye on David and Margaret through her kitchen window. She didn't see much because everything that happened occurred in an old army surplus tent—David's "field hospital." She saw David and Margaret go in, and David go in and out getting rags and tape, but that was about it.

Somehow David had gotten his little sister into the house and into her bed undetected by Eloise. And even though it was very hot, he covered her with a blanket, hiding the taping job he had done on her hands.

The effect of David's "surgery" was not discovered until later in the evening. Thomas came home around 5:00 P.M. Eloise had made a fish casserole and apple turnovers for the family. She was an old maid who had taken care of her father, who had died about the time Margaret was born. Because of her kindness Reverend Sampson asked Eloise to stay and eat with him and the children. Of course she said yes. She was very patient. She hoped some day to be the next Mrs. Sampson.

Margaret was sleeping when her daddy came home. David was reading a book on the sitting room floor. Thomas made some sweet tea. Thomas decided to let Margaret continue sleeping, so he, David, and Eloise ate at the big pine kitchen table. About midway through second helpings, they heard Margaret screaming. The toddler ran into the kitchen screaming, crying, and waving her arms.

Eloise, practical as well as patient, scooped up Margaret and took her to the sink. Her bandaged fists were partially crimson. Thomas was in shock. David, even at seven, sensed the consequences of his "doctoring" were going to be severe.

Eloise carefully unwrapped the bandages. She sat Margaret on the side of the sink and put her feet in the sink. Margaret was screaming and squirming so Eloise had to pin her with her left arm as she looked at Margaret's hands. She wet a sink rag with tepid water and gently stroked Margaret's fingers, attempting to discern where the damage was.

"Thomas, excuse me, Reverend, but I think this situation allows for some informality, call Dr. Jackson and ask him to come over. It looks like Maggie's little fingers, just the tips, have been chopped clean off."

Thomas did as he was told. He began to process what must have happened. *Did David chop off Maggie's fingers? Why?*

David sat very still at the table. His big brown eyes turning from Eloise and Maggie, to his daddy, then back again. He had the urge to urinate, but he knew it was best to sit very still. Maggie kept screaming as if from the depth of her soul.

Dr. Jackson, a short, fat, bald, no-nonsense man, came quickly. He cleaned and rebandaged Margaret's fingers and gave her warm milk to help her go to sleep before the topical painkilling salve wore off. He had asked David as he was cleansing the fingers, "Where are the tips of your sister's fingers?"

And David, now almost catatonic, said, "The dog ate them."

Eloise took her dishes and went home.

When Jackson left, Thomas took David by the hand and led him to the front porch. He sat him in one of the two big weather-beaten rockers. He knelt in front of him. He noted the boy's pants were soaked.

"David, tell me what happened."

David looked at his lap. He tried to cover it with his shirt.

His shoulders slumped forward. He always did what he was told. He never lied. He looked at his father.

"Daddy, I wanted to play doctor. I cut off Maggie's fingers because I thought I could sew them back on. Mama taught me how to sew when I was just a kid. Remember when Ralphie bit the arm off my teddy bear? Mama and I sewed it back on together. She told me I was going to be a fine surgeon. I miss her so much, Daddy."

Thomas had tears in his eyes now. "David, I miss your mama too. Didn't Maggie scream and holler when you cut her first finger?"

"No, Daddy. I gave her whiskey just like they do on *Gunsmoke*. That way she would have no pain, right?"

Thomas was overwhelmed with sadness and love for his motherless son. He picked him up and carried him to the bathroom. He took the boys clothes off and drew a bath for David. He washed him gently. He dried him softly and held him close.

"David, God has a plan for each of us. Sometimes he lets us see pieces of the plan. Part of my plan and part of your plan is to take care of Maggie because she doesn't have a mama. So just like you cared about your teddy bear, you must care about your little sister. You must always protect her, help her, and not harm her in any way ever. Do you understand?"

With tears streaming down his little brown body, wrapped in a dingy white towel and his father's arms, he said, "Yes, Daddy." David always would take care of Maggie, although he thought he would never ever be a doctor who cut people. Thomas put David to bed and checked on Maggie. She was asleep with her hands resting on a small pink pillow Eloise had given her.

Because of this finger-chopping episode, many unanticipated circumstances would play out.

The sun had set. It was very humid. Thomas went on to the porch with a shot of whiskey. He sat in a rocker and put the glass on the table next to him. He stared at the peeling white tabletop. He put his head in his hands and sobbed. "God, whatever your plan is, give me a clue, would you?"

Just then Eloise, plain and tall, in her tan skirt and sparkly, white-lace blouse came across the grass with two mugs of coffee. Six months later they were married.

Chapter 1

Margaret Sampson Sabat cleaned up the kitchen. She could not face it in the morning. Just as she turned out the kitchen light and noticed the dishwasher sounded like it was a diesel truck engine, she heard Eloise say, "Agh, agh," and then a series of thumps. Margaret ran to the foyer.

Eloise, eighty-three and 100 pounds at the most, in a lacy, white, long cotton nightgown was lying motionless in a crumpled heap at the bottom of the stairs. Margaret knelt and felt for a pulse in Eloise's neck. There was none. She turned Eloise flat on her back, and looked and listened for breathing. None.

She sat back on the floor, and extending her legs, leaned against the wall and closed her eyes. *Now what?*

Margaret thought of how the afternoon had begun.

At noon, on this clear summer day, with low humidity, as the plane was descending, out of her window Margaret had a clear view of the Washington Monument. She could care less. She had things on her mind—specifically how to maintain her lifestyle now that her partner in fraud, Fred Firebrand, was retiring. For three years she and Fred, who was employed by the New York Public Auditing Department, had been skimming about $3,000 to $10,000 a month from federal grants awarded to New York for a human service program called Get Ahead.

Margaret and Fred had decided finding her a new partner was too risky. They had met in Albany. They would shut down their skimming operation. She was coming home with no plan. She did not want a new partner. She wanted to go solo on something new. It was less complicated. She would think of an alternative money-generating scheme. She looked down her long, golden-brown legs to her $350 ballerina flats and wiggled her toes. An idea would come to her. Anything could be an opportunity. She would just have to be open and ready for it.

Margaret was a senior auditor for the federal Public Service Agency in Washington, D.C. Known as PSA, it was where grants and contracts for several agencies were processed before they were awarded and from where they were audited. Although there were checks and balances both in state agencies and in PSA, all it took to create your personal financial trickle was two crooks and lazy employees in the chain of paperwork between a state and Washington, D.C. Since any one account could take eighteen to thirty-six months to reconcile at the end of year, as long as you were in the right place, had a partner at the other end, were not greedy, and shifted your dipping pattern frequently, you could do well.

Margaret left the terminal, walked to her Volvo, and threw her bags in the trunk. She drove across the Fourteenth Street Bridge toward Southeast. She was going to see Eloise, her widowed stepmother.

The traffic was bad, which was weird for that time of day. She thought of her fourth birthday. By her fourth birthday, she had a pink gingham bedroom, a brother packed off to live with an uncle in D.C., and her daddy to share with her stepmother, the only mother she knew.

It was a big birthday party at the church with balloons, chocolate cake, and mint chocolate ice cream, games, a banjo player, and tons of presents—all for Margaret. Yet of all the presents and excitement, the little white gloves with ruffles at the wrist that Eloise gave her were what Margaret loved the most because the gloves hid her deformed pinky fingers.

In spite of Eloise's thoughtfulness Margaret did not like sharing Eloise with her daddy. Margaret insisted her daddy put her to bed at night. And at least once a week she would have a recurring nightmare in which David chopped off her hands. These episodes would send her racing for Daddy's arms and bed. Eloise never objected, knowing this repetitive sequence would eventually end. Eloise was right. It did end around Margaret's fifth birthday. By then Margaret thought she was too big to cry and too big to sleep with her daddy.

Eloise had introduced Margaret to nail polish. Every Saturday night Eloise would paint Margaret's nails and talk to her about being a woman, being strong, being independent, and getting what you want. By the time Margaret was ten, she could do her own nails, but every Saturday night, she and Eloise still sat at the kitchen table and talked, and painted their nails. That gave her daddy time to finish his main Sunday sermon. In spite of this ritual, Eloise and Margaret never became close in an emotional sense. There was a practicality to their relationship. Margaret learned the skills associated with manipulation. Eloise increased her control of Margaret, especially Margaret's relationship with her father, which became more formal. As Margaret entered her teenage years, she became aware of what Eloise had brought about. But it didn't matter by then because all Margaret wanted to do was to escape from the small, smothering North Carolina town, and she knew Eloise would pave the way. Eloise wanted the

Reverend all to herself. Then she could unleash her passion and his, or so she thought.

What neither Eloise nor Margaret knew was the Reverend Sampson understood all this. Beginning with the death of his precious wife, through the finger-chopping event, marrying Eloise, and at her urging, sending his precious son to D.C. to live with his brother, the Reverend's heart and soul had slowly died. His life was not what he had dreamed or wanted. He was God's shepherd, but his actions, words, and thoughts were mechanical, were what people expected or needed, not what he felt. He could not change his life, but he would accept it.

Since her father's death, about once a week Margaret would come to visit Eloise, bring her groceries, empty her trash, and pay her bills. She didn't think of this ritual as an obligation or act of kindness, just as watching over an investment. The row house on the corner of Twelfth Street was worth a lot. Someday Eloise would die.

Margaret pulled into Eloise's driveway, which ended in the backyard. She pulled next to the Honda, Eloise's car. It was in tip-top shape. There was a high hedge for privacy that encircled the property, but no garage.

When Margaret entered the kitchen through the back door, she saw the three garbage cans full of empty soup cans, frozen dinner cartons, and Diet Pepsi cans. Crumbs of all kinds covered the dingy yellow tile floor. *I haven't been here in over a week. God help me. It stinks in here. It's also time for Orkin again.*

Margaret went into the living room. Eloise, head tilted toward her chest, was asleep in the lounge chair. She was wearing a yellow jogging suit and matching slippers. CNN was on the TV.

Margaret went upstairs with her bags. She changed into shorts, top, and flip-flops. It was hot in the house. Eloise never used the air conditioners. She was always cold. Margaret went back downstairs and into the kitchen. *Cleaning up this crap is going to ruin my nails!*

In about three hours and after a trip to Harris Teeter at Pentagon City for food, she had everything under control and was frying chicken when Eloise came into the kitchen using her walker.

"Maggie, when did you get here, child? I didn't know you were coming today!" She was smiling. Margaret was almost her only contact with the outside world.

"Ms. Eloise, I just got in from New York. I thought you could use some company and food. How do fried chicken, greens, and hash browns sound?" *It's funny. No one in my immediate family knows I can cook!*

"Heavenly. How about some wine? I have some you know."

"I know. I saw it when I was putting groceries in your pantry. Neither my office nor my girls expect me back until tomorrow night. We can kill as much wine as we want! Who keeps you stocked in wine, anyway? Whoever it is does a great job."

"Don, the new postman. He is a very nice man. A very handsome man."

The air freshener was working in the kitchen, but they ate in the dining room with fine linen, crystal, china, and candles. The room's wallpaper was royal blue with tiny white flowers, faded where the sun had bleached it, and beginning to separate from the wall around the white crown molding. The dining room furniture was solid, medium-colored oak and too big for the long room. Margaret thought it had a smothering effect. Margaret helped Eloise sit in the chair with arms.

After Margaret sat down and had fixed her own plate, Eloise said, "Maggie, please play some of your fine music."

Without saying a word Margaret took a big sip of wine and pushed back from the table and went upstairs and retrieved her IPod and portable speakers. *Eloise looks frail, but clean, thank God.*

When she returned she said, "What do you want to hear?"

"Nat King Cole."

"Done."

As she sat down, before she could get a bite of now-cold chicken to her mouth, Eloise said, "So tell me about the girls. It has so long since we had a good chat!"

"Well, the twins, Shane and Shawna, are going to enter their second year of law school. They have their own apartment now, so I never see or hear from them unless they need money! Baby Bonnie is about to start her senior year in high school. As you know we share the big house in Bethesda, so I see her all the time. Living with a teenager is a challenge. A lot goes on they do not share with adults. She's a good kid, though. She hates to be in the big house by herself."

"Show me your nails, girl. Are you taking care of them?"

Change of subject. Enough on the girls, I guess. Now to Jeremy.

"Of course, just like you taught me." Margaret placed her hands on the table. Eloise smiled. Margaret's nails were perfect down to the customized acrylic nails on her little fingers.

"Now Maggie, what about that husband of yours, Dr. Jeremy Sabat? Is he helping you out?"

I wish. "Ms. Eloise, Jeremy has his own problems. Both his parents have Alzheimer's and are in a private nursing home. His new wife can't work because of their baby twins."

"He had enough children! He didn't need any more. He should help take care of your girls. He should be in private practice and not in some stupid government job focused on disaster relief in foreign countries! Your papa would roll over in his grave if he knew Jeremy skipped out on you!"

"Jeremy never cared about money. He thought his parents had enough to take care of him forever." Margaret opened the second bottle. She excused herself and went to the kitchen, returning with two pieces of lemon pie.

"Ms. Eloise, do you want coffee?"

"No child. I prefer to keep sipping my wine."

Now to money. "Maggie, how do you make ends meet? I am no fool. Law school is expensive. Paying for an apartment is expensive. Bonnie's school is expensive."

"I manage." *Old woman, we have this conversation over and over. I am so tired of it!*

"Ms. Eloise, I never asked you this before, but did Daddy ever talk to you about my mama? You know, what she was like?"

"I was waiting for you to ask about your mama. I am surprised it took this long. Your mother, Ester Windsong Sampson, was with your father and me, even in bed, for thirty-five years!"

Margaret's jaw dropped. She sat her wine down and stared at Eloise. For the first time she grasped the bitterness, sadness, and loneliness Eloise felt. Empathy was not one of Margaret's strengths.

"Your father married me because you needed a mother. I knew that, but desperate fool that I was, I thought I could change him. It did not happen. He shut me out with his kindness and his excuses. He was the one that decided you would call me Ms. Eloise and not Mama!

"I tried everything to make him happy, bring him a measure of joy. All he would do is thank me and look at me with his sad eyes. I thought when we moved here to D.C. to be closer to you, your family, and your brother, your daddy would be happy.

"But then your brother went and told your daddy he hated him for sending him away when he chopped off your fingertips. Of course, it was I who told your father to send him away, but your dad could not say that. Over and over I told your daddy to tell David it was my fault. For whatever reason he would not do that. Every time I would suggest it, your daddy pulled further away. So I stopped trying, and we stopped talking. To make his point about how angry he was, David changed his name to Windson. I guess to honor your dead mother. Shortly after that your daddy had the stroke and then died. But child, you know all this!"

"Ma'am, do you have a picture of my mama?"

"Only one."

"I would like to see it, but first let's go into the kitchen, and I'll paint your nails. I brought you a pretty color." She pulled a bottle of red out of her pocket to show Eloise. Eloise smiled.

Margaret took the two wineglasses and the remaining wine to the kitchen table. Eloise followed her with her walker on unsteady feet. At night the kitchen floor had a lot of traffic—roaches looking for all those crumbs Margaret had swept away.

Margaret carefully bathed Eloise's hands, applied lotion, and massaged them.

"Did my daddy ever talk about my mama?"

"No, but, as I said, I always felt she was with us."

"After my daddy died, did you find any papers about my mama?"

"No, not one."

"When did you find the picture?"

"One day when I was dusting our bedroom, I knocked your daddy's Bible on to the floor from his nightstand. The picture fell out. She was beautiful. She looked like she was Indian. Not surprising, with a name like Ester Windsong."

They sat finishing the last of the wine. Margaret had put on some jazz and turned off the overhead lights. She left the recessed lights on, casting shadows around the room and highlighting the greasy fingerprints on the lower part of the cabinets.

I got to come over here on a weekend and do some serious cleaning.

"You know, Ms. Eloise, when I was old enough to figure things out, I blamed you for losing my fingertips, not David. I thought you were a cheap and lousy babysitter."

"I know. I was."

"I think we need to go to bed. Can you make it up the stairs? I want to clean up the kitchen before coming up."

"Sure. I have railings on both sides and a walker at the top of the stairs. I'll get the picture for you. You can have it. Your mama caused me too much pain."

Chapter 2

Margaret opened her eyes and looked at Eloise. Briefly she felt something—a sense of guilt or a sense of loss. She didn't want Eloise to go yet, not now, not like this. She had to know something more about her mother. There had to be more. *The picture! Where is it?*

Margaret checked Eloise's hands. She looked up the stairs. She raced up the stairs. It was at the top face down. Margaret sat on the top step and picked up the photo. She turned it over. A beautiful young woman with long black hair and big brown eyes smiled back at Margaret. She sat on the grass, leaning against a tree in a flowing white dress, her hands folded in her lap. *Mama, I have always wanted to know you. I could never ask Daddy. I waited too long to ask Eloise. Now I will never know! Never know!* She set the picture down and sobbed. Then she stopped, seeing writing on the back of the picture.

In clear black cursive it read:

Dearest Thomas,

I love you more than words. I will be with you always, not just when we are together but also when we are physically separated. Your soul is my soul. Your heart is my heart.

Love,

Ester

There was no date. In the dim hall light Margaret scanned the back of the photo for a developer's date stamp. If there was one there, it had faded out over time. Margaret pressed the picture to her lips. Then she looked at it again. Margaret looked just like her mama.

Margaret looked down at Eloise. She said out loud, "Eloise, I cannot bury you right now. I need time to think." *I should have tried mouth-to-mouth. Too late now.*

Margaret went down to the basement. She found Eloise's Christmas decorations and her Christmas tree disposal bags. They were long and strong. There were two. She took them upstairs and stuffed Eloise into the first one head first, and then put the second bag over the first. She tied the bags shut, and dragged Eloise down the basement steps and then into the furnace room. The sound of Eloise's head hitting the steps and the cracking sounds were unnerving. She emptied a spray can of air freshener in the furnace room. Margaret locked the metal door to the furnace room and put the key in her pocket. Upstairs she put the air conditioner on sixty-five degrees Fahrenheit and left the basement door open.

She went upstairs and retrieved a legal pad from her computer bag. She plopped on the bed and started a to-do list—get freezer, talk to postman, withdraw cash from checking account, close out post office box for the Albany checks, and schedule the Orkin man.

Chapter 3

Pamela Isadora Planter, known to most as Pip, locked her car and pushed her cart toward the elevator bank. She used the two-bag grocery cart for balance and to carry things. She needed at least eight and one-half pounds in it at all times or it would tip over when she leaned on it to walk. She also hung a cane on the side of the cart with which to steer with her good left hand. The cane was also good for tight spaces.

Sixty, she had short, white, wavy hair, needed to lose ten pounds, always wore black, and stood five-feet-three.

She had brought fresh bagels to soften the blow of making everyone work the Friday before Labor Day. She got off on the top floor and pushed against the glass doors to Forensic Specialists, LLP, a firm she had started six years ago. Sheila, with luscious brown ringlets and a dress about twelve inches long from neck to thigh, the new receptionist from the temp service, came to help her get through the door. Rich was reading the paper. He was six-five, 240 pounds and had strawberry blond hair in a military cut, with a face women loved. He had a flat backside, making everyone wonder how he kept his pants up, even with a belt. Pip looked at him, his legs extending over the sides of an armless chair on wheels next to Sheila's desk.

"One of these days Rich, you are going to (a) fall on your tail and (b) break that chair, or (c) lose weight so I do need not worry about workers' comp."

"Pip, so nice of you to join us on this balmy day before a three-day holiday. If you ever got here before noon, we could actually break a profit. And in the spirit of full disclosure—I didn't want to play golf today. Your cold Starbucks café latte with mocha is on your desk. Everyone is pissed. They think you are a heartless bitch who needs a man, a hobby, or both."

"Rich, what would I do without you! You are so kind, generous to fault, and have such a strong work ethic. Please gather everyone in the big conference room. We have a new case that's packed full of nefarious deeds that we must sort out."

Sheila stood dumbfounded, with the dozen bagels Pip had tossed to her clutched to her chest. *If she's the boss, that guy is crazy, and his days of employment are numbered. Who are these people and what do they do?*

All of them gathered in the conference room, looking rather grim: Pip with a PhD in psychology, a MBA, and cerebral palsy but no speech impediment; Rich, the principal investigator, on medication for a diagnosed bipolar disorder, which he took irregularly; Suzy, Pip's assistant, a knockout brunette working on her master's in organizational development while looking for a husband; fiery Electra, the office manager, with a husband and a blind lover, a phenomenal sense of smell and no sight; Beamer, the handsome street specialist, with no degrees, pursuing a music career and his GED; blond Kit, the forensic accountant, deaf and well-endowed around the lungs, and one heck of a lip-reader; Frank, wearing clothes that looked like they had been left in the dryer too long, with Asperger's syndrome and an uncanny, relentless ability to detect patterns in anything; and Johnny, a sharp dresser, with a killer smile, and Down syndrome, who kept everyone honest.

Sheila stood in the doorway so she could listen for the phone. For the second time today she was dumbfounded. *This must be a government jobs program for the handicapped. I hope the agency gives me something else soon.*

"Good afternoon. I greatly appreciate you all coming in." Pip turned toward Sheila, "Please get my coffee. Then shut the door to the conference room and return to your desk. And, thanks."

"Suzy, you go to the storyboard and write as I summarize." Suzy leaped up and stood almost at attention at the storyboard.

Pip reached into her cart and pulled out two big manila envelopes. She opened them and strewed the content on the table—IDs, business cards, parking permits, passwords. "Find yours and hold them close."

"Here's what we have—I met with Brad Swanson, the administrator of PSA at eight A.M. this morning." She threw a look at Rich.

"The administrator believes there is fraud in PSA that is systemic, going on for two to three years. Before he goes to the PSA inspector general or the FBI, he needs to know where it is and how big it is. They seldom take legal action on any fraud less than one million dollars. We have been hired to find it. Ladies and gentlemen, this means no more charity work for us."

Suzy was writing trying to keep up with Pip. She realized the last comment was editorial and erased it.

"If we pull this one off, we will be set and get on every PSA forensic schedule there is. No more competitive bids, just task orders, where the government calls us, tells us what it wants, and we set the price and set to work. Simple and sweet.

"Questions?"

Johnny said, "What's a forensic schedule? Sounds like something to do with trains."

"Good point, Johnny. The government keeps schedules or lists of companies that do good work. If a company gets on a federal schedule, it is easier to get business from the government, and there is less paperwork."

"That's good. I hate paperwork."

Electra asked, "Do you have a plan? And as an aside, who was the shit that put the salt packets where I keep the sugar packets? Do you have any idea what it is like to take a big sip of salty coffee?"

Pip smiled, "First, the obvious. We need to go undercover and get to know people. Once we know who does what, we can zero in on possible bad guys."

Rich said, "Just what I like—the shoot from the hip scenario. Where do we start?"

"In the Northeast Audit Division of PSA."

"Why there?" Rich asked.

"Well, there was twenty-seven percent less federal auditing in New York in the last three years."

"Oh boy, it's payback time for the last administration!"

Johnny said, "What do you mean, Rich?"

"Well, Johnny, if you were a bureaucrat and your boss says, 'Where are you going to visit next month to see if a state is spending federal dollars in the right way?' Would you pick New York if it were the president's home state?"

"No way. You might find something bad, and the president would be mad."

"Exactly. So now that we have a new president who's not from New York, and it's okay to check out what is going on in New York."

Johnny sat up. "The new president's a Democrat. The other guy was a Republican. Republicans and Democrats don't get along."

Pip smiled. "Kit and Frank will start looking at financial files for northeastern states. If they detect irregularities, we will zero in on the people associated with those records. Suzy, Rich, Beamer, and Johnny will work undercover at PSA."

Beamer said, "What are our covers?"

Pip replied, "You and Johnny are part of the cleaning staff. Your job will be to watch, listen, and check the trash cans of targets."

"And Suzy and me?" Rich asked.

"You and Suzy are graduate interns in organizational development with the division director, Margaret Sabat. Any more questions?"

"I do not know a fuck about organizational development."

"Relax. Neither does Sabat. Suzy will cover you. You owe us five dollars."

Frank said, "Rich said, *fuck* eighteen times in August. If he says *fuck* eighteen times in September, we will have one hundred and eighty dollars for a party. That's plenty."

Rich handed Pip a five-dollar bill. She handed it to Electra.

Electra said, "I have a question, children. Somebody has messed up my supplies. Johnny must help me straighten things out, then help me with invoices."

Johnny said, "Sheila did it, Electra. She was trying to be helpful because this is her first day. I offered to help her, but you know, she thought I was retarded."

"What does she know? Before the day is out, I will see to it she knows you can read, write, and file."

"That's not all. I am taking driving lessons, and I am twenty-one, so I can drink."

"Of course." Electra rolled her beautiful, blue glass eyes.

Chapter 4

Suzy and Rich were in her office. He wanted a crash course in organizational development.

"What is it, Suz? It seems like a lot of mumbo jumbo to me."

Got to keep this simple, short, and entertaining or Rich will lose interest. Being bipolar is not his only issue!

"Well, Rich, think about it like your closet. Let's say you have reached the point you cannot find anything to wear. You do not know what is clean and what is dirty. You cannot find things that go together. You cannot find your baseball glove for the big game."

"How'd you know about my closet?"

"I guessed."

"You should see my refrigerator."

"Let's stick to your closet. Organizational development would help you sort things, organize things, and make rules and procedures so you can find something when you want it the next time."

"Okay. But what do we say or do to convince our 'new boss' she needs to 'clean her closet,' so to speak?"

Suzy smiled. *There's hope!*

Rich thought, *She thinks I am so dumb. Lady you are soooo wrong!*

Suzy said, "I have thought about that. We could offer to develop a training manual for her on something. That would give her a basis for letting us interview her and others. You are a great interviewer, Rich."

Not a bad idea. "Yeah! What are you going to do?"

"I would interview people too. I would also analyze what we learn and identify weaknesses."

"What are we going to 'organize'?"

"How about the process of checks and balances in the auditing of grants?"

"Sounds good to me. I love you Suzy!" He planted a kiss right on her lips. "With your brain and my interviewing skills, we will catch the bad guys in no time."

That went well—I think.

Meanwhile Kit had given Frank a ton of printouts. "Frank, look for irregular patterns in this stuff."

"Kit, what is this?"

"Financial records from local Get Ahead programs in New York and New Jersey for the last three years. See how they spend their money. Are there any big changes from one month to the next? I can give you tons of more printouts, but see what you can do with these first. Thanks." She left.

Frank liked working with Kit and numbers. He wasn't good at small talk. Neither was Kit. *What's Kit going to be doing?*

Johnny went in the kitchen to get a Gatorade. Sheila was sitting at the table crying. When she saw Johnny, she stopped.

"What wrong, Sheila?"

"I can't work with Electra. I do nothing right!"

"You just need to know how to stay on her good side. I had to learn that. You must always do what she says and the way she says to do it. That's all. She needs things in a certain way because she cannot see."

"Will you help me?"

"Sure. I'll help you. I am an expert."

Sheila got up and gave Johnny a hug. "Thanks, Johnny."

He smiled and blushed. *That felt good, but different from hugs from Mom.*

At the other end of the floor Beamer leaned against Pip's door.

"So what is on your mind, Beamer?"

"This is big, isn't it?"

"It could be. You should start using your real name."

"Can't change my name now. The band is Beamer and the First Light."

"Well when you go undercover you need a name."

"Beamer Johnson will work. No one gives a shit about a janitor's name."

"Are you offended about your undercover role?"

"I know my job. Keep an eye on your boy and make sure he does not screw up. What I haven't figured out is why are you complicating things by sending Suzy and Johnny undercover. They don't have a devious bone between them."

"You said it. This job is big. We are a small outfit. I figure we have thirty days, max. The more eyes we have in PSA, the more likely we can deliver on time. Rich has been taking his medication. So I don't think you will have any problems with 'my boy.' As for Johnny, he is very observant and will do what you tell him."

"Well the combo is less than ideal in my opinion."

"Noted. We need to work with what we have."

"Why not just stick to a records review? It's safer, less messy than an a potential undercover fiasco."

"We are using both. Are you in or out?"

"I guess I am in or I would be out. But Pip, we need more time to prepare."

"We have three days."

"Yeah."

"Okay. Go pick up the uniforms for you and Johnny."

"Yes, ma'am."

"Beamer, I trust you. I need you. You have good judgment. You can think on your feet."

"I hear you. Don't worry I'll work it, but I think you are fucking crazy."

"You owe me a five."

"I don't have a five. Anyway that's a deal you have with Rich."

Beamer turned and left, his shoulders hunched, shaking his head.

Chapter 5

"Ted, I don't want TWO dumb interns."

"Maggie, they're graduate students."

"DON'T MAGGIE ME. My name is Margaret! I don't care what they are, Ted. I don't want them. I don't need them. Find someplace else for them to spend thirty days."

"No can do Maggie. The administrator wants them in your division. There is nothing I can do about it. It is only for thirty days, so get over it. Now let's enjoy this lovely evening. What a sunset! And the steaks I just grilled turned out perfectly."

They sat at Margaret's picnic table and began to eat. Ted Morton, Margaret's current love interest and her boss, said, "My son wants to get into George Townsend University next fall. Isn't your uncle dean of the law school? Brad's GPA is only two-point-nine. He is one hell of an athlete, but both he and I recognize that's not enough."

"Why should I help you? You are such a jerk."

"Wait a minute, sister. Who got you your last grade increase? Moi. Who lets you do whatever you damn well please? Moi. So cut out the name-calling."

"You are going to make me take those interns aren't you?"

"Damn it, Maggie, I had no choice. I told you that. Don't be so paranoid. You act like they are undercover agents. Just give them a project and send them on their merry way. The administrator probably owes somebody a political favor."

"Watch your language sailor boy! I'm not paranoid! I have

a lot of responsibilities in September. It's the end of the fiscal year remember!"

"Dammit, assign them to somebody else in your division."

"I'm going to bed. You can take your foul mouth and go home." She threw a plastic wineglass across the grass and stomped into her house and slammed the screen door.

Ted thought to himself, *So much for a romantic evening. She is hot when she's angry! I can't believe the news about the interns set her off like that. There's got to be more to it.*

Margaret decided not to go to work the day after Labor Day. She went to Eloise's house to do some deep cleaning. Her youngest daughter, Bonnie, was staying with her sisters in D.C. Her private school did not start until next week. *No one cares what I'm doing or where I am. The twins think I'm nothing but an ATM machine, and Bonnie just talks to me about extending her curfew.*

Around noon she sat on Eloise's front steps drinking a glass of ice tea, waiting for the mailman. Eloise was now tucked away in a big horizontal freezer in her basement, which Margaret called "the boardroom." Periodically she would go down to the boardroom and chat with Eloise. She knew she would have to come up with a plan for getting Eloise out of the house and buried, and another plan for raising more money. She had drained Eloise's accounts to cover the fall tuition for her girls. So until she came up with a plan, she would be living on her federal salary. She estimated if she had to, she could make it until it was time to buy Christmas presents and pay spring tuition.

She saw the mailman walking up the sidewalk. He was handsome—Bermuda shorts and nice legs, broad shoulders, wraparound sunglasses, baseball cap, and around forty-five.

"Hey, how you doing? I'm Don Pelham. Is Ms. Eloise okay?"

Margaret extended her hand, "Hi, I am Ms. Eloise's stepdaughter. She is fine, just a little weak. She told me about you and how you buy her wine. That's very nice. Unfortunately the doctor says she can't drink wine anymore."

"That's a real shame. She enjoyed it, or so she told me. I saw that big freezer being delivered the other day. Where do you put it?"

Nosy little terd. "In the basement. There is room down there."

"Boy, it must have been a mother to get that sucker down the steps."

Margaret flinched.

"Why did Ms. Eloise get a freezer?"

This little exchange is going on way too long. "I thought it would be a good idea, with the fall and winter coming. I will be able to buy her more food. I travel a lot. It's hard to predict when I can get over here. Nice talking to you. Have to get inside now."

As Margaret entered the house the mailman thought, *Boy, that was abrupt. I guess I drop the mail through the slot! It cannot be safe for Ms. Eloise to go up and down those steps all the time to get food. I will offer to do it for her next time I see her. I didn't get her stepdaughter's name. I should have gotten it and her telephone number too. Oh well, maybe next time I see her. She is gorgeous!*

Margaret poured another ice tea and sat down at the kitchen table with her legal pad. She started a new list—buy lock for freezer, disposable phone, phone cards, and timers for house lights. *Don Pelham better mind his own business or he'll end up in the freezer with Eloise. There's enough room. He could keep Eloise warm! That would make her so happy!* Margaret laughed.

Chapter 6

The Dive was a bar in the basement of the office building housing Forensic Specialists, LLP. It was famous for its bar, imported from a 150-year-old-saloon in Nevada, its circular red-leather booths, its darkness, and its manually controlled, individual spotlights. Everyone in a booth had one, and if they chose to, they could spotlight themselves while they talked. Kit loved the bar because she could still lip-read in the dark. Rich had convinced everybody who was available to meet there after work to compare notes—Suzy, Johnny, Frank, Kit, and Sheila. Beamer had a gig. Rich did not invite Pip. Johnny had invited Sheila. Electra was a no-show.

Rich held court while they waited for the beer pitcher. "I do not ever want to work in the federal government. It is BORING. The boss who was supposed to welcome Suzy and me with open arms didn't show. Some old maid sat us in a room with a bunch of reports and told us to read. Around ten o'clock I went looking for Johnny and Beamer, thinking we could have an early lunch. When I found them, they were cleaning cans out!"

Frank said, "Toilets? How many did you do?"

Johnny said, "Trash cans, Frank, trash cans, not toilets. I don't do toilets."

Everybody laughed.

Frank continued, "We found something today didn't we, Kit? Tell them."

"Yes, we did indeed. There is a federal program called Get Ahead. Anyway the money goes to local schools. Some local schools in New York buy more school supplies than others. Not a lot, but enough to be detected as being strange. It doesn't matter whether the school is big or small. Every school buys between three thousand and ten thousand dollars' worth of school supplies about every four months. That's a lot of supplies! These schools appear to buy school supplies from three sources—one local, one in Albany called Soya Surplus Supplies or SSS, and one in D.C., Robinson Rebate Depot. So the question we have to ask ourselves is why would a school in New York City go to the trouble of buying supplies from SSS in Albany or Robinson in D.C.? Of course they wouldn't. And, SSS has only one address in Albany, nowhere else in New York. So if I were you guys, I'd concentrate on New York and find out more about SSS. We haven't finished looking at Robinson."

Rich raised his beer mug, "Let's toast to Frank and Kit, who may have just made our jobs a hell of a lot easier!" They beamed.

Rich then said, "Hank, bring that dude another drink, but this time a Diet Coke." He pointed at Johnny.

"Why? Is John your designated driver?" Hank laughed.

"Nope. Suzy is. She is a binge drinker, but if she doesn't start, she doesn't have to worry about stopping." Only Rich laughed.

"I can be a designated driver in January, when I get my license," Johnny said.

"One Diet Coke, coming up and looks like you guys could use another pitcher, right?"

Rich said, "Kit, you want to try some shots?"

"Only one round, Rich—no more. We have to work tomorrow."

Three rounds of shots later everybody piled into Suzy's car, a bright red Acura. She dropped Sheila, Kit, and Frank off at the Metro. Then she drove to McLean to drop Johnny off at his parents' house. Rich lived in Arlington but refused, because he was lazy, to ever take the Metro or walk any distance.

When they arrived in front of Rich's building, he said, "Suz, do you think Sabat will come to work tomorrow?"

"I sure hope so. That branch chief, Donna Dawson, sure wasn't helpful."

"Well if she doesn't, why don't we just go see her boss, Ted Morton?"

"Well, I don't know. If we have to work with her for thirty days, we don't want to piss her off. Whether she comes in tomorrow not, we need to find out who handles the Get Ahead accounts in New York. We should be able to do that. I'll pick you up tomorrow morning, since your truck is at work. God forbid you would have to ride the Metro!"

"Great plan, Suz. I was a good boy today, wasn't I?"

"Grow up, Rich. If you would, our lives would be less stressful. All you did today was walk the halls doing, as you call it, 'your recon.' That probably made people suspicious. Remember our objective is to get them to open up."

"I hear you. I know where Morton's office is now. I love you, Suz. Goodnight." He slammed the door and walked off.

Like a brother, right Rich?

Chapter 7

Margaret stomped past Ted's secretary and went right into his office. He looked up from his desk as she put out her hand as a stop sign motion.

"Don't say a word! I talked to Donna Dawson this morning. She told me those two interns want to talk to me about quality control procedures related to grants. They suggested New York as a test case. I won't have it Ted. Do you hear me?"

God, she is gorgeous when she is mad. "Shut the door, Maggie, and lower your voice. Let's try to have a conversation about this like adults, shall we? First, you are in charge. You can have those two interns do anything or nothing. You have control. Second, if you let them do something that appears to have some value, I will not have to deal with the administrator."

Ted got up from his desk and walked around to the other side of it where Margaret was standing and pushed up against her. He put his hand where he shouldn't. "Third, if you keep flipping out about this, I am going to begin to suspect you have something to hide. Do you know the line from Shakespeare, 'I do believe you protest too much' or something like that?" He rammed his finger where he shouldn't and went back around his desk and sat down.

Margaret just stood there in shock. *What a vulgar man.* She walked around to his side of the desk, pushed his chair back, and turned it and him toward her. She pulled up her skirt and straddled him. *When I finish with this guy he's going to have to say he spilled more than his coffee in his lap!*

All the while she was in action she spoke calmly, "Ted, I agree we should deal with this situation like adults. First, assuming you will be able to get out of this chair and walk around without anyone thinking you soiled yourself, you'll arrange with the administrator to have those interns work for you not me. Second, you will not let them see or do anything related to the state of New York. Third, if you ever, and I emphasize ever, want to touch me again, you will do as I say today."

She got up and looked down at his lap. *Too bad he wore khakis today.* She walked out of his office and left the door open. Ted's secretary walked in and said, "The administrator's office just called. He would like to see you in about thirty minutes." Ted nodded. After his secretary left he went into his private bathroom and changed his clothes. *Once a Boy Scout always a Boy Scout. Be prepared—that's my motto. Wow what a ride! But, that woman is dangerous.*

Margaret went back to her office feeling satisfied she had made her point in a way Ted could understand it. She was now sitting across from Rich and Suzy.

"I understand you two are in graduate school at George Townsend University studying organizational development, is that correct?"

"Yes, Ms. Sabat, that is correct," Suzy, said before Rich opened his mouth and put his foot in it.

"We can't use your services in this division so you're going to work for the assistant administrator for human service programs. This change should be arranged by the end of the day. Think of it like a promotion." Margaret smiled.

Rich was too busy thinking. It was fine with him if Suzy handled the small talk. *No doubt about it, Sabat was an alpha bitch. She must think we are going to find something. We don't need thirty days, just a week. Be cool, man.*

"You're right ma'am, that would be a great opportunity and a promotion for sure, maybe even a future job opportunity! In real estate it's location, location, location. In graduate school it is networking, networking, networking. But really, you and I both know this is where the action is. This is where we could truly learn something to help us with our careers. And who knows, if we could stay here even for just one week, maybe we could help you in some small way. Will you at least think about it? We don't want to intrude. We don't want to get in the way of the business of government. But it would be great to learn something about how things are done. Let's face it. PSA is the gateway and the gatekeeper of all federal money. I shouldn't tell you this, but I googled you. You have had a very interesting career and risen steadily. I would value the ability to spend time with someone like you. I think you have a lot to give. One week that's all I'm asking for. How about it?"

Suzy thought, *Where did that come from? I am impressed.*

"Rich—that's your name right?" Rich nodded yes and smiled. "This is a very busy time of year for us, as I guess you may know. It is a sensitive time too. Many competitive awards are made. So you see the dilemma about having outsiders here at this time."

"Yes, I do. But we are interested in the audit process, and what happens at the end of an award not the beginning. What does the reconciliation process look like? Did people spend money on what they said they did? How do you go about verifying that?"

"We have a very strong audit process. We have manuals that cover everything. Staff follow these manuals. We have checks and balances at many levels."

"Could we spend a week just looking at your manuals? What harm would that do?"

"Oh, all right. I guess that would be okay. But the rest of the time you will be on the sixth floor with the assistant administrator. You understand?"

"Of course. You are being very fair and reasonable. Suzy and I appreciate that and will remember your kindness."

Margaret ushered them out of her office, and picked up the phone and called her Uncle Ben, her dad's brother, dean at the George Townsend University Law School.

"Hi, Uncle Ben. This is Margaret. How are you doing?"

"Maggie? I can't believe it's you. I hear by way of the grapevine Shane and Shawna are doing very well in law school, and they are well liked."

"Ah, music to a poverty-stricken mother's ears. I have a big favor to ask of you. I know you are busy, so I'll keep this short. I have been assigned two interns, two graduate students from GTU, unexpectedly. And, if I were honest, they are unwanted. I am suspicious about how they got here. Could you have someone in your office check to see if they actually are on the student roster? Their names are Richard Prichard and Suzy Simon."

"Do you know what college they are from?"

"Not a clue. They are majoring in organizational development."

"That's a start. Can I get back to you by the end of the

week or do you need the information sooner?"

"That's okay. I can keep an eye on them till then. Thanks."

"You, Dave, and I should have dinner sometime. I'll let you pick the date."

"You bet. Bye."

Margaret looked up. Ted was standing in her doorway in a navy blue suit. He walked in and shut the door.

"I just finished a meeting with Administrator Swanson. He suspects there is fraud coming out of your division. Do you have anything to say about that?"

"No, I do not. The reason is simple. There is none. Are the two interns, who you've dumped on me, some kind of agents?"

"That I don't know. How do you know somebody under you is not ripping off the government?"

"It would be too difficult. It would require cooperation here and within a state, and a way around all the controls. It just couldn't happen."

"I tell you what I want. You let those interns or agents or whatever they are document in English all those 'controls' you supposedly have. I want a description of the whole fucking process, something an old navy guy can understand. I'm not kidding about this, Margaret. You need to be straight with me. Helpful. The consequences of you not being straight and helpful are unpleasant to contemplate and would affect both of us.

"And one more thing, next week is a conference on fraud in Medicaid and Medicare. You go. I have to meet a quota, and I am one short." Ted threw a flyer on Margaret's desk, turned on his heels and left.

Chapter 8

Rich stretched his long legs under Pip's conference table. "Pip, that lady is hiding something. I can sense it. She's been having us read manuals all week. That's a meaningless activity unless we can start to interview people. We need to find out if they do what's described in those manuals."

"Do you think you can get her to allow you to interview people?"

Suzy laughed. "I think Rich can convince her."

Pip interjected, "You realize whomever you interview will repeat whatever you say to Margaret Sabat."

Rich said, "Yeah, I know. I'm not worried about that. I think the bitch almost fears us now. She seems almost resigned."

"What gives you that impression?"

"I saw her boss, Ted Morton, go into her office and shut the door. After he left she called us back in. She said she wanted us to describe the controls in the auditing process for grants in layman's terms. Today, she didn't remind us it was our last day, which it should have been. I think that dude told her she was stuck with us. I think he told her what we were supposed to do."

Suzy nodded in agreement.

Rich continued, "One thing bothers me, Pip. I think Sabat and Morton are more than an employee and boss. There's energy between them. A tension. Almost primal. What if I'm right?"

"Rich, all you can do is watch. If what you think turns out to be true, then we probably have less time to get to the bottom of this. If there is fraud, the people involved are not stupid. They will put roadblocks in our way and encourage us to go down dead ends.

"If you can get Margaret to agree to let you interview people, why not start with her boss? That interview may result in some good leads. Also interview the managers under Margaret, at least the one who handles New York.

One last thing—any fraud we find may not be limited to New York. That might trigger a jurisdictional nightmare, take us out of it, and bring in the Feds."

As Suzy and Rich walked out of Pip's office, Beamer and Johnny walked in. Beamer put a six-pack of Corona on the conference table, with some chips and salsa.

"It looks like it is party time, boys. After we talk we can invite others in if there's anybody left here. What do you have for me?"

"According to Suzy, Rich behaved all week. He didn't punch out anyone. Johnny found some interesting pieces of paper in Sabat's trash can. That lady is into to-do lists. Lucky for us she uses a legal pad and not a computer." He spread lists on the conference table.

"Look at this one—disposable phone. Why would she need one of those? Here's another one—lock for freezer. You don't need one of those unless you don't want people to see what you have in your freezer. And finally look at this one—timer for lights – you don't need those unless you are not going to be home."

Pip appreciated the way Beamer thought. She put the lists

in a legal size folder and labeled it Puzzle Pieces.

"I appreciate your work this week. What you found, Johnny, is very important. We just do not know why, but we will figure it out. You need to stay on the job a little while longer. What you find next week, like additional lists, may help us understand the lists we have.

"I have a special request. Keep track of how many times Ted Morton visits Sabat's floor. I suspect when he will go there will be in the morning early, around lunchtime, and at the end of the day. Also, try to keep track of when she goes to his floor. I think it's the sixth. Try not to be conspicuous or obvious. Let Rich know what you find. He thinks Margaret Sabat may be Ted Morton's girlfriend. Now let's eat, drink, and be merry. But, just one beer apiece. We can't have Johnny getting into his mom's car smelling like a brewery."

"I'm too smart for that, Pip. I never spill a drop, and I chew a lot of gum."

Kit walked into Pip's office with Frank. "Pip, you got hear this. Tell her Frank."

"Soya Surplus Supplies is only a post office box in Albany, New York!"

"Well, well, this has turned out to be an interesting day. Come and have a beer and some chips. I think I have to go back to PSA and ask them to modify our contract so we can get some travel money to visit the great state of New York. Who would've thought I would have to do that?"

Sheila came to Pip's office, "Some guy from Franklin Funeral Home is on the phone. He says he's Electra's husband and wants to talk to her. I thought she was on vacation this week? She left here last Friday with some blind guy. What do

I tell him?"

Pip said, "Cheez. Just say you'll have her call him back. Say she's working late on a special project over the weekend, and she'll be home Sunday night. Then come back and have a beer."

Chapter 9

Suzy said, "Rich, I don't think it's a good idea that we inter-view Donna Dawson until after we clear it with Sabat. If we make her angry, we could be out of here before we want to be."

"Relax, Suzy. All ladies love lattes, and that's what we have here. I can handle Margaret. Trust me I know what I'm doing, and I'm the world's greatest interviewer, remember?"

"I don't know, Rich."

Donna Dawson came walking toward them. "Hey, Ms. Dawson, I got you a coffee. May we visit for a few minutes?"

"How sweet. Of course." She unlocked her office door, and they walked in. She had an elephant collection that took up one-third of her bookshelves in her twenty-foot-by-twenty-foot corner office.

"Pull up those chairs so we will be a little closer. This is a first. I have worked for the federal government for thirty years, seen a lot of interns, but none of them ever brought me coffee!"

"And Danish, too, Ms. Dawson!"

"Bless your heart! What can I do for you this morning?"

Suzy said, "As you may know, Ms. Sabat has asked us to draft a manual 'in English' on your grants auditing process. We've done a lot of reading. We would like to ask you some questions."

"I see. Well, I'll try to help. Where do you want to start?"

Rich said, "What do you do?"

"I handle ten human services programs. When a grant or contract has ended in region two, information comes to my branch. I have twenty staff. Everything related to a grant eventually comes to me. Some information is electronic, and some is hard copy. I have thirty days to review the staff report and information on which it is based, and if everything is in order, sign off on it electronically. It then goes to Margaret Sabat. She reviews my report, and if she agrees with it, clears it, and it goes to her boss, Ted Morton, who does about the same thing. If there are discrepancies or problems, the auditing process can take six months to a year or even longer. We use checklists to speed up the review process, but, as I said, if there are issues, the audit could take a long time, with a lot of back-and-forth between us and the grantee."

Rich said, "This is very helpful. Do you handle all states in region two?"

Dawson's phone rang, and she picked it up. "Donna Dawson here." She listened for a minute. "I'll pick it up this evening and thank you for putting on a sticker. I understand, these things happen." She hung up the phone. "Now where were we?"

"My question was do you handle all the states in region two?"

Margaret walked into Dawson's office. "Good morning. I thought you would be off somewhere reading all that material I gave you. Donna, we have to talk about that Caribbean initiative."

"Now? I thought we had about a month?"

"There's been a change. So if Rich and Suzy can get back to their project, you and I can talk now."

On that cue Rich and Suzy got up and left.

Margaret shut the door. "What did they want?"

"They wanted to know what I did for a living related to your 'project'. It would be nice if you told me what's going on."

"What's with the attitude, Donna?"

"I'm frustrated. If you would tell me what is going on, I could be helpful. It's disturbing to get information from interns!"

"Okay. If you want the truth, here it is. Without any warning Morton told me I had to take on those two people. He said the administrator demanded it. Morton expected me to find something for them to do. I think they're not interns. I think they are investigators looking for fraud, so don't tell them anything."

"Oh my God! Are you sure you are not being paranoid? We are squeaky clean. There are so many controls. The only exception is your handling the Get Ahead New York grants by yourself."

Oh great! "Well, I thought I was lightening your load. As of today you can have them back. Just be careful. Don't volunteer any information."

"I haven't told them anything harmful." *Yet.* "It would be good if you would keep me in the loop from now on."

Yeah sure, you are my best buddy. No way!

Margaret left without responding.

At his desk Rich googled Caribbean initiative and found nothing. He decided to walk the halls. He texted Suzy. He and she used texting because they were assigned an open cubicle in which to work.

He found Beamer and Johnny, and they all walked outside. "How you hangin', boys?"

"You won't believe what we found in Donna Dawson's trash," Johnny said.

"Tell me, dude."

"The MSRP for a brand new Honda was in her can. List price was thirty-three thousand dollars. Has a lot of options on it, but it's not fully loaded."

"Interesting. I keep forgetting you were raised on cars. Your dad has three dealerships, right?"

"Yep."

"Anything else?"

Beamer bit into an apple. "Sabat had more to-do lists, but nothing stood out, except for R, close out."

"See any trash on Caribbean initiative?"

"Nope."

After they went back inside, Rich decided to try again with Dawson. He stopped by her office. "Got a minute?"

"I have a meeting to prepare for."

"Okay. May be I can catch you later." All she did was nod.

A cute, little blond walked passed him and smiled.

"Hi, there. I am new, Rich Pritchard."

"Hey. This place is so TOTALLY dull, so when there is a new face, we are TOTALLY curious. Jane Smith."

"Are you free for lunch? It's nice out, low humidity. We could get a burger, and I could take care of your curiosity. Is your name really Jane Smith?"

"Yes and yes. What about your girlfriend?"

"Uh, oh, you mean Suzy. I'll bring her something back." Rich texted Suzy the plan.

Rich and Jane took their burgers to the Botanical Gardens at the base of Capitol Hill. He flirted and charmed, and learned more about grant auditing than he needed. Jane Smith was like her name, dull. As they were back to the PSA, Rich said, "So, Jane, what's the Caribbean initiative?"

She laughed. "Wow. How'd you find out about that?"

"You tell me what you know, and then I'll tell you how I found out."

Later, he gave Suzy her cold burger, fries, and watered-down coke.

"How thoughtful, Rich. Thank you."

"It was worth it."

"Well?"

"Later." Rich put his right index finger to his lips.

Chapter 10

Margaret sat across from her Uncle Ben at the Clos du Bois in Georgetown. Her brother, Dr. David Windson, formerly David Sampson, was unable to join them for lunch.

"Maggie, you look great! Camel and gold are definitely your colors. Sorry about David. That boy works too hard."

"What do you expect, Uncle Ben? He works for the president. What did you find out for me?"

"Oh yes." He reached in his jacket pocket and pulled out a slip of paper. "The information is strange. Suzy Simon is a graduate student in organizational development and in her second year of a master's degree. Richard Pritchard is a new student."

"It looks like they are legit, then. Why do you say the information is strange?"

"My contacts told me neither of them has been assigned an internship, and a new student is never sent on an internship. So I think there is merit in your suspicions."

After lunch as soon as Margaret was in her car, she called Ted on his private line.

"How is my 'Grants Auditing for Dummies' progressing?"

"Your interns are either spies for Administrator Swanson or actual investigators."

"Meet me out front, we got to talk."

"I am in my car on the Second Street side. Don't swear. This is serious. We need to decide how to manage it." *I need to know what Teddy boy thinks?*

"Amen."

Ten minutes later Ted was in Margaret's front seat. "Do you suspect anyone?"

Thank God! Men are so stupid. "Dawson. She just bought a new car and is taking her mom on a cruise."

"So throw her to the wolves, and they will be out of you hair."

"Ted, we must pace ourselves. Do it slowly. Otherwise, they may get suspicious of us."

"Margaret," he put his hand in her lap, "make this go away, or I will."

Margaret removed Ted's hand and kissed him on the cheek. "Get out, Ted. I need to park and get back to work." *Men!*

As Margaret left the elevator on her floor her mind was in overdrive. She saw a janitor lift something out of the trash can.

On the sidewalk outside, Sheila and Johnny had just completed an afternoon jog. "What are you thinking, Johnny?"

"I got to call Rich."

"Okay. I am heading back to the office before Electra discovers I was gone."

Johnny laughed. "Believe me, she knows you're gone. She probably knows what you have been doing! Take her a chocolate milkshake. Then she won't care."

"Will do. Thanks." Sheila ran off.

Johnny dialed Rich. "Rich, this is Johnny. I have something for you."

"You do?"

"Yep. A suit just got out of Margaret Sabat's Volvo. She kissed him on the cheek."

"Describe the dude."

"Armani suit, pale gray, white shirt, red tie, and brown Gucci loafers."

"You are amazing! Was he tall or short?"

"Very short."

"God bless you, dude. Bye."

Rich texted Suzy. "We are going to see Ted Morton." Minutes later as they walked by Margaret's office door, the Do not disturb under any circumstances sign was hanging on her door. Rich said, "Too bad we can't ask permission."

They were lucky. Morton was free. He waved them into his spacious corner office with windows on two sides.

I have never seen so much navy gear in one place, even a stressed leather bomber jacket with a zillion patches.

"Thank you for seeing us, Admiral, without an appointment. My name is Rich Pritchard and this is Suzy Simon, my colleague. I love your Armani suit."

"Uh, good to meet you, Rich and you too, Suzy. You know your threads, huh?"

Rich laughed. "Through *GQ* only."

"I know you're working on a manual for Margaret Sabat. How's it going?"

"Slowly. I think we could accomplish more at this point if we talked to people about what they do. In fact that's why we are here—to talk to you about your role in the grants-auditing process."

"Well fire away. I have about fifteen minutes."

Suzy took over and walked Morton through the electronic side of the clearance process. He seemed clueless. He said he had worker bees to do the reviewing. Then Morton became philosophical.

"At this level a lot happens based on trust. There is too much to do. If you surround yourself with people you trust, then things go as they should, and you have few crises. I pride myself in being a good judge of character, and I think my senior management team has the same talent. Margaret Sabat, for example, is a solid manager.

"Now let's cut the crap. I know why you're here. You are looking for fraud. I don't know whom you're working for, and I guess I don't care. I run a tight ship. If you find anything, you let me know, and I'll make things right. I have nothing to hide. Now get the hell out of here."

Walking down the hall to the elevator, Suzy said to Rich, "Holy cow, our cover is blown!"

"Maybe, but even so only by half. Beamer and Johnny will still be here, even if we leave. I suspect Margaret must have given him a strong assurance or she knows who the culprit is and told him. But I think we can infer from what he said that he and Margaret know we are not graduate students. The question is how did they find out? The simplest explanation is Administrator Swanson told Morton, and Morton told Margaret. I think we should leave early today and go talk to Pip. How's your draft manual coming along? Do you have something we can give to Margaret before we leave?"

"I guess so. I wanted to make a PowerPoint to go with it."

"Suzy! This is not a job! It's a cover! Whatever you have doesn't have to be perfect or even finished. My intuition tells me to get the hell out here, and the quicker the better.

"You know the chick I had lunch with? She said the managers around here have a ton of codes." He looked around and lowered his voice. *Caribbean initiative* means We must to talk privately!"

"Here's what I propose. We go back to the cubicle, you print out whatever you have, we give it to Margaret and say sayonara."

"Why are you so sure Margaret knows what Morton knows?"

"I forgot in all the excitement tell you what happened. Johnny saw Morton get out of Margaret's car. She gave him a kiss."

"Oh my God!"

After Suzy printed out her draft manual, she and Rich went to see Margaret.

The Do not disturb sign was off of Margaret's door, so they knocked.

"Come in."

Suzy said, "Thank you, Ms. Sabat. We have a draft manual for you as well as a disc. We appreciate the time you've given us and the opportunity to learn more about your operation."

"You are leaving?"

"Yes ma'am, we are. It was bad timing on our part. Since you're facing the end of the fiscal year you have a lot to deal with, and we would get in the way. We understand that."

"Yes! Yes! That was very thoughtful of you. Perhaps you could do something with us or for us later in your graduate program. Thank you for this draft manual I will put it to good use." Margaret ushered them out of her office. She leaned her back against her closed door. *Thank you God! I dodged a bullet, I think?*

Suzy and Rich drove back to Forensic Specialists, LLP. They were quiet. Finally Suzy said, "Margaret was overjoyed about our departure, but gave no indication she knew we were undercover. Do you think Ted Morton didn't tell her yet?"

"No. She's smarter than Morton. We will have to work remotely through Kit to resolve this sucker. I don't think Morton is a crook. But in my mind the jury is still out on Margaret and Donna. Margaret is higher up the food chain, so I think she's our perp."

After work Margaret and Ted went to his condominium in Crystal City. Ted was a widower. His son was away on a field trip. Margaret had no idea what her younger daughter was doing, but would track her down later.

Ted looked down at Margaret, "Well, Ms. Maggie, you better be good to me tonight because I got rid of those jerks for you!"

Margaret couldn't talk because she was otherwise occupied. After about five minutes she rearranged herself and him, and said, "What the heck did you say to them to get them to leave so abruptly?"

He took a deep breath and wiped her face gently with a baby wipe and then kissed her on the lips. "I told them I knew they were investigating fraud. I said if they found anything, I would fix it. I told them I trusted my people, and I mentioned you by name. I had no idea they were going to pull out. I don't know what it means. I guess you should keep a sharp eye on Donna Dawson and scrutinize her work. If you find something, we take it to Administrator Swanson. Ideally, everything will just go back to normal. Now let's you and me get back what we were doing, or should I say what you were doing.

At Forensic Specialists, LLP Pip was fascinated by what she heard from her undercover team. They were such amazing people, "her children." They didn't screw up, and they found things she could to take to Swanson. Her inclination was to give him a verbal report. She could see the value of letting Beamer and Johnny continue to be undercover. Those trash cans were gold mines.

Pip talked to Swanson by the phone. "Mr. Swanson, I know it's late. I appreciate your taking my call. Let me summarize for you what we've found so far. There is a personal as well as a work connection between Margaret Sabat and Ted Morton. There is a pattern of payments relate to Get Ahead programs throughout the state of New York, with payments going to one location call Soya Surplus Supplies in Albany and to another location called Robinson Rebate Depot here in D.C. Both companies appear to be nothing but post office boxes. The one for Soya was terminated last week. The one for Robinson was discontinued as of this week. So I think the fraud will not continue, or it is being continued under new dummy companies. Perhaps your authorization of our undercover staff triggered the shut down. The people who are potentially associated with the grants involved are Morton, Sabat, and a woman named Donna Dawson."

"Thank you, Dr. Planter. I know there was a limited amount you could do without involving the inspector general of PSA or other sources of law enforcement. I don't want to know how you did it. Nonetheless, I believe you have identified the fact something irregular is going on and perhaps you have also identified the person or persons connected to this irregularity. I would like to ask you and your team to do two more things before I turn this issue over to other authorities. First, would your forensic records specialists sample the records of Get

Ahead grants in other states to see if they bought supplies from Soya or Robinson? Second, would you be willing to send some of your investigative staff to Albany to identify potential targets there?"

"Yes to both. Also, I would like to keep, but scale back, the undercover work at PSA."

"Sounds okay with me. I'll modify your contract."

"It would be great to be authorized to look at bank accounts."

"Well that involves either Treasury or the FBI, so let's wait on that, shall we? Thank you and good night."

Pip had an intuitive sense about timing. She thought Swanson, though cooperative, was too cautious. The fact two post office boxes, one in D.C. and one in Albany had been cancelled in a week was more than a coincidence. She had Frank look into Margaret Sabat on the Web, and what he found had raised the stakes. She decided to play a card—a card she played rarely. She called an ex-lover, Sam Netherfield, the third highest-ranking man in the FBI.

"Sam, this is Pamela."

"Well, well, what can I do for Dr. Planter, now that I have power and influence, and am no longer a lowly agent?"

"Can we meet?"

"For what?"

"I would rather tell you face to face. I have some sensitive information."

"You like the Ritz at Pentagon City. Let's meet there at eight thirty. Who knows what will happen, right?"

"Thank you."

Later at the Ritz bar Pip found a quiet corner table. When

he arrived, Sam, a big bear of a guy with short, sandy gray hair, a suit that was impeccable, but with pants that looked like they would fall below the hipline any minute, kissed Pip on her head and sat down.

"No more blond hair? I miss it. Now you look like a grown up."

"An old lady. It's good to see you, Sam. I still miss those bear hugs."

"The night is not over, Pamela."

"Let's focus on why we are meeting, shall we?"

"Yes ma'am." He saluted, smiled, and ordered a bottle of Jordan's cabernet.

"A woman named Margaret Sabat, an auditor, a career employee not political, works in PSA. Someone in her division—possibly her—and someone in New York have been siphoning funds to post office boxes for three years. The boxes were cancelled within the last two weeks."

"And?"

"Margaret Sabat is the sister of the president's chief medical adviser, David Windson, aka or formerly, David Sampson."

Sam whistled. "How'd you find that out?"

"On the Web. It is amazing what you can learn if you are willing to spend thirty-nine ninety-five."

"Whom are you working for?"

"Swanson."

"I know him. He is cautious but ambitious. Where do things stand?"

After Pip told him, Sam said, "Play along. Bury your troops in paper reviews. It will take him a week or more to modify your contract. I have an idea, but I need to run some traps first and get you an FBI liaison. In Washington, given the twenty-four/seven news cycle, there is a lot of guilt by association and rush to judgment, so keeping a low profile and being discrete in this case makes sense.

"Swanson is smart. You may not know it, but the guy is in the middle of a power play to bring auditing of entitlement spending and defense spending into PSA. Most of PSA's current portfolio is education, housing, and human services. It would not help Swanson if he contributed to the arrest of the sister of the president's chief medical adviser."

Now it was Pip's turn to whistle, but she could not because of a spastic tongue. She was pleased Sam would try to help her. Over the years she had not often contacted him. In this instance it had been twelve years with nothing between them but Christmas and birthday cards. They had met in high school.

The conversation turned to family. Pip said, "How's your son, Bart?"

"He's a field agent here in D.C. His mother loves that. He doesn't. He is solid. Very straight arrow. No sense of humor. His mother wants grandkids.

"How about you? The last time I saw you, you were the CEO of a chain of community mental health clinics, making a fortune."

"I got bored. Sold them to a corporation, went back to school in forensics, and for several years been operating Forensic Specialists, LLP."

"Do you have a boyfriend?"

"At sixty? Sam, you were my last boyfriend."

After some handholding and smiles between sad eyes, Pip said, "I better spend the night here. I have had too much wine."

"I can drive you home."

"You have had as much to drink as I."

"No I haven't. You were too tipsy to notice."

At Pip's door things were awkward, with her cart, keys, cane, and feelings.

Sam said, "It was so good seeing you, cupcake. He kissed her on the forehead. Do you want me to come in and take off your shoes and put you to bed like I use to?"

When standing and being five-three it is always difficult to look someone six-five in the eyes. Pip said, "Sam, you are a happily married man."

"You got part of that right, darlin'." He kissed her again gently, unlocked her door, and she pushed her cart in. Sam shut the door.

Chapter 11

Pip, dressed in a red tank top and kaki pantsuit, pushed her cart through the glass doors. Rich looked up and then leaped up to help Pip get through the door, the sports section of the *Post* hit the floor. It was 7:30 A.M.

Rich said, "I can't believe my eyes. Do you know what time it is? Look at you—no black, decent make up. What's up?"

"Rich, if you want to find a woman, I suggest you try a less interrogative approach, such as My you look nice today, Pip."

"Thanks for the advice old lady! I thought you and I only engaged in verbal combat in the morning if we had an audience?"

Pip laughed. "One for you. Please get me a coffee and come to the conference room. Where's Beamer?"

"He had a gig last night, I think."

While Rich was in the kitchen Electra came in.

"Hi, Rich."

"How'd you know it was me?"

"Your cheap aftershave."

"Go sit down big Mama. I will bring you your coffee. I know how you like it."

"Oh do you?"

"I am talking about coffee."

"Oh, I see. My mistake.

Rich finished his detour duty and then went to conference room.

"It took you a long time to get here."

"I fixed a coffee for Electra and made us stale bagels. I needed food to go with my pills." He looked at the conference table. It was covered with stacks of printouts.

"What the hell is this? You better tell Electra you depleted her paper supply and tell everyone else we need to shift to toilet paper if we have something to copy!"

Pip, sitting at the far end, said, "Come sit by me, dear one. You are going to have the opportunity to work for a living over the next few weeks. And since I know how you love to read, I am going to give you your personal orientation."

Rich frowned; he was developing a sense of dread, but did as he was told. He made space for the tray as he sat down next to Pip.

Pip spread her left arm. "What you see here are printouts from fifty states of their reports on financial accounts on Get Ahead grants for the last three years."

"And, what does this grunt work have to do with me?"

"Over the next few weeks, everyone here, and I emphasize *everyone*, is going to review financial accounts to look for irregularities."

"You are kidding, right? You know I can't read?"

"That is inaccurate. You can, but you prefer not to."

"PLEASE, Pip, don't make me do this! I'll answer the phones. I'll do the dishes. I'll pick up your dry cleaning. I'll go back to doing Defense Department security clearances."

"Relax, Rich. You will have others to support you. It will be good for everyone to work as a team."

"Bullshit! Are you going to have Beamer and Johnny do this too?"

"Yes. Everyone will have a chance to grow."

"You are crazy. Leave it to Frank, Kit, and Suzy. It will be done in half the time and done right. You always say we each have our individual strengths. That it is best we play to our strengths. In case you forgot, mine is investigation."

"Rich, we have too much to look at. This is investigation. It requires keen eyes and an inquisitive mind. You have both. Suzy and Kit are going to orient everyone with a PowerPoint slide show at ten A.M. We need to help PSA find out how widespread the fraud is. And, Swanson needs time to modify our contract so you can go to New York to do interviews. If you develop a better understanding about grants, it will sharpen your interviewing."

Fuck it. This is what Pip always does—wears me down with logic. I got to play along, but the hell if I like it. I'm good at persuasion, so I guess I'll just have to get my compadres to do my share of the work.

Pip said, "Well, are you going to help on this?"

"Yes, ma'am."

Pip thought, *That was too easy.* "I need you on this, Rich. You are a natural leader."

You got that right, old lady.

Later in Pip's office a second drama played out.

"Electra, what were you thinking? Why didn't you at least tell your husband you were going out of town? I become a nervous wreck whenever I have to cover for you. I am not that convincing. He's got to suspect something."

"You changed your perfume. What's up?"

"Don't change the subject! Is your husband ready to divorce you?"

"No, he's going to try harder to make me happy. He can't,

but he doesn't know, and I am not going to tell him."

"Jeez! If you love Max, why don't you divorce Joe?"

"Pip, you don't understand. You have never been in love. You should try it. It's great. I love Joe, and I love Max, although in different ways. Joe is a seeing guy who loves my glass eyeballs, chutzpah, boobs, and lasagna. He owns three funeral homes. Someone is always dying, so we have plenty of money. Joe swept me off my feet and took me away from my overprotective parents at twenty-one. He took me on trips. He paid for my CPA. He sees himself as Henry Higgins or worse, a savior. But, and it's a big *but*, he is not a good lover. A woman must have a good lover.

"Max, on the other hand, is fantastic in the loving department. He's got hands that could make anything play chimes, if you get my drift. We met in kindergarten at the School for the Blind in Rochester, fell in love, and stayed in love. To give him up would be like cutting off my hearing or sense of smell."

"Does Joe know about Max?"

"He knows Max. He always refers to him as 'my friend, the blind school teacher'. I think Joe thinks people who are blind don't engage in sex with each other because they can't see what they are doing!" Electra laughed.

"Oh, God. I am not covering for you any more. One of these days you are going to slip up. Where did Joe think you were for a whole week?"

"I usually called him every day and said I was staying in town because of work. He was busy with the Metro crash, so he didn't care. On Friday I was otherwise occupied and forgot it was Friday."

"What the heck were you doing that you couldn't make ONE phone call?"

"Do you really want to know? Oh why not? I was in a honeymoon suite in Vegas spinning in a basket with a hole in the bottom hanging over the bed. You should try it sometime. Just remember you need to be attached to something to get the full effect."

Pip put down her coffee and just stared at all of Electra's 170 pounds in her flowing floral dress, auburn curls, beautiful purple glass eyes, two-foot long eyelashes, and perfectly glossed, ruby lips. She thought, *God help me. I am out of my league here. That must have been some big basket. Probably held up by a crane.*

With the extended silence Electra just sat there for a while and then said, "You know what my fantasy is?"

"I don't want to know. Go do something useful."

Electra got up and walked toward the door and then turned, "I wish Max could teach Joe a few tricks."

Pip put her head on her desk.

In five minutes she said a quick prayer and then went to the conference room. Everyone was there but Electra, even Sheila.

"Good morning. Our work with PSA has been expanded to cover all Get Ahead grants, not just those in New York and the northeast. It is too much work for Kit and Frank. We have two months to look at grant files and report any suspected irregularities to PSA."

Pip surveyed the six faces in front of her. She had their attention. "Kit and Suzy, while looking at grant files themselves, will be able to answer your questions. They spent the last several days making tools to help you in the review process. They will orient you now. This is important, serious work. I appreciate your willingness to help." With that Pip left as quickly as she could. She was pleased there was no wisecrack from Rich.

Suzy said to the group, "We have the grant amount and number of students served by each grant for each of the last three years" She showed the first slide. "These are your reference points. When you look at how much something cost, you will ask yourself does that make sense?"

Johnny said, "How will we know what makes sense?"

"You will not know until you look at the spending for a grantee over three years and until you look at grantees in other states with the same size budget and number of students. Johnny, by this afternoon you will start to know what makes sense and every day you work with these files, you will get better at what recognizing makes sense."

Kit worked through examples of what irregularities would look like. She handed out grantee profile sheets and checklists. Suzy assigned pairs of workers—Rich and Frank, Sheila and Johnny, and Kit and Suzy. She answered questions, as did Kit.

Then Rich said, "When I was at PSA, an auditor, Jane Smith, told me PSA auditors have the ability to change files— that is alter numbers—when they're working with a grantee to reconcile discrepancies. So the possibility exists that crooked PSA auditors, without the knowledge of grantees, may have corrupted files. Put another way, without copies of what the local grantees generated, looking at only PSA files may be a waste of time."

Suzy stood there for a minute before responding to Rich. "That is a very good point, Rich. Look at this as the first step. If an item costs too much or if a grantee spends money on something twice in a month, those will be red flags for us. That will give us a reason to then go and look at local records."

"Okay. I see. But I still think we would be more successful if we had some local files to look at the same time we are looking at PSA files. That is, if speed is important here, how do we know the top guy at PSA is doing nothing more than trying to slow us down?"

"We don't. But if Swanson is involved, he would not be paying us to do this, believe me. Okay, let's get started. At least we can all agree we have a lot to look at."

Rich said to Frank, "Well, man, it looks like you and I are working together. How do you feel about that?"

Frank just looked at Rich. Then he said, "I like numbers work. This is numbers work. If you don't want to do it, I can do it for both of us. Our team will still look good. We have New York."

This is going to be interesting. Rich opened the first grant file, took a profile sheet, and entered the grantee's name.

Sheila said to Johnny, "How about you hold the file, I will ask you a question from the checklist, and you will give me the answer from the file. If you're not sure of the right place to look in the file, we can do the first few together. How about that?"

Johnny said, "Sounds good. I am a pretty good reader. I help Electra all the time."

And with that, weeks of analyzing raw records began.

On Independence Avenue at PSA Margaret was in heated argument with Ted in his office.

"Look genius, if you want me to get the goods on Donna

Dawson so we can turn her in, you must take her up here on some temporary assignment so I can have access to her computer. Why can't you agree to that?"

"Maggie this is an escalating situation. My sources in Swanson's office told me he has now expanded the review of Get Ahead grants to a nationwide review. So there must be something very wild going on. This could become a federal fraud case. We may all be suspects. I can't go moving people around. Actions like that will just contribute to the suspicion."

"Ted, I'm not asking you to take Donna Dawson forever. Just for a week. There doesn't even have to be a paper trail on it. Help me out here. If I build a case for a primary culprit, this whole thing could go away. Swanson would look good. You would look good. Don't be so shortsighted!"

"What the hell do you expect me to ask Donna Dawson to do?"

"How about this—she would take that draft guide those interns worked on and polish it up."

"Now, why would she need to be in my office in order to do that?"

"So she would have access the main man, the guy who asked for this in the first place."

"Maggie, it's just too thin. She will see right through it. She'll probably file a grievance."

"Teddy," Margaret approached his desk and kissed his ear, "Just think about it. Please help me out. I'm doing this for both of us."

Before Ted could return a kiss or do anything else Margaret backed off. She had on a very short skirt, too short for somebody fifty years old. "Okay, I'll think about it. You're going to that

Medicaid and Medicare fraud conference tomorrow, right?"

"Not because I want to, but yes."

"Are we going to be able to get together this weekend?"

"No. I'm having a weekend with my girls. We haven't been together for a long time, and I sense they are feeling neglected. I'm sorry."

She went over and locked his door. "Perhaps I can make amends now. I have nothing pending, not even underpants."

Chapter 12

Margaret was excited. Things were looking up. The weekend with her girls had gone well. She told them she was going to spend the next few months in D.C. She was involved in a fraud case and would be staying with a friend. Margaret and her girls "closed up" the house together. Bonnie would move in with her sisters, all four of them would get together for dinner once a week, talk on the telephone every day, and gather at the big house in Bethesda for Christmas. Everyone was in a good mood when they parted; Bonnie would have more freedom and Margaret told the twins they could get a new transmission for their Honda. Margaret gave each girl a $200 Nordstrom gift card.

Margaret's girls stopped going to Eloise's house after their grandfather's death. They were not close to either, and never had anything to do when they went there except sit on the hard couch and watch videos on a small television. There was lots of food, stupid surprises, lots of talk about an Uncle David they only saw at Christmas in Bethesda, and their dad looking either bored or sad. They never asked about Eloise now and were not aware their mother continued to visit Eloise, or more accurately, her house. They would have been blown away to learn Margaret was about to move in with Eloise's body in the freezer.

Margaret felt closer to Eloise than ever. She had twinges now and then about Eloise being cold but would always say,

"Don't worry, Eloise. I'll get you buried. I just need a little more time."

Margaret sat at Eloise's big kitchen table, a big coffee to her left, her legal pad to her right, and the big Medicare-Medicaid fraud conference notebook in front of her. She had taken some time off, much to Ted's chagrin. He loved it when she stopped by his office to argue. He had chosen not to transfer Donna Dawson to his office, so Margaret thought celibacy would help him clear his head and alter his decision. She also had big plans. She was going to start a new business, Landmark Therapies, and defraud Medicare. She had learned everything she needed to know at the conference.

Her first two clients would be her ex-in-laws. Margaret's ex-husband Jeremy never altered their co-power of attorney for his parents' affairs after he divorced Margaret.

She pulled over her legal pad and started her to-do list—download application to be a Medicare service provider, look for David's medical license under his real name, open new post office box, incorporate, rent a van, get sign made saying Landmark Therapies, hire a driver.

David Sampson would be the medical director and Eloise Robinson the CEO of Landmark Therapies. Margaret thought it was nice to keep everything in the family.

Eloise's doorbell rang. Margaret jumped. She looked at herself in the hall mirror. She put her hair behind her ears and thought, *No one will rape me in brown sweats.*

She pulled open the door and saw the hunk of a mailman. It was drizzling, and he didn't have a raincoat.

"Hi, I saw your car, so I thought I would hand you Ms. Eloise's mail and ask how she was doing."

What did he do? Walk around to the back of the house? "How nice." *I need a driver.* "Why don't you come in and dry off. I'll give you a cup of coffee."

Fifteen minutes later, sitting at the kitchen table, Margaret and the mailman had become fast friends.

"I am so sorry you had to place Ms. Eloise in a nursing home in North Carolina."

"I know. It broke my heart. We were very close. But I have had years of nursing home struggles with my ex-in-laws, and Eloise still has her mental faculties. The place in Clinton is so nice, and it's warmer."

"What were Ms. Eloise's issues?"

"She was so frail. I could never be sure she would eat properly, and all the stairs."

"I guess that big freezer was a mistake."

"Yes, it was."

"I would like to send Ms. Eloise a card. Would you give me the address of the nursing home in Clinton?"

"I will. I just have to find it." Margaret forced a laugh and pointed to all the papers in the center of the table. She remembered now this guy was inquisitive. She had to be careful. *Now I have to pray there is a nursing home in Clinton, assuming there is a Clinton in North Carolina!*

"Are you going to be coming here more frequently to clear things out, fix things up, and sell it?"

"I don't know. I have a full-time job, three daughters, and a big house in Maryland."

"Well, if I can help in anyway, I will. I am new to the area and have no family. I like to help people."

Is this guy for real? I need to change the subject.

"How sweet of you. I have a challenge right now that has nothing to do with Eloise's townhouse. Both of my ex-in-laws have Alzheimer's disease and the nursing home in which they live never takes them out. It is so sad. I am in the process of setting up a company to offer excursions and simple getting-out activities for people like my in-laws who live in the Lake and Lawn Nursing Home in Alexandria. I'm in the process of incorporation but expect to have to service up and running by November. I'm looking for a driver who is comfortable around senior citizens with physical and mental problems. Would you be interested in a part-time job?"

"Sure. Look, I need to get back to my mail route. Are you going to be here over the weekend? We could talk more then. Thanks so much for the coffee."

They agreed to get together at 4:30 on Saturday afternoon. After the mailman left, Margaret thought, *That was too easy. What's with that guy? He's just too nice.*

During the week Margaret worked her way through her to-do list. Talked to people in the Medicare regional office in Philadelphia and filed all the necessary papers electronically. She was in a good mood. All she had left was to make a flyer up about Landmark Therapies and rent a van. She had purchased a magnetic sign midweek that looked very professional; it was leaning against the side of the refrigerator. She also had to visit the nursing home to lay the groundwork for taking her in-laws off campus once a week and to recruit other families with her flyer. Given the Medicare reimbursement rates she figures by January she could be pulling in $10,000 a month if she acquired eight other clients.

Her finances were okay because Eloise had received two credit card applications in the mail, each had a $10,000 credit line, with no payments due until February. Margaret had activated both.

She had ten voicemail messages from Ted sounding pitiful.

Saturday afternoon and evening proved interesting. The mailman came on time at 4:30. He brought two bottles of wine, a casserole, and vanilla ice cream. For late September, it was still very warm so they sat outside and drank wine for about an hour on the back steps.

Don Pelham had moved to D.C. from New York about three months ago. He was dressed in a gray sweater, jeans, and a pair of sneakers.

Before too much wine was consumed, Margaret thought it best to find out how much he would charge her to be a driver of the van. He said $15 an hour. She could not believe how reasonable he was. Don Pelham was turning out to be a saint. She had never known a male saint, or any saint for that matter.

Inside at the kitchen table with the second bottle of wine breathing, Margaret asked Don about the contents of his casserole and if he had made it.

"It's chicken breasts with four kinds of peppers, onion, garlic, and pasta topped with sharp cheddar cheese. And yes, I made it."

Margaret enjoyed the casserole. Even the ice cream tasted good with the last of the second bottle of wine.

Now what? Eloise doesn't have the kind of furniture you could make out on. To her surprise Don got up from the kitchen table and started doing the dishes. She just sat there and watched in amazement. Then, when he finished the dishes, he put on his jacket and said, "I enjoyed this evening. Thank you so much, Margaret." And he let himself out after shaking hands. Margaret was dumbfounded.

Chapter 13

At Forensic Specialists, LLP the grant file review was going well. Some of the pairs had been shifted. Johnny had
asked Pip if he could return to PSA to empty trash cans without supervision. She agreed with two caveats: Johnny would
return every day at noon to have lunch with her and then return to Pip's office at 4:30 to be debriefed. In his words "that
was totally cool." Beamer became Sheila's partner.

Rich continued to work with Frank, although Rich took
frequent breaks. Frank had made an interesting discovery.
There appeared to be several states in the southwest that used
contractors for student field trips that had company names
that started with the same letters D and P, although the actual
names varied. Frank made an additional discovery related to
these company names. They had many letters in common.
There were a total of five companies with these interesting
alphabetic commonalities.

Pip and Electra became a team for part of each day, given
the volume of files to review.

Johnny was glad to be on his own. He had his mother drop
him off early every day at PSA. *Pip was smart. Margaret and Ted
did spend a lot of time in each other's offices, at the times Pip said they
would.* Johnny told Pip they always looked a little messed up
when they walked out of an office after they had been together
for a while. Sometimes Ted would come out with different
clothes on! Sometimes one would stomp out mad.

Johnny also told Pip, Donna Dawson was now working on Ted's floor. Margaret spent almost as much time in Donna's office as she did her own. When Johnny reported such news he would say, "Does this help you with your puzzle, Pip?" And Pip would say, "Yes sir, it sure does."

The one thing that disappointed Johnny was Margaret's trash can did not have those legal sheets in it anymore. They were important to Pip's puzzle too. One day Johnny said to Pip, "I think I've done all I can do. I want to stop going to PSA now, but I have a piece of advice for you, Pip. You need to get into those two computers—Margaret's computer and Donna's computer. There's something going on. And I think you need to find out why Donna left." Pip assured Johnny she would do just that.

One afternoon, feeling weary but satisfied, Pip received a call from Sam. "Hi, cupcake. How you doing?"

"Sam, I am beyond tired. We are almost finished with the grant review. There are irregularities within states other than New York. For example, in southwestern states students go on a hell of a lot of field trips. In New York grantees buy twice as many supplies as grantees of comparable size programs in other states. The unknown in this is whether these particular files represent potential fraud perpetrated by locals, state people, or feds, or any combination thereof. We need access to local files before they're sent to Washington."

"I think your best bet is the state-level-fed connection or the local-state connection. I cannot imagine three-way collaboration on fraud like this. Talk to Swanson to get access to local files. It looks to me like you've isolated the problems and things are not too bad. I would get a team to New York."

"I have a team leaving tonight."

"I'm still working on getting you a liaison. But I have to be honest, Pamela, this whole thing is still not big enough to justify many resources or time. You know, it just doesn't fall in the serial-killer category. Want to get together tonight? Edith is at some fund-raiser related to saving the planet."

"I would love to, but I have to meet with my staff before they fly to Albany." *Maybe at another time within the next twelve years.*

"Okay. I love you, darlin'."

Sure you do. A few tears fell on Pip's cheeks. She gently put down the phone without saying good-bye.

Chapter 14

Rich sat in his plaid boxer shorts on the side of his bed drinking. He and Beamer were in Albany.

"Look at this damn room! Enough flowers for a funeral! Do you think that registration clerk thought we are gay?"

"No. We got the last two queen-size beds in the place. I can live with the flowers, considering the alternative—you and me in a king."

Rich opened another beer. "Good point. No offense man, but I can't believe Pip insisted you come with me to Albany!"

Beamer, dressed in a gray sweat suit, said, "It was cheaper. If Suzy had come, she would've had to pay for two rooms."

"Screw you, man." Rich smiled. He threw Beamer a beer.

"What are we supposed to do tomorrow? We cannot just waltz into the director's office of a state agency, wave this letter of introduction, and the guy is going to tell us everything. With a letter of introduction, I feel like I'm in the middle of a fucking Jane Austen novel. This place is cold. Are we up somewhere near the Arctic?"

For Beamer making conversation with Rich sometimes was a challenge. Topics could change frequently. His main goal was not to alienate Rich. He knew Rich saw him as a babysitter. So he felt anything could set him off.

"On your first point, we have more than a letter. Swanson called the director of the state agency today and told him we were coming. On the second point, dude, yes, it is fucking cold. We are north of D.C., south of the Canadian border, and a long way from the Arctic."

Rich turned toward his pants laying on the bed and reached into his pants pocket for one of his new business cards, real engraved ones, not ones made on an office printer. "I like the new cards, top quality. Mine says I am a principal investigator, what does yours say?"

"Context specialist."

"No shit? Whose idea was that?"

"Mine."

"Not bad. I thought it would say bandleader or guiding light."

Rich did two successful bank shots into the wastepaper basket with his empty beer cans.

"What's your real name, Beamer?" Rich turned out the light and lay down.

"John Peter."

"That's okay. My adoptive parents hated me. They had to... to name me Richard Prichard."

"What's your middle name?"

"So glad you asked. Francis."

"See your point, Fran."

"Shut up! Don't get any funny ideas. Remember, I have a black belt in karate."

The next morning Beamer got up before Rich, showered, shaved, and dressed. He went to the free breakfast buffet and brought a paper, two coffees, two bagels, and two doughnuts back to the room. *Hope that drama queen takes his medication.*

Rich came out of the bathroom with a towel wrapped around himself. "Put some cream in my wheat! As my grandma use to say. You look like Obama, except you're better looking. I have never seen you in anything but two-hundred-dollar jeans and a hundred and fifty-dollar white shirt, starched, hanging to your two-hundred and fifty-dollar running shoes."

"How do you know what my threads are worth?"

"Johnny. He knows all that shit."

Beamer and Rich had no trouble getting in to see the director of the New York Public Auditing Department. He did not even ask for their cards. He was short, fat, with a hairpiece but a good dresser. His name was John Brown. Rich thought to himself, *He's probably Jane Smith's uncle.*

"Swanson and I go way back. He's from New York, you know. What can I do for you guys?"

Rich said, "Thank you for seeing us, Mr. Brown. My colleague, John, and I appreciate the fact you have made time to see us with such short notice. We're investigating only one type of grant at this point, the New York Get Ahead program."

"Do you expect to look at others as well?"

"I do not know the answer to that. Right now we are just focused on Get Ahead. Could you tell us who audits the local records for you?"

"Yes I can, but I don't think it would do any good. The guy who handled most of it for thirty years just retired—Fred Firebrand. And, to make it even more interesting, rumor has it he moved to Mexico."

Beamer whistled. "Well, maybe we could start with people who worked with him. They might know something."

"Sure. You can start with the division director, Jerry Jones—a real piece of work. He has a Napoleonic complex. He and Fred did not get along. I'll call him and tell him you're on your way. His office is on the second floor, the first door on the right after you get off the elevator. Good luck guys. Jerry may know where Fred is."

On the elevator Rich said, "This may be an even shorter trip than we planned, Beamer."

"That John Brown was comfortable in his skin. I suspect he was thinking or hoping this is your problem and not mine, boys. Let's see what we can find out from Firebrand's former coworkers, and then I have some low-tech ideas to run by you."

Well how about that! A bandleader telling me how to do my job.

In Jerry Jones's office Rich said, "So, Mr. Jones, what can you tell us about Fred?"

"Nothing, unless you tell me why you want to know."

"Mr. Jones," Beamer said, "This is a federal investigation of fraud. Financial records related to Get Ahead grants in this state suggest grantees on a regular basis bought an enormous amount of supplies. Some of which were purchased in Albany, some in Washington, D.C., as well as some from local suppliers in the towns in which they were located. That's a lot of supplies."

"I see. Are you with the FBI?"

"No, we are private contractors working for PSA."

"Well, then I do not have to tell you squat."

Rich stood up. Beamer did too. Beamer said, "If you think of anything that might help us, here's my card."

Jerry dropped it in his trash can.

Rich went over to Jerry's desk, swung his chair around, and stood him up and gripped his arms. He was a little guy. He did not weigh more than 150 pounds. "Jerry, let me give your tiny ass a piece of advice. This fraud case is not going away. It would make so much more sense for you to be helpful right now before we come back with the FBI, got it?"

He threw the guy back into his chair. He did it with such force the chair rolled about five feet to a bookcase and knocked over a vase. The vase shattered and water went everywhere, as did the yellow carnations. "I can't help but wonder—you must have something to hide. Am I right?"

Rich's unexpected explosion worked. The guy started talking. "Okay. Okay. I get it. I don't want any trouble. I have a wife and kids. I took over this division two years ago. It was a promotion. Fred was a problem from day one. He constantly reminded me he had a friend high up in Washington, D.C., and not to mess with him."

"Didn't anybody check his work?"

"Yes. But just to make sure the numbers came out right, not to review where the money went or how much was spent on any one item. We do not have enough staff for that." Jerry was shaking. He was wide-eyed, apprehensive.

Rich said, "Do you have any idea about how Fred lived? You know, like above his means?"

"No. You can talk to Maria Belafonte. She and Don Pellingham were his only true friends in the office."

Beamer said, "We'd like to talk to Don, too."

"That will be pretty hard. He quit about the same time Fred retired."

"Do you have any idea where he is?"

"If I did, I would tell you. I am strongly motivated to keep my body intact."

Rich said, "Touché. Where do we find Maria?"

"I'll take you to her. She is a real looker."

In the hall Jerry said, "Nothing personal, but after I take you to see Maria, I hope I never see you guys again. You ought to go to anger management class, dude."

Rich turned to Jerry and gave him a bear hug and lifted him two feet off the floor.

"I love you, man. Don't you know that?" Beamer and Jerry both looked terrified. *I don't think he took his medication.*

Maria was beautiful. She had an angelic face, bright red hair with waves and golden highlights that fell to her shoulders. The red was stunning. It had to be natural. She sat in a wheelchair.

My luck. Hair, a face, shapely shoulders, arms, boobs, and no engine!

Jerry introduced Rich and Beamer to Maria and left. They each gave her a business card.

Maria smiled up at both of them. "If you go in the hall, you can find a second chair. It's a little cramped in here." Maria had an office with a door. Beamer returned with a chair and closed the door. Rich seemed speechless.

Beamer told Maria enough about why they were there to satisfy her. He then said, "Did you work with Fred Firebrand?"

"Yes. He helped me get this job when I graduated from Syracuse."

"How did you meet him?"

"He dated my mom."

Rich recovered and asked the next question. "Is he still in touch with your mom?"

"No. He broke up with my mom about three years ago."

Beamer said, "Do you know where Fred is now?"

"No idea. The grapevine has him in Guadalajara, Mexico."

Rich said, "Why did he stop dating your mom?"

"Who knows? Mom thought he met someone else—someone outside of Albany. My mom is the martyr type. She didn't push Fred to find out."

"Did Fred seem to have enough money?"

"Yes, but he was not a big spender. He had an ex-wife and three kids."

"Did you ever go to his house?"

"Yes. He had a two-bedroom, furnished apartment, not a house. When he dated my mom, he spent a lot of time at our house. My mom is a very good cook. Fred slept in the guest room."

Sure he did, Maria.

Rich said, "Is Fred's ex-wife in Albany?"

"No. I think she lives in Texas."

Maria looked at her watch. "It's time for me to go to Mass. Do you want to go with me, and then we can get some good, homemade pizza?"

Without a pause, Beamer said, "Okay." *Maybe prayers will help if Rich forgot his medication. If I didn't know better, I would swear he is in love.*

Maria said, "I'll drive. As long as I bring Jerry some pizza, we can take our time."

Rich was very quiet. Beamer had no idea what Rich was thinking. He wasn't thinking, he was having a conversation.

God, Maria is so beautiful, so sweet, and so innocent. Why did you cripple her up? I have not been to Mass since I left home. I am going to go. I am going to pray for Maria. You give her a good life, you hear?

They went in Maria's van. She had hand controls for the accelerator and brakes. She drove well, within the speed limit. Neither Rich nor Beamer had ever ridden as a passenger with a chick driver.

Sitting, kneeling, and standing in the church amazed Beamer. It reminded him of calisthenics. Last time he was in a church he was ten and had gone with his grandmother. He remembered the shouting, singing, and hand raising, but not much else. Beamer looked at Rich. Rich seemed absorbed in his own thoughts. Maria looked radiant. *God, this is Beamer. It is good to be in your house again. Please help me make the right moves till I get Rich, unarrested, back to D.C. Thank you, Man. Amen.*

After Mass, Maria took them to *Tony's Pizza* about two blocks from the church. She drove. They walked.

"You a Catholic, huh, Rich?"

"Yeah. Was an altar boy. Maria is a good person."

"Yes. Don't mean to shift to business, but maybe Maria can give us some local grantees to talk to before we fly back tonight. Also, we could check the phone book for addresses for Fred and Don and talk to their neighbors."

"Yeah, whatever."

"What's wrong, Rich?"

"Beamer, don't you see it? Maria is gorgeous and sweet, but she can't walk. That's so sad!"

"Rich, get a grip. Maria is happy, strong, and a take-charge lady. Let's just focus on why we are here."

Rich seemed to snap in the right direction. "That car is following Maria's car. Pick up your speed." They started running.

As Maria pulled into the parking lot, the car pulled up beside her. The driver got out and stood by Maria's driver's window.

"Hi, Maria, how are you?"

"Well, what a surprise. How are you? Where are you?"

"D.C. I'm here for the closing on my condo."

"What are you up to?"

"I am having pizza with some investigators from D.C. They are trying to find Fred. You want to have lunch with us, since you knew Fred?"

"I'd love to, but I've got to get to that closing. You take care. I'll call you later."

Rich and Beamer ran into the parking lot as the car that had pulled next to Maria's left. Maria was laughing when they got to her car.

"Why were you running?"

"Who was that?" Rich said.

"Oh, a guy I know. Were you jealous, Rich?"

Beamer couldn't help himself, and he laughed.

Lunch was fun. Maria told them about life in Albany—local political intrigue, her pumping iron in the local gym with guys who always want to help her, learning how to cook Mexican, playing basketball, and volunteering at the local library. She promised to give them addresses for local grantees.

Rich volunteered, with his mouth half full; he was a slob, exercised every twelfth Wednesday, and was married to his job.

Beamer talked about his band and his love of rock n' roll.

Toward the end of the pizza, after her cousin Tony brought another pitcher of peach ice tea Maria said, "Rich, what did you do before this job?"

"I was with Special Forces in Afghanistan."

"Wow. That had to be so hard!"

"Yeah. But it is behind me."

"Sure. Sure. How about you Beamer? What did you use

to do?"

"I worked in a mental health clinic."

"Did you guys know each other before your current jobs? You seem so close."

Without thinking Beamer said, "We met at the clinic."

There was silence.

Then Rich said, "Did you know Don Pellingham well?"

"Yes indeed. Don always gave me rides in bad weather, even to church at lunchtime! I called him my St. Bernard."

"He was close to Fred?"

"Yes. They were always scheming to create a company to make big money. I avoided those conversations, believe me."

"Do you know where Pellingham is now?"

"Yes. I know he is in D.C. now, but today he is in Albany selling his condo."

Rich and Beamer leaned in and said at the same time, "He's here!"

Maria laughed. "Yes, he is, but I don't know where."

Beamer said, "Do you have his cell number?"

"No. Don dropped the one he had here."

Rich said, "What did he do when he worked here?"

"He was an auditor like Fred and me."

"Do you have a picture of him?" Beamer asked.

Maria smiled, "Somewhere. You almost met him today. I invited him to have lunch with us. He was the stalker you were chasing!"

Maria took Jerry pizza. Rich and Beamer went back to her office. Maria said they could look at her grant files going back three years. She had the original files from grantees, as well as the versions she cleared, as well as Fred's version. Fred had been her supervisor. Looking at files there meant they would not need to visit grantees. Maria set them up in the conference room. It took a while, but they determined Fred had altered some expense categories. His were not as the original files or Maria's files. So it looked like Fred was the New York culprit. What they didn't know was—was there a D.C. partner?

Beamer had an idea: why not check Pellingham's files too? Jerry gave them what they needed. After two hours, they decided Pellingham's files were clean. So they packed up, kissed Maria good-bye, and headed for the airport. Neither thought to ask Maria if she was going to see Pellingham after work.

About the same time Rich and Beamer were boarding the plane to return to D.C., Pellingham was pulling into Maria's parking lot in front of her apartment building. He had rocky road ice cream and flowers for his "angel on earth." He needed to know what she told those guys. It should be easy.

Chapter 15

Margaret and Don, the mailman, settled into a comfortable routine. Don would come on Saturday afternoon at 4:30, bringing wine, dinner, and something sweet. He and Margaret would laugh about the excursions he conducted for the Landmark Therapies. They were able to start operation in mid-October. They had eight clients. He tried to mix things up, sometimes going to a park, sometimes the mall, sometimes movies. Going out to lunch was too complicated with eight people with Alzheimer's. Also bathroom stops were a challenge. Being a guy he couldn't go in with the ladies, but he was pretty good at getting strangers to help him.

The problem with this rosy scenario with Don was Margaret was falling in love for the first time in her life. He was kind. He was respectful. He never put a move on her. He never tried to manipulate her. And, he always was able to anticipate what she needed and deliver.

The first glitch came right after Veterans Day. As usual Don arrived at 4:30 on Saturday afternoon. Margaret had gotten her first reimbursement check from Medicare. *God bless electronic filing. It is so fast.* She had not paid Don yet, so she wrote him a check for $1,000 because she was in an expansive mood. *Not bad for three hours a week for six weeks.* Don, on the other hand seemed stressed and did not even look at the check when she handed it to him. He just put it in his wallet and said thank you.

"Don, what is wrong? You seem down."

"Margaret has something happened to Eloise?"

"No. Why do you ask?"

"My card was returned. The nursing home said she didn't live there."

Oh my God! "Oh, I'm so sorry Don. I forgot to tell you. She's moved in with her brother. She's doing better. A nursing home was a big expense."

"I wish you had told me. I care about Eloise. I am glad she is okay."

Margaret embraced Don. He kissed her on the cheek.

Margaret had purchased new comfortable living room furniture and given Eloise's furniture to the Salvation Army.

After a dinner of short ribs, asparagus, and steak fries, they did the dishes together. All that wine was gone. Margaret made a suggestion, "Let's raid some of Eloise's stash. I think it's a three-bottle night!"

"No way, Margaret, I have to drive home." So Don put on his coat and headed out the door.

Margaret was so frustrated. Here was the sweetest guy on earth, and he did not want to jump her bones. *May be he's gay! That would explain so much—the cooking, the cleaning, and the caring about Eloise. Just my luck.*

She went down to the basement and sat on the bottom step with the third bottle of wine she had opened. She poured a glass.

"Eloise, you won't believe it. I think you're gorgeous mailman is gay. Guess I'll have to go back to Ted, the 'bam bam, thank you ma'am' guy, huh?"

Chapter 16

November was proving to be a low-drama month at Forensic Specialists, LLP. Suzy and Kit were writing the report to submit to PSA. Rich was doing security background checks for the Departments of State and Defense. Frank was scrutinizing tables and charts for the report for PSA. Johnny was helping Electra. Pip had hired Sheila, who seemed to have a positive and calming effect on everyone. Right now she was helping Johnny and Electra. Beamer had completed his GED, and was teaching saxophone at a charter school in D.C. and loving it. Pip was trying to figure out how to sustain her motley crew without dipping into her own money. She thought they were on the verge of something big, but the question was what?

Social activity was interesting. For Frank's birthday, everyone had bought him dancing lessons. He turned out to be a phenomenal dancer—you name it, he could do it. One of the young ladies in the office went with him to each lesson. Each came back with a glowing report. Frank and Kit had entered a contest, the final event for Frank's dance class.

Rich had taken to calling or texting Maria Belaforte every day. She and Rich covered many things—work-related stuff, movies, music, sports, and food. She encouraged him to work out, so he got a membership at a gym down on Fourth Street and was exercising. He didn't drink as much, had tried some wine, and was taking his medication. He hadn't changed his eating habits. Rich and Maria did not talk about being in a wheelchair or being bipolar, although Rich was curious about being a paraplegic and dating. She still hadn't sent him a picture of Don Pellingham, but she had told Rich that, in addition to being so nice, Pellingham was good with computers, a real techie. Marie also told Rich she had told Don about the fraud investigation, told Don to contact Rich, and gave Don Rich's business card. Maria did not have Don's current phone number. Rich thought that was strange.

Johnny liked Sheila, but he had no one to talk to about it.

Electra's husband wanted to sell his business and move to Arizona so he and Electra could have "fun in the sun."

Suzy was still hoping the man of her dreams would show up.

Kit had a new boyfriend—a reporter who could sign in American Sign Language but wasn't deaf.

Pip had not heard from or called Sam.

The Friday before Thanksgiving Rich finished his scheduled interviews early, bought a couple of lattes, and went to Pip's office. Somehow he wanted to work the conversation around to dating by mobility-impaired individuals.

"Hi, there. Are you up for a drink and some company?"

"Sure. How has your week been?"

"Boring. People who apply for government jobs lead dull lives and have dull references, or everybody I talked to this week was a good liar. I guess once that PSA report is done, I'll be the only breadwinner in this family."

She did not say anything for a minute. Then, "Rich, I am an intuitive person. I feel soon we will be knee deep in more work."

"Come on, Pip, there has to be more to it than you intuition, as good as it is."

"Connections and probabilities too. Do you have some time for brainstorming?"

"Sure."

"Question one—why would two post office boxes, associated with suspected irregularities, be canceled within a week. Because…?"

"Four possibilities, Pip. One, the bad guys got a heads up on what was coming down, two, for some other reason, three, there were other fraud opportunities awaiting, or four all three."

"Rich, regardless, you will agree that someone in New York was partnering with someone in PSA?"

"It looks that way."

"Let's set aside your *other reason* for a minute, Rich, and look at your heads-up theory, which suggests someone above Margaret Sabat and Donna Dawson found out from Swanson or someone in his office. This person warned one or both of them. The person between Dawson and Sabat and Swanson is Ted Morton. And?"

"Morton is sleeping with Sabat, not Dawson, so he would warn or try to protect Sabat."

Pip leaned back. "Yes, but if Dawson's work is reviewed by Sabat, they could be collaborating. Morton told Sabat. Sabat then told Dawson. And less we forget, Sabat and/or Dawson told the New York partner."

"We do not know enough about the relationship between Sabat and Dawson, Pip."

"We know more than you think.

"Think about this, Rich. Dawson now has an office on the sixth floor, according to Johnny. We do not know what she is doing up there. Also, according to Johnny, Sabat is spending as much time in Dawson's division office as she is spending in her own office. If Sabat and Dawson were collaborators, would Johnny have seen what he saw?"

"Who knows, Pip? Sabat could be scrubbing files to protect Dawson and/or herself. What about Morton? Couldn't he also be involved in the fraud itself?"

"I doubt it, Rich. He is a retired admiral and a political appointee. It would seem to me he would be motivated to keep his record clean. Remember what he said to you. 'I run a tight ship. If you find anything, let me know, and I'll fix it.' You're right we have no real data, but I do not think Morton is in on the fraud. He may have warned Sabat, but that is about it."

"Now Pip, let's return to my other reason scenario. It could be a factor here too. When Beamer and I went to Albany, we found out Fred Firebrand had recently retired, and his best buddy, Don Pellingham, quit at the same time. We don't know when, but it was around the time the post office boxes were canceled. If Fred was Sabat's partner, and she didn't know how to find a new one without exposing herself, she, too, would have canceled her post office box.

"Pip, the someone-warned-Sabat scenario and the other-reason scenario could work together. They do not conflict. Neither does my final probable scenario—another fraud opportunity.

"I'm going out on limb here with regard to Sabat's motivation. I think her motivation at the beginning and now was to maintain a lifestyle above her means. Johnny would give me a price tag on her daily outfits. Everyone was over five hundred dollars. Assuming she has a family, car payments, college tuition, and a mortgage, how can she afford to spend what she does on clothes? It would be fantastic if we could get access to her financial records. The only thing we know about anybody's finances is that Donna Dawson bought a new car and that is because Johnny found the MSRP sheet in her trash can.

"Pip, if Margaret has shut down the Get Ahead caper, she has found or will need to find another illegal cash cow. We need to find a way to put a tail on her and get access to her financial records."

"Rich, my second question has to do with Swanson. What is his motivation in this whole thing? I know through an unimpeachable source he's trying to expand his domain. What he wants to do will require cooperation from the White House and action by Congress. If he has any messes that hit the public, his efforts to expand will be doomed. I think that's why he hired us, a small, unknown firm, to do his detective work and keep the lid on things. Based on what we find or don't find, he can slow things down so they do not derail his empire expansion."

"Pip, why in hell would the public have an interest in fraud in the Get Ahead program in New York?"

"If the perpetrator was the sister of the president's principal medical adviser, they would, Rich."

Rich sat back in his chair, his eyes wide. "Wow!"

Pip leaned forward, "What do you think Swanson will do when he gets the report on Get Ahead grants?"

"Pip, the report suggests shenanigans are going on in southwestern states as well as in New York. So the problem is bigger than he thought, and he can't just sweep it under the rug, fine somebody quietly, or fire her."

"Rich, we have no information linking Sabat in any way to the southwestern states. We haven't talked to anybody who handles the southwestern states in PSA. Letting us do that— interview people in the division responsible for southwestern states—would appeal to Swanson because it would slow things down and keep them from going public for while."

"Yeah, Pip, that's probably true. That would be a logical next move for him."

"I can see it now, Rich. He will suggest to me we do just that—interview people in the division responsible for the Get Ahead grants in the southwestern states. And with the holidays coming on, he will tell me we can wait until January.

"Rich, my last question has to do with Sabat. How will she divert attention from herself? She knows something is going on, and the blame has to be placed somewhere other than on her. She would not be inclined to make her boyfriend the fall guy. She would be inclined to make Dawson the fall girl. Now how will she do that? While she's attempting to blaze a trail to Dawson's ass, what if Dawson finds out?"

"Pip, Sabat is first and foremost a bureaucrat. She understands the checks and balances in the software with which she works. Because she is a manager, she can tell IT staff she needs access to passwords in order to investigate fraud. She could put anything on Dawson's computer to make her look like the guilty party. I bet there is nothing to stop her. She is clever enough to keep Dawson from finding that out. What we need is a Frank-style analysis. We need to get a copy of Dawson's hard drive BEFORE she went to work on Morton's floor and a copy of her hard drive now. Any changes on Dawson's hard drive were likely put there by Sabat."

"And," Rich leaned forward, "If Dawson finds out what Sabat has been up to, she is going to report it. The unknown is will Dawson tell Sabat before she reports it? If Dawson is stupid enough to tell Sabat before Dawson reports it, Sabat will try to stop her. This could become more than a simple fraud case in a very short time."

"I agree, Rich. That's why I wanted to brainstorm. The outcome I came to when I thought about this by myself scared me."

"Look, Pip, I think you should have another conversation with your unimpeachable source and get him to invest some resources so this thing ends before anybody gets hurt. Don't worry about Swanson. He's toast no matter how this ends."

"There's one more piece to this puzzle—Don Pellingham, the friend of Fred Firebrand. Remember he quit the same time Firebrand retired. One of the people I interviewed in New York told me Pellingham had moved to D.C. I'll have Frank see if he can find something out on the Web, okay Mama?"

"Okay. If Frank comes up with something, we will add it to the mix, but we just don't want to spend too much time on extraneous paths given everything else we have to do.

"This has been very helpful, Rich. You have a very good mind. Why did you come in here? I know it wasn't to talk about this case." Pip smiled.

Rich looked around the room—the night lights out the large windows, the degrees, wall plaques and awards, the books in the bookcase, the little cart next to Pip, her lifeline. *What's this little lady who pushes a cart and has never been married know about sex?* "Why nothing old lady. Can't a guy just come in and hang out with you? You have lived in D.C. too long, not every encounter has to have an agenda!"

As he left Pip's office, Johnny approached him and asked if he wanted to go for a drink at the Dive.

"Well, I'll be—why not?"

"Is that a yes?"

Rich laughed. "Yes, sir."

They huddled in a booth, didn't use their personal spotlights, with the pitcher beer between them.

"Rich, I need to talk to you about something personal."

"If someone's messing with you, Johnny, I'll punch their lights out! Tell me who?"

"No, nothing like that. I need some advice about a girl."

Rich sprayed beer all over the table. He wiped it up with napkins. "You got a girlfriend?"

"No. I have a friend who is a girl."

This guy is no lightweight. I don't know if I would be capable of that distinction. "So what's the problem?"

"I would like the friend who is a girl to be my girlfriend, but I do not know how to talk to her."

"I see." *Now what genius!* "What do you do with this girl now?"

"We work together and run together."

Once again Rich sprayed beer all over the table and wiped it with napkins. Composing himself, he asked, "It's somebody at work?"

"Yep."

"Well, as a general rule it's not good to date somebody you work with."

"Why's that?"

"Because if you were to ever to break up, you know, get mad at each other, it would be hard to see each other after that every day."

"But if you didn't get mad at each other, it would be fun to come to work every day."

Shit now what. "Who is it, Johnny?"

"You promise you won't tell her?"

"I promise."

"Sheila."

Rich ordered a shot and a Diet Coke for Johnny. "Well, Bud," Please, help me here God. "Does Sheila like to hang out with you? We know she likes to run with you. She has to work with you. Does she eat lunch with you? Does she do favors for you? Does she ask your opinion?"

"Rich, that is too many questions at one time."

So they took the questions one at a time. The answer to each one was yes.

"The lady likes you, Johnny. The next step is to ask her out on a date. You could ask her what movie she likes and then suggest you both go to it together."

"I don't drive yet."

"Sheila can drive. When you get your license, you can drive. It's no big deal."

Rich proceeded to have three more shots.

Johnny said, " How's your love life, Rich?"

"Funny you should ask. I am in love with someone who cannot walk."

"It cannot be Pip, right? She can walk, and she is too old."

"You got that one right."

"Where is your girlfriend?"

"New York."

"That makes it a little bit hard to date, doesn't it?"

"Yeah, but that's not the only problem."

Rich ordered another shot. He was slurring his words.

"What's the other problem, Rich?"

"Ah, I don't think she can fuck—you know make love. You know what that is, right?"

"Yeah, I know what it is. Have you ever asked her if she can do it?"

"Well, no."

"Then you should. If she says she can't and it's important to you, then you need to find another girlfriend."

The bartender came over and told Johnny the car service was there to pick him up.

Johnny said the Rich, "My dad's car service is here. I'll take you home first, and then I'll go home. You are too drunk to drive, Rich."

Rich got up, patted his new best buddy on the shoulder, and smiled. They walked out together, arms around each other's shoulders.

Chapter 17

Margaret learned through the grapevine that Donna was not coming back to Margaret's division. Donna, much to Margaret's surprise, had left Ted's suite and was working for Swanson as his special assistant. Margaret stewed over this set of facts and then decided to go talk to Ted. Perhaps her celibacy policy had backfired.

She had no idea how she was going to play it when she walked into his office. After working out in the gym on the second floor of the PSA building, Margaret showered and dressed in a white sweater, chocolate skirt, and chocolate boots. She wanted to get to Ted's office before Donna got to work. At 8:30 A.M. she breezed passed Ted's secretary and marched into his office. Ted looked up from his newspaper. A steaming cup of coffee was by his right hand. He took a sip. She could not read his state of mind, and he didn't say anything.

"Hi, Ted. I thought it would be good if we had a little chat about my detective work and about if you've learned anything more about Swanson's plans associated with his suspicions about fraud."

Matter-of-factly Ted said, "Why don't I start? Swanson is waiting for a report from a contractor. He gave the contractor three years' worth of files from all states. He assumes fraud activities will surface elsewhere. If so, he will have the contractor interview additional people. He has not given me any more information about your division.

"With no warning Swanson offered Donna Dawson a position in his office as a special assistant, and she has accepted.

"What detective work were you referring to, Maggie?"

The old boy is playing hardball.

"You may recall I suspected Donna Dawson was involved in fraud associated with New York Get Ahead grants. It has been going on for three years. If we can get access to local financial records before they were submitted to the state, we will be able to identify those that were altered at the state level and then submitted here or submitted unaltered by the state and altered by Dawson."

"There are lots of reasons why records are altered and some are legitimate. I have read your draft manual, believe it or not, and so unless you've identified a pattern of irregularities, you may have nothing with which to charge Dawson or anyone else."

"I have identified a pattern of irregularities. Grantees in New York bought three to four times as many supplies as grantees of comparable size in other states in Region II."

"Why don't we talk to Dawson about this now, Margaret?"

"Since she is now working for Swanson, I'd rather have a chance to look at some local financial records first."

"Why Ms. Sabat? Because you think Dawson may be only negligent or God forbid innocent? You said it yourself Maggie, it may just be a case of within-state fraud, with sloppy auditing at our end. Both Dawson and you, and possibly me, may be at fault. When somebody gives you a grant file to review do you ever look at expenditures for specific budget categories, or compare expenditures from one quarter to the next or from one year to the next or one grantee to another? I know I don't because I assume you do it."

"Ted, auditors at Dawson's level are supposed to bring discrepancies like those to my attention so I can alert you. She has never done that."

"Why do you think she failed to do that, Margaret?"

"Because she's engaged in fraud, Ted."

"Or maybe she reconciled things with the state auditor according to your damn procedural manuals!"

Ted got out of his chair and walked toward Margaret. A light bulb could have been lit with the electricity bouncing between them. He stopped when he was about two feet from her. "You know what I think? You have nothing on Dawson. You are still fishing. Until you have something specific, concrete, and tangible I am not buying it. Not for one minute. And you are right. Things have changed. She works for Swanson." He put his hands on his hips.

Margaret went to his couch and sat down, put her head in her hands, and started crying. With tear-stained cheeks, she looked up at him and said, "You are such a jerk. I am trying so hard to give you what you want, Ted. To do what's right and make this whole thing go away. I thought I had to do it on my own, not to abuse our friendship, to make you happy, to make you proud. And then you treat me like you did just now. What's the point?"

Ted, still cold as ice, walked over to her and put his hand on her shoulder, and said, "Maggie, we need to finish this conversation later. I have a meeting with Donna Dawson in ten minutes, and I don't think it would be good for her to see you in here, since you're upset. We'll talk later." Margaret dried her eyes and got up and walked out without saying anything.

Back in her office Margaret shut the door after putting out the Do not disturb sign. She sat at her desk and pulled out a legal pad and started a new to-do list. The first item was something specific, concrete, tangible—do Christmas shopping for the girls, find out the name of Swanson's contractor, google those interns, find out what Dawson is working on, get a portable hard drive and copy Dawson's files, have IT close down Dawson's division computer, order a copy of the book *Hacking for Dummies*. She put the list in her purse.

Margaret remained distressed all day. At six o'clock she decided to go to the gym again to get rid of some of the tension. She seldom went in the evening. Donna Dawson went every evening. Dawson was on a treadmill. The one next to her was empty. Margaret got on and said, "Donna, congratulations on your new job. When does it become official?"

"Not until the first of the year. I'll be back in the division tomorrow and start working on cleaning up my files. I had planned to tell you myself, but Ted was very demanding, and Swanson is as demanding, I have not had a free minute. I saw you leave Ted's office this morning. I came down to see you later, but you had your Do not disturb sign out so I didn't knock.

"My transfer upstairs to Ted's office was unexpected and quick. The opportunity to work for Swanson also came quickly. You and I never had a chance to go over my workload and talk about how it should be redistributed in my absence. I suspect the files have just sat there. I can use from now until January one getting everything caught up. Whenever you want to talk about my files, me orienting somebody who'll get them, and anything else, just let me know."

"Okay, maybe we can talk next week. Once again, congratulations."

"Thank you. I bet you never expected this outcome did you, Margaret?"

"Nothing surprises me, Donna."

By the time Donna left, Margaret was feeling sorry for herself. *I have no understanding or sympathy from Ted, the guy I like is gay or I think he is, and this fraud thing is becoming bigger, not smaller. Ted would sell me down the river in a minute. I'll give him something specific, concrete, and tangible. I'll charge Christmas presents for my kids on the office credit card with Donna Dawson's authorization identification number. That should send him over the edge, and get him back on my side. It would also fix Miss High and Mighty Dawson.* Margaret went to her car in the garage. Ted was standing next to her car.

"I know we need to finish our conversation. You want to get a bite to eat at the Holiday Inn?" Ted's question was put to Margaret like he was asking her about what kind gasoline she used—no affect whatsoever.

"Whatever you want, sir!"

"Margaret, we must talk our way through this as adults. No cheap theatrics. You must develop an appreciation of the consequences of what could happen if we don't solve this in a responsible way. We could both lose our jobs."

Margaret just looked at Ted. She followed him to his car, and they drove together to the Holiday Inn.

At the dinner table Margaret sat on one side of the table and Ted sat across from her. He had a brief lapse and thought, *No hand activity under the table tonight. It's for the best.*

They ordered salmon and arugula salad, and a bottle of

Smoking Dove chardonnay.

"Why do you think Donna Dawson is engaged in fraud?"

"She is living beyond her means. She has a new car. She is taking her mother on a cruise."

"You told me that already. She's single and a senior manager. She can afford both."

"The files say something is going on. If she's innocent, as well as smart and competent, which is what you think because you probably helped her get the job with Swanson, why didn't she spot the irregularities?"

"Because you're damn jobs are mind numbing."

Margaret pushed her chair back with every intention of leaving. She would not tolerate foul language.

"You are not going anywhere."

Margaret pushed her chair back to the table.

"Good girl, Maggie. Now I am going to ask you a question, and I want a truthful answer. The only person who looks guilty to me is you. You bitched and moaned about getting those two interns, you told me you didn't want them looking at New York grants, and you too quickly said Donna was the culprit. Okay, here's the question. Did you screw up those Get Ahead files? Are you the one behind the fraud?"

"If you're so sure I did it, why do I need to tell you anything? If you're interested in the truth, the actual truth, then I'm willing to sit here and continue the conversation."

"For God's sake, Maggie, if you know the truth, tell me!"

"I'm not convinced you want to hear it. And if I tell you, I suspect there's nothing you can do about it."

"This conversation is not going anywhere. It's not your responsibility to decide what should be done with the truth—

just to provide the truth. Tell me, God dammit!"

She pushed her chair back, got up, and walked out of the restaurant. Ted quickly followed her. He caught up with her and grabbed her arm and took her to his car. He threw her into the passenger seat in the front. They drove back to the PSA garage. He stopped by her car. He dragged her out of his car. Found the keys for her car in her purse, open the driver side door, and forced her in behind the steering wheel.

"Maggie, this whole thing has gone too far and escalated because of your behavior and lack of judgment. I want you to think about the things I have said today and tonight. It is my hope that tomorrow you will tell me what you know. No more games or this relationship, which is hanging by a thread right now, is fucking over!"

Margaret looked at Ted. She then slammed the door, started her engine, backed out of the parking space, and peeled out of the garage.

Ted got in his Mercedes and put his head on the steering wheel. His shirt underneath his suit coat and topcoat was soaked with sweat. *Unless she comes and tells me the truth tomorrow, I'm going to talk to Dawson, and then I'm going to fry Margaret's ass. She is not going to take me down with her. I'm going to blow this thing wide open and take credit for it.*

For the first time in Margaret's adult life she was scared. She could not have Ted as an enemy. She would give him Fred Firebrand. That would buy her some time to think up a long-term strategy to get out of this mess. She called him on his cell phone and said, "Don't say a word just listen. Meet me at the Crown Plaza in Bethesda tonight. I will leave you a note at the registration desk." She hung up.

Ted was still sitting in the garage. *I shouldn't go, but I need to know what she knows. I can control the situation. Bethesda is so far, but I have no choice. I have to go. Maybe then I will be able to bring this thing to an end.*

When Ted knocked on the door of room 1515, Margaret opened it in a gold bra and thong. She took his hand and drew him in. She sat him on the bed and undressed him. Neither of them spoke. Her hands and lips did most of the work. At the moment of climax she said, "The person engaged in fraud in New York is a man by the name of Fred Firebrand." She got up got dressed and left without saying another word.

At that moment, Ted knew Margaret was back in control.

His cell phone rang, and he answered. His son said, "Dad, where the hell are you? We keep missing each other. I need to know whether you have made any progress in getting me some help to get into George Townsend University. Dad, are you there?"

Margaret has the upper hand. "Tommy, I'll be home in an hour. And yes, I am making progress. By the time the Christmas holidays are over you will be in. You have my word on that. You go to bed now."

Chapter 18

Pip hated snow. It impacted her independence. She could not go out alone. It would be great if it held off till Thanksgiving because then she would not have a need to go anywhere or do anything for four days. Nonetheless, the sky looked threatening and even the air in the office felt heavy.

Rich and Beamer had done well in Albany. Their success had an unanticipated effect. Swanson was about to terminate their contract. He said he would handle things from now on. He would pay for a report on the southwestern grantees that seemed to fund too many field trips. Kit and Suzy were working on that.

With Thanksgiving coming and then the Christmas holiday, there was no point in mining for new business. She had transferred funds from one of her personal accounts to cover operating expenses through January. Electra would see what she had done and be relieved.

She decided to walk around and find out what everyone was doing for Thanksgiving. She needed the exercise. Her first stop was the reception area. Electra was telling Johnny and Sheila a story. It was not X-rated.

"Looks like it might snow, huh? Electra, what are you and Joe doing for Thanksgiving?"

"I am cooking. We have invited my schoolteacher friend, Max, to join us." Electra smiled.

Pip sat down in a chair. "That's nice. How about you, Johnny?"

"My mom invited Sheila, and she is coming!"

"Awesome. I just wanted to let you know that you can have Friday off too."

"Great. Sheila has agreed to take me for some driving practice in the parking lot of the high school near my house. What are you going to do, Pip?"

Pip got up. "I don't know yet."

Electra said, "You are welcome to join Joe, Max, and me."

"Thank you, but I don't think my nerves could take the excitement."

Johnny said, "What are you going to do Electra?"

"That is to be determined. I haven't decided yet."

"I don't understand."

"Well, I am fixing a big bird. After I stuff Joe and Max with food, they will be too full for any fun, so I am trying to decide what to do with them to get them up and moving...something fun, something exciting, like a threesome—"

Pip cut her off, "Enough, Electra."

Electra laughed.

Sheila couldn't believe what Electra tried to say. *She couldn't be talking about sex! She is too old, big, and blind.*

Pip asked Sheila and Johnny to get her a snack from the bar on the first floor. When they left she said, "Electra, you are incorrigible. I can't believe what you planned to say to those little innocents!"

"Wait a minute sister. I was going to say poker!"

"Right!"

"*Strip* poker. You know you need a man in your life. Join

e-Harmony or something! On another matter, thanks for filling the coffers. My offer still stands for Thanksgiving. I'm going home now. See you tomorrow."

"Okay. See you tomorrow."

Pip walked to the kitchen. Rich and Beamer were eating leftover Chinese.

"Well look who's here. The CEO. Have a seat, Doc," Rich said.

"I was thinking of cooking. You guys want to come over to my place for Thanksgiving?"

"Funny you should ask. I am going out of town." Rich looked at his watch. "In fact, I would like to leave now!"

"Uh, okay. Where are you going?"

"I'll tell you when I get back, if things go well." Rich ran out of the kitchen.

"Beamer what is he talking about? Why the mystery?"

"It's complicated. The answer to your initial question—I am going to my Aunt Lily's. You want to come?"

"Thanks, but no. I have a standing invitation to go to my neighbor's, so I'm covered."

Beamer said, "Guess where Frank is going? The Poconos with Kit! She said they could practice their dance routines because her brother has a powerful sound system. You know Kit needs vibration for her spectacular moves."

"That's great. Can we return to your buddy, Rich? What's complicated? What's in New York?"

"First, Rich is not my buddy. I endure him. Sometimes I admire the SOB. But he stresses me out, even when he acts like a normal human being. He is going to Albany to see a chick—a chick we met in the state auditing department."

"Well, why are you so disturbed by that?"

"In the past her mom dated Fred Firebrand."

"How recently?"

"Three years ago."

"Um, that is interesting. That's when Fred must have met his D.C. partner. May be it was more than a business partnership. But back to Rich—why are you concerned?"

"Because the chick is sweet, innocent, and beautiful, and Rich is a mess."

"It's not our choice, Beamer."

"You don't understand. She is really a good person. She goes to church EVERYDAY! Pip, she is a paraplegic."

Beamer got up and left the kitchen.

Pip sat back in her chair.

Wow, that was unexpected. I bet that is why Rich came to see me the other day—for advice. I talk too much. I need to listen more, listen more with my heart. Oh, Rich, take care, dear boy.

Suzy came into the kitchen. "I was looking for you. I am taking you with me to my parents' for Thanksgiving. I won't take a no."

"Sweetie, I need some time to myself. Caroline, on the other side of your condo, will feed me."

"Aunt Pip!"

"Relax Suzy, I'll be fine. I need to do some thinking. What you and Kit are working on is the end and last of the PSA contract."

"What! I thought we would get to do interviews after we finish the report."

"Swanson wants to handle things internally after he gets your report."

"I don't understand. He does not know who is involved or who to trust."

"You are right, but we cannot force him to keep us under contract."

"Too bad we can't find a whistle-blower."

"Interesting thought. That's why I want some time to think about what to do next. I have some contacts who may help us stay involved.

"I think it would be great if we could continue to work as a team on this. This is the first case on which we all worked together."

"When are you driving home for Thanksgiving?"

"Thanksgiving morning."

"Why don't we have breakfast before you leave? You know how I love your egg and cheese sandwiches. I'll supply the ingredients, and you can do the cooking."

"It's a deal."

Suzy left for the day. Pip went back to her office and found her snack—a tuna sandwich on rye, chips, a Diet Pepsi, and a chocolate chip cookie—her standing order.

Pip's message light was blinking on her private line, which only rang in her office.

The message was from Sam. He said, "A heads up—Edith is going to call and invite you for Thanksgiving." Pip hung up the phone

Great.

The phone rang. "Hi, Pip, this is Sheila. Johnny and I are leaving. An Edith Netherfield is on line one. No one else is here. Will you be all right? Beamer went somewhere to rehearse with his band."

"I'm fine. Thanks for taking the call." *Now for the sparring match.* Pip pushed line one.

"Hi, Edith, what a surprise."

"Pamela, Pamela. How are you?"

Which means how is the poor little cripple girl who is old and hopefully fat.

"It's been too, too long. Can you come for Thanksgiving?"

"Well how nice. You know I would love to, but I have an invitation I have accepted."

"Now, Pamela, I am going to Africa on Friday! You must come. You can wear comfy clothes and bring your toothbrush in case the weather is bad, and you need to stay over and keep Sam company. And Bart is going to try and come. And it means so much to me."

Which means I am doing all of this for Bart, so cooperate you bitch.

"Wouldn't it be simpler just to feed your boys and pack for your trip?"

"Oh, Pamela, that is so typical of you, always worrying about everyone else. I'm all packed. The turkey is stuffed and ready, and I've fixed everything else. If I only have Sam and Bart, all they will do is watch football. At least with you with us, they won't dare turn on the TV or at least no watching TV all day long."

Which means you and I know you have nothing better to do, so just say yes so I can get off the phone.

"Okay, you are so persuasive. But then again, you always have been, haven't you? One caveat, if we have a blizzard, I am staying home!"

"No you are not. Sam will pick you up in one of those big,

black SUVs the FBI has tons of. I'll make sure of it. Bye now, dear. I am so looking forward to laying eyes on you. Our Sam will get back to you with the pick up time." Edith hung up.

I can just seeing her checking call Pamela off her to-do list. Maybe I'm being unfair. Perhaps she is not a bitch now, and I'm just jealous. She got what I wanted. It could be as basic as that. Well let the games begin—again.

Pip made several phone calls, sent an e-mail to everyone letting them know they had Wednesday and Friday off, and then grabbed her cart and began the trek to Pentagon City for some shopping.

Chapter 19

Margaret sat sipping her morning coffee, watching the snow out the kitchen window falling steady and thick. The pies were in the oven, to be followed by her turkey. She had a twinge of guilt. Her family thought she could make only sandwiches, but nothing else.

She and the girls had gone out to dinner the night before. They would spend today, Thanksgiving, with Jeremy, Angela, and their toddlers. According to the girls, the only cooking Angela had mastered was what went into a microwave. Jeremy was a great cook. He had become one because Margaret chose not to cook.

Today's the day. I am going to find out whether Don is gay, and if he isn't, boy is he in for a treat!

Margaret basted her turkey some more and checked the pies. Don would not be there until 4:30, so after putting the turkey in the oven, she decided to determine her financial status. Last night she had given each of her daughters a $500 check to do their Christmas shopping. That would have been okay if she had not also given Don $1,000 and the guy who redid the dining room $5,000—both in cash. She might need to transfer funds from the Landmark Therapies account, although she was trying to reserve that money to pay tuition bills in January.

She had expanded what Landmark Therapies "offered" to include physical and occupational therapy, as well as outings.

She did this when Don said he was willing to drive on a weekday, as well as Saturday. All he did was outings, but she billed the second day as therapies for which she got a higher fee. Don did not know this.

She loved the remodeled dining room. It was now her office. Painted white, it had one wall with floor-to-ceiling cabinets and bookcases. The accents were chocolate and gold. The furniture, also white, was simple, sturdy, and modern. She financed much of it by selling everything in the old dining room on eBay. She had all the necessary technology to run an office. Don had helped her set everything up. He even suggested a strategy for remembering and changing passwords.

He was a man of many talents, but a man of mystery too. After all these months, she did not know where he was from, where he lived, or with whom he lived. He always called her. No telephone number showed on her phone. He always wore sneakers, jeans, and a sweater. He had a nondescript watch, but a beautiful black leather jacket.

Margaret poured another cup of coffee and went to her desk. She opened the blinds so she could keep an eye on the snow. It was falling more heavily now. *I think I'll take a bubble bath, when I finished here.*

Her cell phone rang. Caller ID said it was Ted. Margaret was no longer interested in Ted, but she was curious. And if Don were gay, Ted would do until someone else taller came along. In fact, she had been flirting with a very handsome security guard at work—George Jones. George Jones would be less trouble than Ted. She picked up the cell.

"Hi, Ted. Where are you?"

"Hi, Maggie. I miss you. I am skiing with my son. We are

in West Virginia. The holidays are always hard for him, so we go away.

"You have been scarce lately. Swanson shut down the fraud contractor. Whatever they are finishing up has nothing to do with your division."

"That's good news. What's he going to do about Firebrand?"

"I haven't told him yet."

"What's he going to do about Dawson?"

"Nothing. He likes her and can't wait for her to work full time after she finishes working for you."

"So, that means he thinks I am linked to the fraud?"

"I don't know. He seems preoccupied with Defense and asks me about my contacts—Medicaid and Medicare too."

"Why?"

"I have no idea. He is starting a working group on entitlements. Why don't you volunteer for it and get on his good side."

"So, you are assuming I am on his bad side."

"I said I don't know."

"I'll think about it. Why did you call?"

"What do you have on?"

Margaret hung up the phone. *Phone sex and foul language are not in my repertoire.*

She went back to her accounts. After about twenty minutes she had become concerned. She had made three payments to Dew Point Graphics, totaling $427 since November 15. Who were they? What did she buy? She had no recall on Dew Point Graphics.

Chapter 20

In Alexandria in a snowstorm that just kept snowing, Sam stopped in front of Pip's building, and put up his red light and put on his flashers. Pip buzzed him in and he went to her floor.

He rang her bell. It took awhile, but she opened the door. Sam fell back in shock. Pip had had a makeover. She had on a tight-fitting, pink, leather jacket, pink turtleneck, pink scarf and gloves, fitted black slacks, and black boots. She was now a blond.

"Look at you! You are gorgeous." He leaned over her cart and kissed her.

"I took time and lots of work, but I like it. Let's go, Sam, before it gets any worse out there."

"Pink, you look so good, darlin'." He picked up her suitcase, and they headed for the elevator."

The ride to McLean took forever. The conversation took a few turns.

Pip said, "How is this SUV in snow?"

"Relax, cupcake, it will get us there. You do look gorgeous. How's the contract with Swanson?"

"About to end. He is about to pull everything back in-house."

"I'm not surprised. He wants to postpone problems until he has his legislation drafted. He is already talking to David Windson on how to sell his power grab of Defense and

Medicare auditing to the Congress."

"How do you know?"

"I have my ways of finding out, when the information is important to someone I care about."

"Sam, why do you bring everything back to our relationship? It hurts because to you it's just a line."

"That's not true. I love you. I always have and always will."

"So your expression of love includes me having Thanksgiving with you, your wife, and son?"

"Yes, if that is the only way I can spend time with you today."

"Do you have any idea how stressful it will be for me?"

"Only if you let it. Edith won't eat you alive. How'd your conversation go?"

"Fine."

"See. You have nothing to worry about."

"Why did you marry Edith?

"Whoa! I didn't expect that one." After a pause, "But since you asked, Edith was available, and you were not."

"What's that suppose to mean?"

"You were too busy asserting your independence and striving for success to worry about me or anyone else."

"That's not true."

"Oh yes it is, darlin'. Every time I would see you or talk to you, the conversation quickly turned to what you were doing or planned to do. Not much of turn on. Nothing about us. Nothing about how you felt about me."

"Oh, Sam, that is so not true. I loved you so much. I was afraid. I feared you needed more than a poster child. I could not be an equal partner in a physical sense. I thought you would become disappointed and stay with me out of pity. I couldn't face that. I was proud, and I had to be strong."

"How was I to know that?"

They didn't talk anymore.

Edith met them at the garage door to the kitchen. "Pamela Planter you look like a bowl of sorbet from Neiman Marcus. How are you, dear?"

"It's good to see you, Edith. I can't wait to hear about your trip to Africa." *A bowl of sorbet? Suck it up and smile. Edith of course is still tall, blond, and elegant. Probably six million-ply cashmere and pearls straight from China. How can I compete with that?*

Once everyone was in the kitchen Sam said, "How about if I open some cab?"

"I did already, Sam. It's breathing in the great room, and the fire is just right."

Sam took Pip's arm an escorted her into the great room. Edith followed with shrimp and crab dip, and crackers, dragging Pip's cart behind her.

"Edith, have you heard from your son?"

"Our son is not coming. He is in New Mexico—a kidnapping case."

Pip then said, "Oh that's too bad. The last time I saw him was at his graduation party."

"I am so sorry it's been that long. Life just interfered didn't it? To better efforts from now on!" Edith offered a toast.

"I can't believe you run a detective agency, Pamela. Sam told me. Have you caught any bad guys?"

"We are trying, although our current person of interest is a woman."

A cell phone rang. Edith reached under her sweater. "Happy

Thanksgiving, Bob. Why the call? Oh, I see. Two hours? Okay, I'll be at the end of the driveway."

"You won't believe it. I am leaving in two hours for New York by train. Bob's concerned about the weather."

"Do I need to drive you somewhere, Edith?"

"No, just clear a path to the curb. They are picking everyone up in some kind of Hummer-like vehicle. Enjoy the wine kids, I must go change clothes and finish packing. Everything will be ready to eat around six."

"I'll drive you to the street. It's not that safe in the driveway. Besides why should we freeze our butts off waiting for the Department of State cavalry to show up? Is there anything I can do for you?"

"Two things. Bring my bags down when I finish packing and pray the snowstorm heads out to sea before it hits New York!"

"Yes ma'am."

After Edith was occupied and out of earshot Sam said, "God works in mysterious ways doesn't he, darlin'?" He raised his glass, kissed Pip on the cheek, popped a cracker in his mouth, leaned back on the bronze-colored, leather sofa, and looked into the fire. "Cupcake and ole Sam get to play house. It's been a long time."

Chapter 21

Margaret had fixed a bubble bath in Eloise's big, claw-footed tub. She had a glass of champagne on the stool next to her. She was imagining what would happen over the next twenty-four hours because of the storm. She heard banging at the kitchen door.

It can't be Don. He never comes early. I am not moving. The banging persisted. Margaret got out of the tub, put on her robe, and went downstairs ready to commit murder. She looked out the kitchen door bars. There stood Don covered with snow and a huge dolly with a big box on it. She unlocked and opened the door.

"Hi there, Margaret. I know I am early. I brought you a surprise—a new dishwasher. I wanted to hook it up before we ate. You go back to whatever you were doing. Boy, it smells good in here. I also brought some wood to build a fire and to keep you warm."

"Ah, sure. Thanks. This is a surprise." *I have myself a Boy Scout, probably a gay Boy Scout.*

Margaret did as Don suggested. She went back to her bubble bath and drank the whole bottle of champagne. *A mailman can't afford a dishwasher. A mailman would never even charge a dishwasher on his credit card for a chick who had not yet put out. Unless...*

When Margaret returned to the kitchen, Don wasn't there, but the new dishwasher was installed. He came through the kitchen door with wood in his arms. He smiled, "You look good enough to eat."

Maybe, just maybe, I can only hope it is true.

"Chocolate velour is very flattering on you."

"Thank you, Don. You look good enough to eat, too."

Don winked. He walked passed Margaret, carrying the wood to the fireplace in the living room.

Margaret followed him in with a bottle of wine and two glasses. She went back to the kitchen for the cheese and crackers. Don had a fire going. Margaret put on some soothing background music. She went over to Don, unzipped his jacket, and took it and his ski cap off. He smiled. She threw both in the office on a chair and came back into the living room, took Don's hand and led him to the soft, gold microfiber couch. He sat and looked at the fire. "It's a good one."

Margaret sat next to him, opened the wine, and poured two glasses. "It is indeed."

Don fixed a cracker and handed it to Margaret. He fixed another and put the whole thing in his mouth. "I got to tell you Margaret, I am starving. I can't wait to try your tuna casserole."

Margaret laughed. "Yeah, I made it with Miracle Whip. I have hot dog rolls with garlic butter for the starch."

"How'd you know I loved hot dog rolls with garlic butter?"

"You said so in your sleep."

Don filled their wineglasses. "It doesn't get much better than this." Don turned toward Margaret to hand her, her glass, she was leaning back in the corner of the sofa, propped on two red accent pillows, her velour V-neck covering very little. She reached for her glass. Don put it on the coffee table, leaned over, and kissed the V in Margaret's top.

Thank you, God.

Don straightened up. "Ma'am I would very much like to make love, but later, after we eat."

Talk about control! What an unromantic twit!

"Sure, Don. It is so much fun to make love on a full stomach of tuna casserole!" She sat up and took a gulp of wine.

What happened next she could not have anticipated. He threw her over his shoulder and went up the stairs. He went to the first bed he saw. He sat her up, stripped off her clothes, and threw her naked on the bed. "Don't move."

Margaret was terrified and thrilled. She did not move a muscle. She heard him go downstairs. He was gone for about twenty minutes. She knew he had not left because she could hear activity in the kitchen.

He came back in the bedroom, covered her eyes with a towel, and bound her arms and legs spread-eagled. He proceeded to put a plate of mash potatoes and gravy on her chest, a plate of string beans and almonds on her navel, and a plate of turkey and gravy on her private parts. He proceeded to eat, using a knife and fork. He did not say a word. Neither did Margaret, but she had never been aroused before from vibrations coming from plates. When he finished, aiming a can of whip cream with special care, he said, "Now for dessert!" Later, he carried her to the bathtub, once again full of bubble bath and sat her in the tub. Finally, he said, "I am very good at solving conflicts. You got what you wanted, and I got what I wanted." Margaret smiled and fell asleep. Don opened a second bottle of wine, sat on the floor, and leaned against the tub. He kept looking at Margaret to make sure her head was above water. After he finished his wine, he stripped, and got in the tub. When he entered her, Margaret opened her eyes wide and said, "It doesn't get any better than this." She leaned up and kissed him. Don started humming *Bolero*.

When Margaret awoke in bed in the middle of the night, Don was right next to her, but she was cold. The power was off. She got up and found more blankets, and then got back in bed with her awesome mailman.

Chapter 22

Edith went off in the Hummer. Sam fixed plates full of five-star food for the two of them. They sat in the dining room at a table that could seat sixteen. Sam lit candles, poured wine, and sat next to Pip. He took her left hand and looked into her eyes, "Darlin', I have dreamed of a chance like this." He kissed her.

Pip pulled back. "Sam, you are a total romantic aren't you? You know what is going through my mind? Any minute Edith will march through the door and see what you just did. I can't pretend otherwise. I am sorry." She laughed.

"Dr. Planter, before this night is over I will bring you around to my way of thinking—the seize-the-moment scenario or God-wouldn't-have-let-this-happen-if-it-were-not-to-be scenario."

"I don't think so. Let's enjoy this delicious food and wine, and forget about your scenarios."

"Pamela, you are a piece of work. All I need to do is get you drunk, and then I can have my way with you, woman! Your invincible will power will crumble, and you will succumb to my charm. No doubt about it. I can't wait."

"Hah. We'll see."

Two bottles later they were cuddling on the couch asleep. The fire was down to embers. Sam's cell rang and woke them up. Edith let Sam know she was on the train, thirty minutes out of New York City, and they were ahead of the storm. She should be back for Christmas. Sam thought, *Almost thirty days, I need to take my time.*

Sam carried Pip's cart upstairs and took it to the guest room. He then helped her up the stairs. He then went back downstairs and cleaned up the kitchen. Later, after he had put his pajamas on, he went to Pip's room. He opened the door. She opened her eyes when the door creaked. "Hi, cupcake, how are you doing?"

"Oh Sam." She started crying. "We can't do it in your house!"

Sam thought, *Ah progress. We CAN do it, just not in my house.*

He went to the bed and peeked under the covers. He pulled the covers back. He wanted to ravage the woman in the sexy pink gown, but all he did was take off her boots. He kissed her and left.

Three hours later, the power went off. Sam took his blankets and went to Pip's room and got in bed with her. "Darlin', I will do nothing but keep you warm so you do not freeze to death."

"Promise me, Sam."

"No."

Chapter 23

The D.C. area was shut down by multiple snowstorms until the Thursday following Thanksgiving. It meant everyone stayed where they were, tried to stay warm, and "camped out." Power came back on most places by Sunday night. Pip's complex never lost power so she and Sam took up housekeeping there. Sam went to work everyday because of the storms. They were considered "an emergency" so government "essential" officials were required to work. Pip cleaned, cooked, and pretended this "temporary situation" would never end. She liked it and loved Sam.

Margaret was the happiest she had ever been. She and Don roasted all kinds of things in the fireplace. They talked about futures in far away places. Don would and could do anything, things she asked him to do and things he anticipated she would like. They did not talk about family.

Don walked all over town, bringing back wine and food. He shoveled the driveway. He made bread. He said he was not scheduled to work until a week from the Monday after Thanksgiving. He washed her hair, gave her massages, and made love for hours. Every night he would lay his clothes on the floor, take a shower, wash out his underwear and socks, hop into bed, and kiss Margaret with a mint chocolate wafer on his tongue. Margaret was usually too drunk to consider having a routine at bedtime. She had no interest in talking. The mint chocolate kiss was always the beginning of a sensual high she wished would never end. Lovemaking ended when she fell asleep.

By the Wednesday after Thanksgiving, Margaret was beyond happy, beyond being in love. She was addicted to Don, especially his touch. She decided Wednesday not to drink and use all her powers of persuasion to convince Don to go away with her and start fresh.

"Don, you moved around a lot, haven't you?" She was sitting at the kitchen table watching him baste short ribs.

"Some."

She opened a bottle of wine, poured him a glass, and handed it to him.

"Thanks. Why did you ask?"

"I admire your ability to move, to try new things."

"It's easy when you have no family, few possessions, and are motivated by simple things."

"What motivates you?"

"You won't believe it. You may laugh."

"No, I want to know."

"Okay. Bringing joy to others, helping others unconditionally."

"I believe you. I don't think it's funny. On the contrary, I think you are unique and special."

"What motivates you, Margaret?"

"What motivates me today is different than what motivated me before I met you. Taking care of my family was my first priority, heightened when I divorced my husband. Now I realize my three girls and I have grown apart. Now they prefer to spend time with their father, who contributed little to their wellbeing for the last four years, than with me. I have become an ATM machine to them. It is stressful and not fulfilling.

"After Christmas I want happiness, peace, less responsibility, perhaps a new start somewhere else." She filled Don's wine glass. He had sat down across from her. She was drinking soda water.

"That's a sad story."

"No, it is enlightening."

"Margaret, helping others brings peace and happiness— not pulling in, not becoming self-centered."

Margaret didn't like this turn in the conversation. She poured herself some wine.

"Don, I do not want to be alone. I want to be with someone I love and who loves me I am capable of unconditional love, lasting love, but have not been a recipient of the same for most of my life."

"I am so sorry. Our actions have consequences. Perhaps you do not or did not have the ability to accept or see unconditional love."

Margaret poured both of them the last of the wine bottle. She started to cry. It was not an act. Don arose and came to her side of the table and massaged her shoulders. He then opened another bottle of wine.

"Margaret, Ms. Eloise loves you."

Margaret stopped crying. She turned and looked into Don's eyes. Her own were piercing black dots. "Be careful, Don."

He put up his hand. "Sorry."

"I don't understand you. I know nothing about you. What are you hiding? You are not real. You say you are motivated by helping others like a saint. Yet you help me defraud the government. That doesn't bother you?"

"No. I have learned not to judge people's relationships with government. Fred told me what you and he were doing in the Get Ahead program in New York."

Margaret dropped her glass; wine went all over the table. Don retrieved the paper towels and cleaned it up.

Margaret's antennae were activated. She was shocked and fascinated. Don was off his pedestal. "So you know Firebrand? Why did you come here?"

"Fred asked me to look out for you. He thought the best way to connect with you was through your stepmother. And here we are." He raised his glass.

Margaret's version of a future with Don was crumbling. "So all we have been through is because your friend, Fred, asked you to do it?"

"You know it's more than that. Fred was a catalyst."

She had a glimmer of hope. "How do you feel about me, Don?"

"I think you are beautiful and smart. I think you are a wounded person. I think you build relationships on manipulation. I tried and am trying to show you an alternative."

"That is so clinical, so righteous, so unfeeling."

"It's the truth. I care about you."

"Do you love me?"

"Not yet, but I could."

"What do I have to do?"

"Be honest with me."

Margaret laughed. "Tell you what, let's eat, drink, and be merry one more time, and then I'll decide."

They ate in silence. They went upstairs. Don went to take

a shower. Margaret looked in his pants pockets—a disposable phone, a New York driver's license for Don Pellingham not Pelham, a flash drive, a comb, and three Visa cards, each in a different name. *Well, well.*

She put everything back in Don's pants and hopped in bed. She was sober. Facts can do that to you. *I love the crook. What do I do? I can't live without him. I think I need to show him what I can do for him, and sprinkle in some honesty. He is either one of the greatest cons or delusional, or both! He needs to get out of town as much as I do, I suspect.*

True to her intent Margaret made Don's night. At one point she thought he was going into cardiac arrest. False alarm. Later when they we cuddling, he said, "Ms. Sabat, I had no idea you were so talented and versatile! I would like to experience it again—after I recover."

"When do you think that will be Mr. Pelham or is it Pellingham?"

He pulled away from Margaret. He wasn't angry. He smiled. "In about a week. Since we are playing Truth or Dare, it's your turn."

"Eloise fell down the stairs. She died. I put her in the freezer in the basement so I could use her name and credit for a while."

Don seemed to look into Margaret's soul. She was scared. He made love to her, without tenderness. When she awoke to get ready for work, Don was gone.

God, what will he do? Will I ever see him again? Do I want to see him again?

Chapter 24

Margaret was stressed by the time she arrived at work. She felt in the grip of a dangerous situation, and her mind reeled with the perceived loss of control, anxiety, and fear. Making her realize she needed to-do lists for multiple contingencies. Don was the unpredictable element. He knew too much. She got a cup of coffee, went to her office, put out the Do not disturb sign, shut her door, and began her lists.

Within ten minutes, Donna Dawson knocked and walked in.

"Margaret, we need to talk."

"Look, Donna, I hang out that sign for a reason. How about three? I should be finished by then."

"No. We need to talk now."

"Shut the door." Donna entered the office, closing the door behind her. Now, what couldn't wait?"

Donna sat down across from Margaret at her desk.

"The New York Get Ahead grants. I worked on reviewing the files from home, once the power was restored. I talked several times with Jerry in New York. Did you know Swanson sent investigators to New York? I came in early this morning and asked Swanson for his take on things. He said you, Ted Morton, and I were implicated. I told him you had handled the New York grants for three years, not me."

"I plead guilty. I guess I didn't thoroughly check things given my other responsibilities."

"Then why did you get my passwords from IT and change

the log to remove your name and replace it with mine as the first-line reviewer for the last three years?"

Careful. "Donna, as I said, I didn't scrutinize the files as I should. When I learned about the investigation, I suspected Fred Firebrand in New York. I told Ted, but I don't think he has told Swanson yet."

"You didn't answer my question."

"I thought the changes, if checked, would show you and I 'did things by the book,' and we would be less likely to be implicated. It was a judgment call. Look, why don't we have dinner tonight and just hash everything out. I owe you that much."

"All right, we need to clear the air. It would be better to do it somewhere other than here. You know we have choir rehearsal tonight—why not eat somewhere in Chevy Chase?"

"It's a deal. How about *Charlie's* off the circle at seven? We can eat fast and then go sing our hearts out at St. Joe's. Sound like a plan?"

Donna nodded, got up, and left Margaret's office. Margaret looked at her Blackberry; she had a message from Shawna, one of the twins.

It read: Hi, Mom. We have had some wild weather, haven't we? We stayed with Dad for five days. It was too long. If I never see another Spaghetti O or animal cracker I will be a happy camper! Attached is the Christmas wish list for your three children, lots of electronics. Ask Santa to do what he can. When are you moving back home? We all want to come over and help you decorate. Love, Your favorite child.

Margaret opened the Staples catalog, copied down the items she wanted to buy and then went online to purchase. She entered Donna Dawson's information. Donna had changed her password. Margaret entered her own information, completed the transaction, and charged the electronics to the division credit card, not a personal one. The electronic receipt said she would receive her items on Monday next. She scratched Buy Christmas gifts off her to-do list. She went back to her list making. One item was very critical; it was not on all lists—close up Eloise's house.

She went to Eloise's house at lunchtime. She cleaned up the kitchen. She sorted through her clothing and threw the favorite items in a bag, and then she was about to empty the trash. She saw the bill for the dishwasher. It was for $427. That number bothered her. She put the receipt in her purse. She heard the mail come through the mail slot, she rushed to the door and opened it, and saw a female mail carrier walking down her path to the sidewalk. She yelled, "Hi there! Where's Don? On vacation?"

"No. He just up and quit. I got word this morning that this block is now part of my route."

"If you can take a minute, I'll be glad to offer you a cup of coffee."

"Why, thank you. It is very cold today."

The mail carrier's name was Joan. She had a big chest, big brown eyes, and beautiful white teeth. Margaret made her a sandwich.

"Joan, did you know Don?"

"Just to see him. It seems he pretty much kept to himself. He was quiet and polite, not much of a talker. He was handsome. I guess the strong, silent type."

"He was a very nice man. I got to know him on Saturdays

when I was home."

"You run some kind of business out of here?"

Why did she ask that? All the Landmark Therapies mail goes to a post office box.

"This is my stepmother's house. Why do you ask?"

"One time a bunch of us went out for drinks after work, and Don said he had a part-time job taking old people on field trips. When I saw the sign on the side of your van parked in your driveway, I assumed you ran the business, and Don worked for you."

"Oh yes. But I've stopped operation for the winter. It is not easy to take older people, some have Alzheimer's, out in this kind of weather." *I must get rid of that sign and van.*

"Well, if you decide to restart your business in the spring, I would not mind a part-time job."

"Thank you. I will keep you in mind. Did Don ever say where he was from?"

"No, not specifically, but I believe it was somewhere in the southwest. Thank you for your hospitality, but I need to get back my route."

"You bet. It has been great talking to you."

Margaret packed up her Landmark Therapies laptop and files, and took them along with her clothing to her car. She took the sign off this side of the van. She had one last thing to do—go visit Eloise.

She went down the steps to the basement and sat on the third step from the bottom, staring at the freezer. "Eloise, I have to leave for a while, but I will be back, and I will bury you. I promise. Unfortunately, your boy, Don, was a mistake.

You take care."

Margaret decided not to go back to the office. She drove straight home. She wanted her own bed, her own things, and time to think before heading for dinner with Donna. About midway home her phone rang, "Maggie, where the hell are you?" It was Ted.

"I have a migraine, Ted. I'm going home to sleep it off. Then I have choir practice. I will be back in the office tomorrow. Perhaps we can see each other then."

"What's with you, chick? I want to see you. My son is hounding me about school."

"Of course, I haven't forgotten about your son. I'm trying to decide what kind of angle to use with my uncle. I'll take care of it. I'm just too sick to talk right now, Ted. Please understand." She hung up the phone.

She stopped by the grocery store and picked up some food to hold her over until she did the Christmas food shopping. She was pleased with the migraine story; she would use that again.

After she lugged everything into the house, she poured a glass of wine, and opened her laptop in the great room. She needed to calculate the status of her financial situation. The receipt for the dishwasher had fallen out of her purse and was sitting on the coffee table. She picked it up and studied it. It did not have Don Pelham's name on it. It had Dew Point Graphics.

She found Dew Point Graphics on her electronic bank statement. Margaret had paid Dew Point Graphics for the dishwasher. Don had not bought it for her. She was scared. Don could drain her accounts, and she would not know it until after he did it. She changed all her passwords, but she knew that that would not stop him. She was desperate. She rested her head on the back of the couch. She closed her eyes and let the tears slide down her cheeks. She had no idea what she was going to do to extricate herself from the mess she was in. She sensed whatever she did would require drastic measures—she would have to disappear. That was a scary prospect because she had no support system.

Chapter 25

You would think the main topic of conversation at Forensic Specialists, LLP would have been the big snows and what everyone did, but that was not the case. The main topic of conversation was "the new Pip." She was a blond. She wore colors. She looked hot. And, she seemed happy. The speculation was wild. She had won the lottery. She had found a man. She was up for political appointment. Nobody had the nerve to ask her why she had gone through such a dramatic transformation. Everybody wanted to be the first person to find out the reason why they now had the coolest looking boss in town—cart or no cart. She even looked like she had lost some weight! And on top of everything else, she pronounced that she would be leaving the office every night no later than six.

Suzy and Kit were in Pip's office. Suzy was the first person to try and get the scoop. "Aunt Pip, you look great! Care to share any secrets?"

"No secrets. One day I just looked in the mirror and said to myself, it is a time for a change, and this is it. It is that simple. Now how are you two doing on that report? You look disappointed."

"Oh, not about the report. The irregularities appear to be limited to Texas, Arizona, Oklahoma, and New Mexico. In those states the irregularities are limited to metropolitan areas. The number of grantees involved is limited to a total of about twenty. What is interesting in each case is there are two audit reports for each grantee for each year for a five-year period."

"I don't understand."

Suzy said, "You take over, Kit."

"Each of the twenty grantees submitted amended reports each year for the years involved. The total amount of money for a given year did not change, but the amount allocated for field trips went up by fifty percent and some other category or categories went down to compensate for that change. Many of the field trip vendors a grantee used had a name that began with the letter D and has a second name with a letter P. All amended reports were submitted electronically, although initial audit reports were sometimes in hard copy. This pattern suggests to us someone was doctoring the books, probably at the state level. But maybe not. A hacker could have done it from any location. At least that's what Frank said. One more thing, all corrections occurred within ninety days of the next fiscal year. That is no payments to vendors were adjusted downward."

"You lost me again."

Kit said, "There was always enough money in the bank account, so to speak, to cover the increases that went to field trip vendors, without going through the process of taking money back from others who had been paid."

Pip said, "Let me see if I get it. Funding in year two was used to cover the increase in costs in year one."

Kit nodded. "It became a rolling adjustment over the five-year period. No one was looking for it, so they didn't find it. It could still be going on."

"Is that in your report?"

"Yes, ma'am."

Beamer stuck his head in the doorway. "Sorry to interrupt you foxes, I ordered the exercise equipment for our small conference room. It won't be here until after Christmas. That means Kit, you and Frank can continue to practice your dance moves and make the building vibrate for a couple more weeks!"

Pip said, "Beamer, it was supposed to be a Christmas surprise!"

"Oops!" He turned and left.

"Well, now you know. Don't tell anybody else. I want it to be a surprise at least for somebody. Rich could stand to tone up his muscles. Frank can discover whether he has any. Johnny is in good shape because he works out with his dad. I know I could use some exercise.

"When you expect to have the report finished?"

Kit said, "We are almost finished. It's hard to give you a date, but before Christmas. It will be a hell of a Christmas present for Swanson."

Kit and Suzy left and Rich came in. He looked tired, but his eyes were different—kinder, less intense.

"Mama, what happened to you? I feel like I'm talking to an avatar. My old Pip is all gone, and I'm communicating with some hot chick from Second Life!"

Pip laughed.

"I'm not kidding. I feel like I'm talking to a stranger, like I said, a hot one, but still a stranger."

"How was your holiday, Rich?"

"That is complicated. I have some information about the case I want to give you first."

"Okay."

"A woman who is an auditor in New York has a mother

who once dated Fred Firebrand. I spent Thanksgiving with them. Fred called the mother from Mexico on Thanksgiving to say hi.

When I realized who was on the phone, I asked Maria, the auditor, if she would ask Fred a few questions, when her turn with Fred came. I wrote the questions out for her."

Rich reached in his pocket and pulled out his questions.

"Tell him you saw Don Pellingham. Ask if he has heard from him. Maria's answer was yes.

"Ask if he has been in touch with anyone in the 'grant world' since he retired. Answer was no one.

"Ask if he plans to come back to visit. Answer was no plans.

"Ask if he has been to Texas to see his kids since he retired. Answer was no.

"Ask how he uses his time. Answer was arranging field trips for U.S. students to farm cooperatives in Mexico. Bingo."

"So, we can assume he knows about the investigation. We don't know his D.C. partner, but we could surmise he still is into fraud."

"Yep."

"Maria went to work on Monday, Tuesday, and Wednesday. There was no snow in Albany. I went with her. Effective Monday, her federal point of contact was listed as 'to be determined.'"

"Who was it for this before the change?"

"Margaret Sabat."

"Wow! I would love to know if she handles the southwestern states' Get Ahead grants. We have no way of finding out. Swanson has pulled the plug on our contract."

"Shoot. Too bad. I may have a way of finding out. Give me a couple days. Don't worry, I'll be careful, discreet."

"So, when you weren't working, how was your Thanksgiving?"

"Look, Pip, I know you care, but I am not ready to spill my guts in detail on that topic. I am okay. I need time to think through things on my own. I'll tell you this much, she is a beautiful, angelic virgin, who is saving herself for marriage. She cares about me, but she can't believe I care about her."

That sounds familiar. If he only knew. "I understand. If you ever want to talk, I am here. Beamer told me she uses a wheelchair."

Rich thought, *Why am I not surprised?* "Thanks. One more thing—no more *fucks*. You'll have to find other ways to underwrite office parties."

The floor started to vibrate. Rich said, "What was that?"

They both went in the direction of music and booming. Rich put his hands over his ears. Pip couldn't do that. She had to push her cart.

In the second conference room Frank and Kit were practicing their rock n' roll number. Beamer and Electra were watching them. Beamer was describing their moves to Electra. Johnny and Sheila were dancing on the other side of the room. Suzy came up behind Rich and Pip. She said, "They are good! I ordered pizza for all of us."

As she promised, Pip went home at six o'clock. Everyone else dispersed, Sheila had a class; Beamer had rehearsal; Electra was meeting Max and Joe for a night out; Frank and Kit had a dance class; and Johnny, Rich, and Suzy went to the Dive for some drinks.

Rich said, "I'll be the designated driver tonight. You two enjoy yourselves."

Suzy said, "I think something is wrong with my hearing.

Did you just say *you* would be the designated driver?"

"Yes. I am not kidding. One beer—that is all I am going to have."

Johnny said, "How was your trip, Rich? Can your friend make, you know, the 'f' word?"

Shocked, Suzy said, "What the hell is he talking about?"

Rich ordered a pitcher of margaritas and one beer. "One question at a time children. Johnny, the politically correct way to ask your question is -- Can your friend make love. Fuck is out. The answer to your question is -- I have no idea."

Johnny took a sip of his drink. "Why didn't you find out?"

Suzy interrupted, "Could I have some background here?"

Johnny said, "What do you mean by background?"

Suzy, frustrated, said, "I have no idea what you and Rich are talking about."

"Oh that's easy. Rich fell in love with a girl who uses a wheelchair. She lives in New York. He doesn't know whether he wants to date her or not because he does not know if she can make love."

Rich smiled. "I could not have said it better myself."

"Boy that is heavy. I can't even see you being attracted to someone in a wheelchair much less dating her."

"That's not a very nice thing to say to a big brother!"

"Sorry. You are such a macho kind of guy."

"Say bro, how was your Thanksgiving with Sheila?"

Suzy interrupted again, "Now what's that about?"

"Tell her, Johnny."

"It's complicated. Sheila is a girl. She is a friend. I wanted Sheila to be my girlfriend so we could make love. Sheila got snowed in with me and my mom and dad. We were together for five days. We talked a lot, but that's about it. She said she would be my friend forever, but never my girlfriend. I want to continue hanging out with Sheila. That's all I know. So I have a friend forever. That's better than nothing, right?

"There's hope, man. Maybe someday she'll see things your way. How about you Suzy, how is your love life?"

Suzy took a big sip of her drink. I have no love life. What's wrong with me? You guys are doing okay."

Rich said, "That is debatable. You know what your problem is, Suzy?"

"Tell me."

"Guys like vulnerable women. They like damsels in distress. You come across as a damsel in charge. You need to dumb it down a little bit."

Johnny said, "Rich, I didn't understand a word you said. Remember I am part of this conversation too."

"I'm sorry, Johnny. I just told Suzy she's too smart for her own good. Guys like girls who need help. Suzy never needs help."

"Sheila's smart, and I like her."

"Yeah, but Sheila knows to ask you questions and ask for your help now and then. Suzy doesn't know how to do that. Suzy also worries too much. She always thinks about the future rather than having a good time right now."

"Speaking about a good time," Suzy interjected, "something is up with Pip. I offered to cook her dinner tonight, and she said she had other plans. That has never happened before."

Johnny said, "Some guy named Sam called her twice today while I was watching the phones. Do you think that's her boyfriend?"

Rich slapped Johnny on the back. "Son of a bitch! If we had had a pool on what was going on with Pip, you would have won!"

Rich's phone rang. He saw it was Maria. He got up and walked into the building lobby. "Hey, pumpkin, what's shaken?"

"You." Maria was whispering. "Guess who is here?"

"Santa Claus, asking if you've been a good girl all year and have gone to church every day. Why are you whispering? Are you in church?"

Maria giggled. "No. Don Pellingham is here! He is on his way to Mexico to spend Christmas with Fred. He brought mom and me each a laptop—a MacBook Pro!"

"Did you tell him about my visit?"

"Give me a little credit, I'm not an idiot. My mom didn't tell him either."

"Sorry. How long is he staying, Maria?"

"He is leaving tonight, I think."

"Can you get him to stay longer?"

"I doubt it. He's not stupid."

"Look, Babe, this is important. See if you can get him to stay just a few days. You can think of something. Then call me back when you know what his plans are."

"I wish you were still here, Rich. I miss your hugs and your kisses."

"I miss you too—more than you know and more than I expected. We have a lot to work on, but it is hard to do long distance. I got a go, cupcake." He hung up.

He dialed Pip on her home phone. Pip picked up the phone and smiled at Sam, who was setting the table for dinner. "Hi, Rich, what's up?"

"Pip, my friend in New York just called me. Don Pellingham is at her mother's house. He is flying to Mexico tomorrow. Can you pull some strings? We need to stop this guy and find out what's going on. You know, bring in the feds. Does your 'friend' Sam have any pull?"

"What are you talking about? If the guy is leaving tomorrow, there is nothing the feds can do between now and tomorrow morning. Can your friend persuade him to stay in New York longer?"

"She is going to work on it."

"I'll get back to you."

"Sam, we have a problem. The troops know about you. I have another problem. A potential fraud operator in New York who is connected to the case on which we are working for Swanson, is flying to Mexico tomorrow morning."

"Cupcake, let's eat and drink. And then I'll think about your problem and our problem. I love playing house with you sweetie. It's never dull." Sam took Pip's arm and escorted her to the dining room table, where cranberry-scented candles were burning. He had fixed filet mignon. "You can give me all the boring details while we eat. Then I'll pull a rabbit out of a hat and save the day. How's that sound?"

Chapter 26

Charlie's was an upscale bar and grill. It had lots of dark mahogany and minimal lighting. People came there to start affairs, end affairs, threaten, plot, and not be seen. Margaret got there early and sat at in a booth in a back corner. She had dressed in camel slacks, red cashmere sweater, and opera pearls.

When Donna came in Margaret waved.

"Nice booth. You disappeared this afternoon, what happened."

"I went out at lunchtime to do some Christmas shopping, got a migraine, and went home."

"I've never known you to have migraines."

"They're a new thing."

They ordered apple martinis.

"Is it okay for you to drink?"

"We'll find out, won't we? We can always take a taxi to the church."

Donna laughed. "Of course!"

"How's the new job? Word is you have been working long hours."

"It's a challenge. I am spearheading two things for Swanson, establishing a task force to learn more about Medicare billing and establishing a work group to audit small-time Medicare vendors in D.C."

The drinks arrived and Margaret took a big swig of hers.

"Why Medicare? We don't handle Medicare in PSA."

"There appear to be some seismic shifts in the works with regard to auditing, more centralization coming. Swanson is a real player. You didn't hear any of this for me.

"I understand. How far along are you in setting things up?" Margaret finished her martini, looked at the wine list, and ordered an eighty-dollar bottle of chardonnay. She looked at Donna and smiled. "Relax girl, this dinner is on me. Now how far along are you?"

"I have the files for the D.C. pilot test. But, I am still in the process of staffing. Swanson wants me to get people by borrowing them from other offices on a short-term basis. Even that involves a lot of paperwork and given the sensitive nature of what's being implemented, I don't know if it is the best strategy. Swanson's primary motivation is to move fast. He thinks hiring people will take too much time."

"I am willing to help you. Do you want me to take a quick look at the D.C. files?"

"No. I think I have to do that myself. In fact Swanson told me to review the files and give him a report before Christmas. That is why I'm not spending as much time in our division as I would like. I promised you I would finish up everything before the holidays, and that may not happen."

"Don't you worry about the division work. I can handle that. You focus on your new job. Can I treat you to a pedicure on Saturday before our Christmas luncheon at church? Consider it a going away present."

"Why, Margaret, that is downright sweet. Thank you so much."

The rest of the evening was uneventful. Donna could

not believe how friendly and kind Margaret was turning out to be. Perhaps when Donna changed jobs she and Margaret could become friends. Who knows, since Margaret's brother was a big shot in the White House maybe he could help with Swanson's projects? She would have to tell Swanson about that connection.

When Donna got back to her condo in Crystal City she was wide-awake. She decided to take a look at the files she had and started her review. She poured herself a glass of milk, retrieved the files, and plopped down on her couch. Everything in the files seemed rather straightforward and boring. Nothing stood out. She was about to pack up and go to bed when something caught her eye; the medical director's name for Landmark Therapies was David Sampson. *David was Margaret's brother's first name, and Sampson was Margaret's maiden name. Shoot. What a mess if this means something.*

The next morning she met with Swanson. She had not slept all night.

"What's up, Donna?"

"Mr. Administrator, I have uncovered something I want to share with you, but first must give you some background.

"Margaret Sabat and I started in the federal service at the same time. Although she is not a friend of mine, I am aware of some of her personal circumstances. For example, I have met her children, I know she is divorced, and I know her brother, David, is the principal medical adviser to the president. She shared that last fact with everyone when he was selected for the job. His last name is, of course, Windson, not Sabat. However, Margaret's maiden name is Sampson. I do not know why they have different last names."

Swanson's antennae were up. "I can't wait to see where this is going."

"I appreciate your patience. Last night I started reviewing the D.C. files, as you directed. There is a small vendor named Landmark Therapies. The medical director is Dr. David Sampson. We might be able to chalk that up to a strange coincidence, but then I noticed the CEO's name, Eloise Robinson. Margaret's stepmother's first name is Eloise. I think we are beyond coincidences, don't you?"

Potential leverage with the president's chief medical advisor How sweet it is. "Donna this is very interesting information. Given its implications I must consider what to do next. Please return all the D.C. files to me, give me your assurance you have made no copies, and you have shared this information with no one else."

"Here are the files. I brought them with me. I have not shared any of this with anyone."

"Good. You concentrate on setting up the task force on Medicare auditing. I am suspending any work on the D.C. pilot until I have had time to think about what to do about what you have shared with me. And one more thing, do not under any circumstances share your speculation with Margaret Sabat. Is that crystal clear?"

"Yes sir."

Chapter 27

"Well, did you pull some strings last night?" Rich asked Pip in the office kitchen. She was all dolled up in a pink and gray outfit. Rich was trying to figure out how she got those boots off at the end of the day. *Maybe Suzy helped her since she lived next door in Pip's condo building.*

Pip smiled. *I did pull something last night. But, I'll not be talking about that.* "The FBI checked names for scheduled departures—no Don Pellingham or anyone similar. Do you have a picture of this guy?"

"Not yet. I am working on it." *Shit. The old woman has connections. Sam?*

Rich went to his office, shut the door, and called Maria.

"Maria, is Pellingham still there?"

"Good morning to you too, Rich. No."

"My luck. Did you ever find that damn picture?"

"No. But if you stop being so obnoxious and check your e-mail, you will see I sent you a picture I took yesterday."

"Hold on, I'll check." He did and there was no e-mail from Maria.

"Nothing there. When did you send it? How did you send it?"

"Oh, no! Don said he would load it and send it to you from my new laptop, so I handed him my camera and gave him your e-mail address."

"Darn, that was totally stupid, Maria! What does the guy

look like?"

There was no answer on the other end for about thirty seconds.

"Maria, are you still there?"

"Yes, I am. I am trying to process a side of you I have not seen before, a side I do not like. First, when he offered to do what he evidently didn't do, I did not know how to say no. Second, when I got off the phone with you last night, he was gone. Mom said he heard me on the phone talking to you. Third, I tried to call you to tell you, but I couldn't get through because we are having a raging storm. I'm with my mom, and cell phone reception is not good in her neighborhood. Finally, Don Pellingham is light-skinned, forty-five, six-foot-three, about two hundred and ten pounds, square jaw, brown eyes, clean shaven, medium brown hair, military cut, very muscular, and very nice. Have a good day, Buster. You sure messed up mine." She hung up.

Chapter 28

The Christmas luncheon of St. Joe's choral group was over. Margaret joined Donna as she was walking out. "Nice luncheon, huh Donna?"

"Yes it was, even though it was chicken. Fried at that."

As they walked toward the parked cars, Donna said, "Damn, I have a flat!"

"No problem, I'll give you a ride to the gas station off the Circle. It's on my way to the gym."

"I thought you used the one at PSA."

"My kids gave me a membership at a gym near my house as an early Christmas present, so I thought I would try it out."

"Nice. I appreciate the ride." *Be careful Donna. Remember what your boss said!*

Donna was surprised, but pleased at Margaret's offer. Ever since dinner at Charlie's Margaret had been friendly. Margaret did not sit with her at the luncheon, but engaged her in an extended chat afterwards till everyone else had left. Also, Margaret had treated Donna to acrylic nails the same color as Margaret's that morning. *The Christmas spirit was seeping into Margaret. I once thought she was a cold-hearted witch. I wonder if it is guilt, manipulation?*

Margaret parked her car on a side street next to a cluster of trees. Donna said, "Why didn't you pull into the gas station?"

"I wanted to avoid making a left in the traffic when I leave, and I want to put on my exercise clothes while you are arranging to get your flat fixed. Can you get me the key to the restroom?"

Donna rolled her eyes but walked toward the entrance to the station office. While she was gone, Margaret, for the second time that day, surveyed the cluster of trees, the gulley she had found, and the abundance of ground cover. She smiled. *It was thoughtful of Donna to wear muted autumn colors today!*

Donna brought Margaret the key and headed back to arrange for her flat. Margaret went into the restroom, but on her gray running suit, and a black and gray knit cap to cover her hair. After tying her shoes, she made sure the ten-pound free weight was in the top of her bag. She rushed out to see Donna looking ticked. "What's the matter?"

"Since they are short handed, they can only lend me a jack. Can you believe it?"

"Don't worry. We'll call AAA from my car, but come with me, I have something to show you in those trees—a litter of puppies with no mother."

"Oh no!" Donna followed Margaret into the thick foliage. Margaret let her get ahead, after pointing toward the gulley.

"They are at the far end down the slope. You'll need to remove the leaves to see them."

Donna did as she was told. Donna bent down and started brushing leaves aside. "How did you hear anything from—"

Donna was cut off in mid-sentence. The dumbbell went crashing into the back of her skull. Donna tumbled into the gulley. Unfortunately, she fell in head first with her legs flexed. She looked like she was doing stretching exercises with her butt in the air. Margaret pushed Donna's butt with her foot, slipped because of the wet leaves, and fell in the gulley on top of Donna, who was now prone. "God!" Margaret stood up, dusted herself off as best she could, and climbed out of the gulley. She took the rake base out of her gym bag, knelt, and used its prongs to cover Donna's body with leaves.

Margaret returned to her car shaking all over. She drove her car a block from the church. She got everything she needed out of her trunk. It was overcast and cold. She headed to the parking lot on foot. She repaired Donna's tire with the portable pump and patch. She sat behind the wheel and put her head on it. She stopped shaking. *I did it!* She put the car in drive and headed toward Donna's condo in Crystal City. She wanted to check it out. She needed a new place to hide from Don, and she wanted to find those D.C. Medicare vendors' files. She hoped Donna kept them at home. And, Margaret was banking on no one discovering Donna's body till spring. *I hope she's dead. I should have checked. I wouldn't want her to die of exposure. Oh well, it's too late now.*

Chapter 29

Saturday was the big night, the night of the big dance competition. Frank and Kit were ready. Everybody from Forensic Specialists, LLP, Frank's grandmother, and Kit's boyfriend, Jack Danielson, were to there to cheer them on. They had made it to the Clarendon ballroom in spite of an ice storm. Rich was the only person who was in a somber mood. Kit and Frank were competing in two categories—the tango and rock 'n roll. Frank's grandmother had made their costumes. Their costumes were the best.

They came in second in the rock 'n roll category. Kit was ecstatic. Frank was pissed. It seemed everyone knew Frank's partner was deaf. During a break in the competitions one TV station reporter asked Kit if he could interview her after the competitions were over.

Kit and Frank were the last to compete in the tango category. In the middle of their routine the power went off. Out of nowhere came about thirty candles that were quickly lit. Staff started the music over in a battery-operated boom box.

Kit looked at Frank. She had tears in our eyes. "Frank, I can't do it without vibrations."

Frank said, "I'll take care of everything. I have every detail memorized, just follow my lead. We are going to win. I promise you, Kit."

Frank was right. They won first prize. They received lots of cheers, lots of hugs, and Kit was interviewed—not only by the television station, but also by her boyfriend.

Because of the weather everybody went home after the competition, except for Rich. He went to a bar, got drunk, got in a fight, and was arrested. After being processed, he called Pip. It was about 1:30 A.M. Sam handed her the phone.

"Hello?"

"Pip, it's Rich. I'm at the Arlington Police station on Eleventh Street. Can you come bail me out?"

"Bail you out? Have you been arrested?" With that Sam was out of bed and putting on pants and a sweater.

"Where is he, cupcake?" She told him. He was out the door before she could say another word.

Sam returned about two hours later with Rich. They went to the kitchen, and Sam made some coffee. Pip heard them, got out of bed, and went to the kitchen.

"You two have met I suppose?"

Sam said, "Yes we have. I told your boy here if he ever did something like that again I'd break his neck, so he assured me he would not."

Pip said, "What about the charges?"

Sam said, "What charges?"

Smiling, Pip replied, "Oh thank God!"

"Rich, what is the matter? Did something happen with your friend in New York?"

"Yes it did. I acted like an asshole on the phone, and she hung up on me."

"And your response to that is to go out in an ice storm, get drunk, and beat somebody up?"

"I was out of medication."

Sam rolled his eyes. "Dear hearts I need some sleep. I'm leaving. Going back to bed. Don't fight, but if you do, do it quietly." Sam left the kitchen.

Pip made Rich a peanut butter and jelly sandwich on whole-wheat toast. She went to her medicine cabinet in her bathroom and came back with her reserve stash of Rich's prescription. She gave him the pills and a glass of milk.

"Lady, who is that dude?"

"Somebody I love madly, who I've loved since high school, who is very married, and very powerful."

"What! Well, that explains the makeover. He saved my ass. I'm grateful for that."

"Rich, you need to talk to that girl in New York."

"I don't know what to say to her."

"How about something like I'm sorry or I was a jerk or both, and ask for forgiveness. How hard is that?"

"You think that'll work?"

"Saints preserve us! You're not stupid. Of course it will work. Now go to bed in the guest room. And don't sleep naked!"

"Yes ma'am."

When Pip got into bed Sam kissed her on the cheek. "Where do you find these people?"

"He's good, and he's smart. He just needs a little help now and then. Thanks for what you did Sam, I love you for it—it and so much more."

"Cupcake, I got to go home tomorrow, clean up, and buy groceries. Edith is coming in tomorrow night."

Even in the dark Sam could see tears on her cheeks. They made love.

Chapter 30

Margaret had never been to Donna Dawson's condo in Crystal City. When she arrived she found the parking space for 1212, Donna's condo, according to her driver's license. She went from the garage to the twelfth floor. There was an elevator that went to the units without a stop at the lobby level—only in the D.C. area do builders think of discretion over convenience.

The condo was decorated throughout in white with green accents. Donna had many books on self-improvement. And like her office, she had elephants of different sizes and shapes all over the place – on bookshelves, tables, and the floor.

On this first visit Margaret did not want to stay too long. She emptied Donna's purse on the coffee table. She found Donna's Blackberry and sent Swanson an e-mail with a copy to Margaret, explaining Donna's plans had changed, and Donna would be taking off the week before Christmas, rather than the week after. She put everything back in the purse, planning to take it with her.

Margaret searched the condo for a laptop, a PC, or files, but did not find any of them. She sat down on the couch and looked around. *This could be a good hideaway for a week at least.* Then Margaret's eye caught a collection of photos on a bookshelf. *Donna's mother! I wonder if she is still alive? Easy way to check.* Margaret picked up Donna's phone and looked at the phone log. There was a consistent pattern of calls to a

202 number at around five o'clock every evening. *What do I do about her mother?*

She drove to Eloise's instead of going home to Bethesda. The roads were still icy. She had given Don a key, so she had a fear of him showing up unannounced, but Margaret was more tired than scared.

Later, lying in bed Margaret couldn't sleep. She kept thinking about what she had done to Donna. Eloise was one thing; her falling down the stairs and dying was not Margaret's fault. Donna, on the other hand, was Margaret's doing. Margaret again rationalized Donna had left Margaret no choice. She was too close to finding out about Landmark Therapies. Donna had to be stopped. Donna became a checked-off item on the to-do list in Margaret's mind, the kind of to-do list Margaret would never write down.

Margaret's thoughts turned to Landmark Therapies. Margaret had told the nursing home outings would stop the Saturday before Thanksgiving and resume in the spring, although Margaret kept billing Medicare electronically for therapies. *Maybe I should stop. After the holidays.*

Margaret lay awake all night. By morning she knew she would need to come up with an exit strategy. She would need to disappear. She didn't want any loose ends. The question was, how much time did she have?

When she got to her office Monday morning, she had bags under eyes, her nails were ragged, and her hair was flat and greasy, but she had her to-do list.

As she had anticipated, Ted was in her office. "God, what happened to you? Did somebody die?"

Margaret started laughing and could not stop.

Ted was alarmed. "Maggie, get a hold of yourself! What's wrong?"

She sat down in her chair. "If I told you, you wouldn't believe me. Donna Dawson is gone."

"What do you mean gone?"

"Gone."

"She does not answer her cell phone. She does not respond to e-mails. Look at this message she left me at one thirty on Sunday morning."

Ted looked at the message Margaret had sent to Swanson and herself from Donna's Blackberry.

"Do you know what she was going to do for the holidays? Does she have a family?"

"I don't know."

"Okay, you calm down. I'll see what I can find out."

"Do you think there may be something in her division office or in her office in Swanson's suite that might give us a clue?"

"Good point. I'll alert security."

"Ted, I am sorry I went hysterical. Why don't I check Donna's two offices, and you find out if she has family? Maybe I am over reacting."

"Okay. But Maggie, why do you think something bad has happened to Donna?"

"Think about it, Ted. She is so responsible, reliable, and predictable. She is working on two big projects for Swanson and trying to close out her role in my division before she goes with Swanson full time. There is no way she would take off the week before Christmas."

"How do you know she is now working for Swanson?"

"You told me! Now go check if she has family."

"Yeah. I'll get a family contact. You check the offices. We will meet back here in an hour. For now we will keep it between the two of us. One more thing, do you think her disappearance is linked to the Firebrand fraud thing?"

"Who knows? All I can say is I have a bad feeling." *Item one on my to-do list worked like a charm. So glad Teddy boy has such an active imagination.*

Chapter 31

In his office on the sixth floor, Swanson was unsettled. He had been so happy. Over the weekend anytime he considered his potential leverage over Windson, discovered by Dawson, he smiled. The guy might be engaged in Medicare fraud, and he worked for the president.

As was his policy, Swanson turned his Blackberry off on Friday night and back on, on Monday morning. He was unsettled because according to her e-mail message to him, Donna had decided to take a week off.

Why? It makes no sense. What if she shared what she shared with me with Sabat, and Sabat shared it with her brother, and then somebody made Donna disappear? Stranger things have happened in this town. And, for every cover-up exposed, probably ten go undetected. This is too hot.

Swanson called Sam Netherfield at the FBI and arranged to meet him later in the day. *Screw leverage. Let the damn FBI sort this mother out.*

Netherfield was operating *on* reserves. Edith had talked his ear off day and night since she returned about the success of her trip to Africa and the numerous water purification projects they launched in eight countries. She was the State Department liaison to the Agency for International Development and the United Nations for water projects.

Talk about a niche! Thank God the only thing she complained about was the house being dusty and my not spending more time with our son. I wonder why Swanson wants to see me? I need to slip out of here early, and go home and take a nap. Maybe I could go to Pamela's and take a nap? That could be fun if she would join me!

When Swanson arrived, he shook Sam's hand, handed Sam the D.C. Medicare files pertaining to Landmark Therapies, and sat down across from Sam at his desk.

"Brad Swanson, it is good to see you. I have to admit I sense an element of mystery is involved, since you would not even tell me the topic on the phone."

"I appreciate your seeing me on such short notice, Sam."

Swanson proceeded to fill Sam in on hiring Forensic Specialists, LLP, what they did, what they found, his concerns about Margaret Sabat and Ted Morton, his high regard for Donna Dawson, what she discovered, and now her unexpected absence.

"Brad, why were you planning to do an audit pilot on some D.C. Medicare vendors? Medicare is not part of PSA's portfolio, right?" Sam knew all of this from his sources, but he wanted to see what Swanson would say.

"David Windson wanted to see how good we are at detecting fraud before he would consider or push for legislation giving PSA jurisdiction over Medicare auditing."

"Who picked D.C. for the pilot?"

"I did. I thought it would allow us to save money and do things quickly."

"So Windson had nothing to do with your picking D.C.?"

"That's right."

"What about Dawson? Would she have told Sabat anything?"

"I doubt it. Why would she?"

"You have reservations about Margaret Sabat and Ted

Morton? In essence, you do not trust them."

"That's right."

"There are two issues here. First, the question of fraud and who is behind it with regard to Landmark Therapies. Second, why is Donna Dawson missing?"

"On the first I would suggest you go back to your initial contractor, Forensic Specialists, LLP and have them review all the online transactions between Medicare and Landmark Therapies. Have them verify with other parties, for example, nursing homes, what occurred, and when it did. Have them talk to Eloise Robinson. If she is collaborating with David Windson, under the name of David Sampson, she will tell him, and he will do something to try and cut off the investigation. At that point, the FBI would become involved.

"On the second, I would have Forensic Specialists, LLP talk with Dawson's relatives. After forty-eight hours, the FBI can become involved because it will be a missing person case."

"Sam, forgive me for being blunt, but if I hear you correctly, you want to distance yourself from this case."

"No. I just think the best move at this point is to let the contractor do low-key snooping to remove some of the speculation and get us more facts.

"I will be glad to assign an FBI liaison to Forensic Specialists, LLP, who will have the power to bring FBI resources into play when they're needed.

"And because I take you seriously, Brad, I intend to share with the FBI director what you have told me and what's going to happen next.

"Look, no one wants to take on the president's chief medical adviser without hard facts. What complicates everything is the fact even if the medical adviser is innocent, his sister may be as guilty as hell. We don't know what he will do to protect her. We need to move slowly. We need to move methodically. We need to recognize we are approaching Christmas week. All I'm asking is you use your existing contract with Forensic Specialists, LLP to gather some facts. The FBI will be on call and ready to take over when the situation warrants it."

"Sam I'll have to amend the contract."

"Do it and do it quickly, and then set up a meeting with the head of Forensic Specialists, LLP. Give her a briefing, tell her what you want, and give her the Landmark Therapies files."

"How do you know at the head of Forensic Specialists, LLP is a woman?"

"We went to high school together. I've known her a long time. She has good judgment, knows how to be discreet, and has the right kind of staff to do what needs to be done." *That last point may be a stretch!*

"What if David Windson is implicated in Donna Dawson's disappearance? Should we bring in the local police?"

"Look Brad, you are political. It is in your best interest to move slowly and cautiously. If Windson is cleared, you will have not lost anything but a little time with regard to legislation to authorize centralization of Medicare auditing. You just don't want this thing to be in the media. That could happen if local jurisdictions get mixed up in this thing now. If it ends up in the media before we have the facts, it doesn't matter what the truth is, you are screwed and so is Windson.

As Swanson left, Sam believed Swanson saw the value of moving slowly and using Pamela's outfit to get more facts. Sam called Pip and summarized the conversation with Swanson.

He also said he missed her.

"That's nice, I'm glad you miss me. I look forward to seeing you in another twelve years."

"Edith will be back on the road within a month, and then we can play house again."

"No. No more. It is too stressful, it is wrong, and it is too risky."

"Look, Pamela, I cannot talk about this, I'm too tired. We have to deal with it face to face. What are you doing for Christmas? You can come over and have Christmas with Edith, Bart, and me."

"You are flaming crazy! You want all four of us to discuss what we should do?"

"Of course not! I just want to see you soon."

"I am never setting foot in your house again. You have to decide what you want out of life Netherfield, and then you tell me. I am no longer going to support, no matter how I feel about you, the-you-can-have-your-cake-and-eat-it-too scenario! You can have me or you can have Edith, but you cannot have both of us. I suspect if I asked Edith, she would agree with me."

"Is that a threat? Because if it is sweetie, it will not work. Time has a way of working things out. You have to be patient and not disregard our feelings for each other, while you wait for things to turn out the way you want them to be."

"Your phrasing is unbelievable! If I were a thirty-something, I would think you were contemplating a divorce. But I'm not thirty-something. I'm old, and I don't like to be lonely. I am looking for more certainty in my life, not some time in the undefined future. Even during the happiest moments we were together between Thanksgiving and last weekend, I still felt a deep sadness because it was temporary, and I want more than that. Don't say anything, Sam. Good-bye."

By the time the conversation ended Sam was not only tired but also very sad. Pamela always did this to him. Cut him off.

Sam dragged his body to the penthouse floor to talk to the director, and tell her about Swanson's problem and what was going to happen.

The director concurred with Sam's plan. In fact, she suggested he use his son, Bart, as the liaison with Forensic Specialists, LLP.

Sam thought, *Why not? That could prove interesting.*

Sam drove home. Bart was at the kitchen counter eating leftover lasagna and talking to his Mom. Sam slapped him on the back and gave his wife a kiss on the cheek. Edith fixed Sam a plate.

Sam described to Bart what he would be doing starting tomorrow.

"You are telling me, Dad, I'm being hung out to dry?"

"No, you're too far down the food chain for that to happen. If any heads roll, it will not be yours. Just do things by the book."

"Do you know if Forensic Specialists, LLP has a history of doing things by the book?"

Sam hesitated, thinking about his trip to get Rich out of jail. "Yes they do. You have nothing to worry about, and I have your back.

"Oh, and one more thing. The CEO is Pamela Planter." Edith frowned.

"You mean Aunt Pamela, whom I haven't seen since my high school graduation?"

"The one and the same."

"She's into the detective business?"

"Yep."

"But Dad, she's handicapped!"

"The politically correct term is *disabled*, which she is indeed. But, that in no way interferes with her ability to catch bad guys. Right, Mom?"

Edith gave a weak smile.

"Dad, I want a few days to read the files and finish up the paperwork on my last case. Can I start next Monday?"

"At this point there is not much in the way of 'files.' As things progress, we can decide what kind of files we want to maintain. As for starting Monday—no. Go talk to your Aunt Pamela tomorrow. Call her Dr. Planter when other people are around. After that, you can finish up on your other case. I don't have to tell you this is sensitive. You were picked because you have good judgment and go by the book."

"If the files are going to be limited, mostly verbal, need-to-know, how can I go by the book?"

"That's where you let your creative side come into play. Consider this assignment as a career enhancer."

"Yeah, right. I am assuming if I need a warrant, I'll need documentation?"

"If an FBI agent is involved."

"But not if a rent-a-detective is?"

"You have the hang of it."

Bart got up from the counter and kissed his mother good night and then looked at his dad, "I have a headache already." Sam smiled.

"Dad, I'm staying here until this case is over, I think."

Edith smiled, "I'll make it worth it, Bart."

Later in bed Edith said to Sam, "It will be good to have our boy home, huh Dad?"

"It will."

"Rosita said you canceled her cleaning service while I was away. Why?"

"I wasn't home much. Why waste the money?"

"You didn't touch the frozen homemade dinners I had for you."

"I ate out."

Edith reached down and picked a pink negligee in a plastic bag. "Rosita found this under the bed Pamela slept in at Thanksgiving and washed it. Do you want Bart to take it back to her?"

Sam turned out the light.

"No, mail it, and send her a note." *I have got to get her to shut up.* Sam rolled toward Edith and kissed her on the lips. Edith's lips parted.

Chapter 32

Margaret put on her coat, scarf, and hat. She looked at her watch. It was 7:30 P.M. She assumed it was safe to leave, but her stomach was churning. The reason was obvious. She was committing overt theft, not remote, electronically based fraud on the computer. She looked at the four bags on the floor. She lifted them slowly. They were not too heavy; the handles seemed sturdy. She had put tissue paper on top of the bags and bow bags on top of the tissue, to conceal the contents. She thought about using a cart, but that would be too conspicuous. She turned out the light, pushed in the door lock, and shut the door. *She could do this. It was for a good cause. A Merry Christmas for her girls.* She looked in the wall mirror she donated to the office by the main door of the division suite. *Camel and gold outfit and chocolate boots—my favorite combo. Hopefully I am the ONLY one in the building at this hour!* She checked and smiled at her perfectly manicured nails.

Margaret felt no regret about using the office credit card. It was one funding source she knew Don Pelham could not easily access. And, Donna was alive when Margaret made the online purchase of the electronics for her kids. When or if the need arose, Margaret would say Donna did it. Margaret would say Donna had access to Margaret's authorization ID.

Margaret made it to the elevator. She was relieved she was alone. She sat the bags down and put her head back against the wall. She pushed the B-one button. Then she jumped. On the first floor the elevator stopped and the door opened. George Jones, the handsome security guard with whom she had flirted on several occasions got in.

"You are looking mighty fine and warm tonight. Can I help you get the bundles to your car? They look bulky."

Oh no. "No, I can handle them, thanks. I'm in a hurry."

"Margaret what's with you? I'm going that way anyway."

At the B-one level, the door opened, and Margaret and George fought over the bags; one handle ripped, the bow bag and tissue flew out, exposing DVD players.

George gathered the spilled stuff and put it back in its bag. He gripped that bag from the bottom and picked it up, as well as one more bag by the handle. Margaret followed him out of the elevator in silence, carrying the other two bags and fishing for her car keys. *Thank goodness my car is right near the door. I do not want to have an extended conversation with this guy!*

"Thank you, George. I'm just tired, and I have much to do tonight. I appreciate your help."

"What is all this, Margaret? It looks like you did some damage?"

"Oh it's for Christmas. I had it delivered to the office. The challenge will be to get it into my house and to a safe place before anybody in the family sees it."

As she approached her trunk, balancing the two bags, she hit the clicker and the trunk lid opened. She put the first two bags in the trunk, and George put in the other two.

Without saying anything more, she went to the driver's door, clicked it open, and got in. "Thanks again, George. I'm out of here." She started the car, put it in reverse, and took off toward the exit ramp.

George walked back toward the elevator bank, wondering if his charm was slipping. In front of the elevator that they had used was a receipt. He picked it up and looked at it—Staples, Public Service Administration account, total $1,365. Margaret's name was at the bottom. *This explained everything. The question is what to do about it?* He would not mind a nice cozy liaison with the pretty divorcee. Perhaps with this leverage, he could get what he wanted. He would have to think about whether it was worth it, but not too long.

By the time Margaret hit the expressway she was a wreck. She had the urge to barf. *What have I done? Should I go back? No, I will run into George. Relax woman! He's only a dumb security guard. Anyway, what would your division do with three digital cameras and all the other stuff such as two digital recorders?*

When Margaret arrived home she pulled into her garage. She pushed the trunk open button. She carried three of the bags into the house. The fourth, with the broken handle, she would retrieve later. Her older two girls would not come home till Friday night or Saturday morning, and Bonnie was at a school event. Margaret sat on the couch. *I need to find the receipt and put it in a safe place.* She went through the bags, no receipt. *It must be in the fourth bag.*

She went upstairs to change her clothes and then went out to the garage in her robe and slippers. There was no receipt in the fourth bag. *Where the heck was it? Was it in the hall or elevator at work? George? Well, it could be anywhere. It's probably in my office.* She carried the fourth bag into the house and put all four in the far side of her bedroom behind the loveseat in front of the largest set of windows. She had windows on two sides and a sliding door to a deck off her bedroom.

Maybe I should give some of this to St. Joe's. The twins can share some of it. She went down to the kitchen and poured some already-opened chardonnay and looked at the mail—catalogues, spring tuition bills, and the Amex bill. She sat looking at $56,000 worth of obligations.

The phone rang. She picked it up without looking at the caller ID, assuming it was one of the girls.

"Hi, Margaret, it's George Jones. I wanted to make sure you got home. I found the invoice for your contraband. I think we should get together, don't you?"

Margaret put her wineglass down slowly. *Oh my God!*

"Margaret, are you still there?"

"Why not tomorrow night?" She pulled out Donna's driver's license and gave him that address. *An unanticipated loose end.*

"Fantastic! I am looking forward to it."

Chapter 33

Bart Netherfield got in the car and headed for Forensic Specialists, LLP, wondering what he would find. His dad said he was to 'liaison' with his aunt's outfit as a contractor helping PSA decide if it had a missing person case. His dad said he was picked because he knew the rules, was analytical, had great interpersonal skills, and was discreet. All crap, but Bart was curious.

As Bart opened the glass door of Forensic Specialists, LLP, the first thing he saw was the cutest little butt in a great pair of jeans and a pink turtleneck. She turned and smiled at him. "Hi, my name is Suzy Simon, may I help you?"

Will you marry me? Focus. "Uh, yes. I am Bart Netherfield. I am with the FBI, and I am here to talk to Dr. Planter."

"Right this way, Mr. Netherfield." *He is adorable. No ring. That's a good sign.*

As they entered Pip's office, she smiled at Bart. *Oh my God, Sam sent his son!* Bart looked just like his dad but was about two inches shorter. "It's good to see you, Bart. Have a seat."

Pip knows this guy?

"Suzy, why don't you stay? I assume you two have met. Suzy is working on her master's in organizational development."

Suzy and Bart smiled at each other. Pip thought to herself, *Real chemistry!*

"Now, Bart, let me recap for you. We had been investigating fraud for PSA in one grant program. Suzy will get you our two reports. Now our contract is being expanded in two ways—to look at the electronic transactions of one Medicare vendor, Landmark Therapies and to interview the CEO, Eloise Robinson, and to do some preliminary work on a potential missing person Donna Dawson. In essence, interview her family. She has not responded to e-mails from her boss. She was not to be off this week. She did send an e-mail to her former supervisor, Margaret Sabat, and her current boss, Brad Swanson, giving a change in plans, but she gave no explanation."

"Anyone could have sent those e-mails."

"You are right about that. Early this morning I received a call from Swanson telling me Margaret Sabat charged about $1,300 in electronics on a PSA credit card. He wants us to do some interviewing around that as well. What makes things dicey is Swanson does not want to confront Sabat until we have more facts."

"My dad told me her brother is the president's medical adviser."

"Yes."

"Well, I don't think there is anything you need from me right now, Dr. Planter. If Suzy will give me the reports, I'll look them over, but their relevance is marginal. We can meet again the week after Christmas."

"Could you get us authorization to check for any activity on Dawson's credit cards?"

"Uh, I guess so."

"Do you anticipate a problem?"

"I don't think so, but I think we may need to give your company an FBI contract in order to give you access to Dawson's credit card activity, and we may need formal approval higher than my pay grade. This stuff takes time."

Pip nodded. *His Dad was right. He is a by-the-book guy.* "Bart, before you leave come meet the rest of the staff."

After introductions, Rich pointed out the connection between Sabat and Morton. He indicated he felt Donna Dawson was too much of an old maid to be crooked; Morton wasn't involved in anything criminal, other than to warn Sabat; and Sabat had the smarts, the motive, and the opportunity to engage in fraud.

Bart thought, *Interesting take. How much is based on fact and how much on observation?* "Unfortunately, I must leave now. I wish I had time to hear more about what you have done for PSA. I would start reviewing the files on Landmark Therapies, interview Dawson's family, and go talk to Sabat's boss. Dr. Planter, I would recommend you do that one, since he knows Rich. I also recommend Rich interview the guard who found the invoice."

After Bart left, escorted out by a smiling Suzy, Rich said, "What's the Boy Scout going to do for us other than boss us around?"

Pip said, "Hopefully grease the wheels and get us a consulting contract with the FBI so we can do more."

Johnny said, "Why did you call that guy a Boy Scout, Rich?"

Beamer thought, *I can't wait to hear Rich's answer to that one!*

"Well, Johnny, he's tall, straight, and his suit looks like a uniform."

"I don't get it. He had on a Brooks Brothers' suit and no badges."

"Well, maybe it was because he was so serious."

"Wouldn't you be serious if you worked for the FBI?"

Pip said, "Gentlemen and ladies, sorry to interrupt, but we have a lot to do. Frank and Kit you tackle the Medicare files. Rich, you arrange an interview with Dawson's mother. Here's her address. Beamer and I will try and go talk to Morton. Hopefully, he won't recognize Beamer in a suit. Suzy can interview Eloise Robinson."

"What am I going to do, Pip?" Johnny asked.

Pip thought, *I didn't see that one coming. I guess helping Electra is no longer Johnny's main mission.*

"Johnny, if you would come with me, we can talk about the new categories of files we need to set up. You will be in charge of them."

"Okay."

"You go get both of us a drink, and I'll join you in my office."

Everyone else had dispersed, except for Rich. Pip knew what was coming.

"Pip, does the name Netherfield ring a bell?"

"And?"

"I hope the dude turns out to be as resourceful as his old man."

"I agree. Anything else?"

"Relax, my lips are sealed."

Pip did not respond.

"Look, Pip, your friend saved my ass. I will be forever grateful. I am not sure his sending, I assume, his only begotten son here to keep an eye on us, to help, or both was a wise move. And as far as I can tell, junior did not offer to do anything for us yet. Am I right?"

"As he said, he is going to try and get us a consulting

arrangement with the FBI and with it, the ability to review credit transactions and perhaps phone records."

"I know his dad could and would be able to pull that off, but not junior. The unanswered question is, will junior ask his dad to help? And, lest we forget, Christmas is this weekend. What are we doing for Christmas, by the way?"

"We, as in you and me, can spend it together, unless you have a more attractive offer. Everyone else is taken care of."

"Sounds good to me. I enjoyed last year."

"You have not been in contact with your friend from New York?"

"Nope."

Chapter 34

Over at PSA Swanson was talking with Ted Morton.
    "Now you have the big picture. I want you to be my liaison to the Department of Defense and run the auditing pilot on DOD Family Services contracts for the northeast. You need to focus on this full time. You will be temporarily reassigned to my direct staff, set up a task force, use the five auditors coming over from Defense, and pick some good people you know here who can work well, hard, and fast. One thing, Margaret Sabat should not be recruited to join the task force."

Ted couldn't get out of Swanson's office fast enough. On the way back to his office he tried to arrange to have lunch with Margaret. She agreed to drinks at 4:00 P.M. He needed to find out what she had done now.

At 4:00 P.M. Margaret sat back in the booth, feeling relaxed, sipping some Wente 2007 Southern Hills cabernet. This was the first time Ted had arranged to meet her out in the open, and at such a fine bar—Topaz on Nineteenth. *Where was he? He was never late. It's the navy thing.* Just then, he slid in the seat across from her. Looking at the waiter, "A double, Daniels black on the rocks."

He looked at Margaret. No smile. His deep blue eyes cold, piercing. Margaret did not say anything. They sat in silence till Ted's drink arrived. He drank half of it with one swallow. "Maggie, you know I love your tight little behind, right?"

"What are you talking about, Ted?"

"Have you done anything you would like to share with me such as pissing off Swanson?"

"Ted, you are making no sense!"

I better stop drinking. I have said too much already. "All I'm saying is Donna Dawson better show up. You need her in order to deflect suspicion from you. You haven't heard from her today, have you?"

"No." *Ted is hiding something.* "Look, Ted, I am as concerned about Donna's mysterious change of plans as you, or perhaps you don't remember my reaction to her e-mail to me. You seem distracted. Let's talk about something else for a while, and then maybe your head will clear. What are you and your son doing for Christmas?"

"We are going to West Virginia—another skiing trip. I'll be back Christmas night. We can get together after that."

Margaret looked at her watch. She wanted to know why Ted was being so accusatory, but she had to rush and get to Donna's so she could fix dinner for George Jones, the security guard who had found the receipt for the electronics. She finished her wine and got up. "Have to run Ted. A previous commitment. Don't worry—it's not competition. You are one of a kind. Oh, one more item, Suzy Simon and Rich Pritchard, the interns you forced on me, work for a detective agency. The agency head is some cripple with a Ph.D." Margaret blew a kiss, and rushed off.

George Jones put on his favorite slacks and cashmere jacket. He could not believe his luck. He was spending the evening with the hottest, albeit cold sometimes, divorcee in the PSA. That invoice did the trick. Now he regretted turning it over to his boss. Fortunately, he had made and brought a full-color copy, in case Margaret brought it up. *Margaret won't know the difference.*

Margaret was busy. She had stayed too long with Ted. Even so, she was amazed at her coolness, her calm. She looked at her watch, 8:00 P.M., then, she looked at her five-foot-ten frame. She smiled and slipped into her camel-colored outfit; it was so soft and smooth. She was chilling the champagne in the freezer, and had taken out the cheese and arranged it with black olives and crackers, two wineglasses, and flowers on the coffee table. The main dish was a casserole. *I don't want too much to clean up after the evening's events.* She put the date rape drug into George's glass and kissed it with her bright red lipstick so later she would know which one to give George. She put the two glasses in the freezer. She looked at the open bottle of wine on the counter; it was almost empty. *Pace yourself! Otherwise, you may end up sleeping with rather than killing the security guard.* Margaret laughed out loud and tossed the remaining wine down her throat.

She put opened chardonnay in the ice bucket; put Donna's cream-colored satin sheen sheets on the bed; and put the Velcro strips and blindfold in the nightstand drawer with Donna's butcher knife. She put *Charlie Brown's Christmas* on the CD player, set up Kenny G on the iPod in the bedroom, where scented Christmas candles were lit everywhere. *One, two, three, four, five, six, seven, eight, nine, ten, eleven, twelve, thirteen...how appropriate! Must remember to put them all out.* She turned on Charlie Brown, poured a glass of wine and popped an olive in her mouth, rolling it around with her tongue—*exercise of one's muscles is good*—waiting for George.

George rang the doorbell at 8:30. Margaret had given his name to the security guard in the lobby. Margaret opened the door with a broad smile and a wineglass in her hand, "George, finally! Come in. Come in." She gave him a little peck on the cheek.

George was beside himself. He noticed the plastic gloves on Margaret's hands. He smiled back, handed Margaret the wine and flowers, and kissed her cheek. She retreated to the kitchen. *Where in heck are Donna's vases?* George followed her. "Where do you keep your vases?"

"Let's put them in this aluminum pitcher."

George was disappointed. He had dropped fifty dollars on the flowers and thirty dollars on the wine. "You don't have a vase?" *I thought she lived in a house?*

"Oh, George I took them all to the church for a luncheon. I promise tomorrow the roses will be placed in a crystal vase commensurate with their beauty and value." She took off the plastic gloves and threw them in the trash.

George looked appeased, but he was not sure what she had said. *I shouldn't have had two scotches while getting ready to come here. I hope this lady dumbs down her verbs!*

They went to the couch, hand in hand. "You pour the wine, George. Tell me about the guy behind those big brown eyes."

"Not much to tell. Raised in southeast. Joined the marines after high school. Served in the Gulf War. Have an application pending with the Capitol Police."

"No girlfriend? No ex-wife?"

"What's important to me, Margaret, is I am here with you now." He reached over, took her hands, and kissed them ever so gently. "What happened to your little fingers?"

Margaret pulled her hands back. She had not had time for a new manicure or a do-it-yourself touch up. *Should have kept the gloves on.* "I was born with most of my nail missing on those fingers. I try to hide them.

"Margaret, you don't need to wear gloves. You are beautiful. Don't think like that." George leaned over and touched her lips with his and then, with cooperation, had an opening.

About twenty seconds later... *Shoot that felt good. Lover boy Ted is so mechanical and always in a hurry. George may have some talent to make the evening worth it.* She pulled back and smiled, took a big gulp of wine, and fixed two crackers.

"What's your story? You mentioned kids. Any husband who will come rushing in any minute with a gun?"

"I have three kids and an ex-husband. I assure you no one will come rushing in on us."

"This place seems too small for three kids and a mom." *I am sure she said she had a house, when I helped her with her loot the other day.* "What is this place—two bedrooms and two baths?" George put is arm behind Margaret, and kissed her ear.

"My oldest daughters are in law school and have their own apartment. So, there are just two of us—one of which is a high school senior."

"That does not make sense—this place is way too neat!" George laughed.

"George, why don't you look around? I'll put the rolls in to heat up and toss the salad."

"In a minute." He pushed Margaret back and proceeded to send chills through Margaret's lower extremities. After about five minutes she pushed George back, poured more wine, finished it in one gulp, and headed for the kitchen.

Well I guess I am going to eat dinner at a table! I had other options in mind. George left the couch and walked around the condo. *This place is too organized, and there's no evidence of a high school kid. Strange.*

Margaret called from the kitchen, "Come give me a little help, George. I can't get our second bottle opened." George entered the kitchen and pushed Margaret against the dishwasher. She had put on gloves again. "Margaret, I'll be glad to open anything you want opened." His left hand made an illegal U-turn. Margaret jumped and reached for the wine opener and turned to the counter. George leaned into her, hard.

We should be in the bedroom in thirty minutes, tops. Now act interested, man. Ask lots of questions. He kissed Margaret on the neck as they proceeded through the door to the dining room. Margaret tossed the second pair of gloves in the trash. The dining table was lit with gold and red candles; there was no overhead light, and a green salad, the casserole, and the rolls had already been placed neatly on red square dishes on a white tablecloth.

"Margaret, given what day it is, I am surprised you do not have a tree up. Why not?"

"I know. I should have one up, but with no husband and older kids, it is just not that important. I know that sounds like a lame excuse, but the girls also visit their dad on Christmas. He has a tree, a young wife, and two toddlers, so you get the picture." She finished her second glass of wine. *Whew, I need to slow down and not sound so pitiful. I must remember the next item on my not-to-be-written-down to-do list.*

"I understand, but tomorrow I am going to buy you a tree

and help you decorate it. Every girl needs a Christmas tree and some mistletoe too!"

"Oh, George, that is very sweet, but not necessary and not your responsibility."

"Screw it, Margaret, I want to do it. You sound like a bureaucrat. "I want a reason to see you again."

Margaret was shocked. *I am not the only one being affected by the wine.* "George, I do not appreciate or tolerate foul language. If we are going to spend time together, it is worth remembering, when around me, to drop all words like that from your vocabulary. This is not a request, I demand it."

Bitch. I knew it. Now, I'll have to do the dishes to get her into the bedroom. "Margaret, I am sorry. I hear you."

The tone of the evening had been altered. George offered to help with the dishes, so the two of them cleaned up in silence. Once again Margaret donned gloves. She did not start the dishwasher.

When they were finished, Margaret knew she had to recalibrate. She turned to George and kissed him as if it were his last. He thought, *Jesus, I do not get this bitch.* She pulled away and took the champagne, frosted glasses, and chocolate covered strawberries out of the fridge. She marched out of the kitchen, swaying her hips, with a renewed commitment and confidence. *Men are sooooo stupid.* She went into Donna's bedroom. George followed, sensing he would get what he came for, although he also sensed he may have lost control, the advantage.

Margaret said, "Take off your clothes and lie down. I plan to pour champagne for you and feed you strawberries, and then the sky will open, and you will see a million stars and float to heaven."

I can live with that! What a woman. George did what he was told. Margaret turned on the iPod speakers. The effect of music and candles was soothing. She popped the cork. She poured the champagne into both glasses, drank a big swig of hers, turned, and took the glasses and one strawberry to George, in all his magnificence lying on the bed. She pulled the sheet over him. He took his glass. Margaret fed him a strawberry. They toasted and downed the champagne.

"Margaret, why does your glass have red streaks on the side of it?"

Margaret laughed in an unhinged way. *The lipstick ran. I DRANK FROM THE DATE RAPE GLASS! Get a grip girl! You have only five minutes max.* Margaret ripped open the bedside drawer. She threw the blindfold and Velcro strips to George. "Put these on, sweetie." He did his left hand and slid on the blindfold. Margaret velcroed his right wrist to the bed post. "That's it. Good boy. Now Margaret's going to get ready."

She ran to the bathroom, stripped, and put on the clear plastic gown. *A knife is too messy. I'll just use the dumbbell.* She ran to the closet and grabbed the dumbbell from her gym bag, which she had left during her first trip to Donna's. She looked at her watch—sixty seconds left.

George called, "What are you doing Margaret?"

Margaret swished to George's side. She leaned over and kissed George softly. The sheet made a little tent. Margaret was dizzy. She slurred, "Babe, think stars." With that she brought the dumbbell down hard on George's head. She heard something crack. She then passed out and fell on George. The tent folded.

Chapter 35

The sun was shining brightly when Pip pulled into the PSA garage. Beamer hadn't come with her. He feared Morton would recognize him, suit or no suit. When Pip scheduled the appointment with Ted Morton, she had asked him to arrange for parking, and he had. She knew her way around the building since it once housed Health and Human Services, where she had once worked.

When she arrived in Morton's office, he immediately stood up and walked to greet her. Once he made it to Pip's cart, he didn't know what to do. Pip extended her right hand to be shaken. One of the few things it did well.

"Dr. Planter, I must confess I googled you. Quite a diversified career path!"

"Admiral, I did the same for you! After your naval experience, how do you like your land-based job?"

"It's okay. I have creaking bones."

They sat in high-backed chairs with arms across from Ted's couch.

"I greatly appreciate you seeing me so close to Christmas."

"No problem. So what can I do for you?"

Driving over Pip had decided to use the direct, honest approach. Morton did not seem to be implicated other than as a "warning system" for Sabat. Maybe he would warn her after meeting with Pip, and Sabat would make a mistake.

"My firm, Forensic Specialists, LLP was hired by

Administrator Swanson to investigate potential fraud in one of your divisions. Our contract was expanded to look for fraud in all of your divisions."

"What did you find?"

"Selected patterns of irregularity in Get Ahead grants in New York and several southwestern states. We were not tasked to establish who might be involved in the fraud activity."

"Your role with regard to Get Ahead grants has ended?"

"Yes, but our contract has been extended to do work related to one Medicare provider in D.C. and Donna Dawson's unexplained absence."

"Whoa! You lost me. PSA has nothing to do with Medicare providers."

"PSA was authorized by the White House to conduct an auditing pilot of Medicare vendors in D.C. Donna Dawson found some interesting names associated with a vendor named, Landmark Therapies—a CEO named Eloise Robinson, Margaret Sabat's stepmother, and a medical director named David Sampson, aka David Windson, Sabat's brother."

Ted almost wet his pants. He did not have to fake his shock. "Oh my God!"

"Admiral, yesterday Swanson learned Sabat is implicated in the misuse of a PSA credit card. My firm is investigating that as well."

Pip knew she had Morton in her grip but had no idea what he would say or do. "Do you have any information about these matters you care to share with me?"

"None. I have no knowledge of any of this?"

"How about Dawson? Any knowledge of her reasons for being absent?"

"No."

Ted wanted to end the interview. Pip sensed he did. She gave him her card and asked that if he thought of anything or heard of Donna's whereabouts, he would contact Pip. He agreed to do so.

When Pip had left, Ted sat on his couch, put his head back, and ran his fingers through his hair. *No more contact with sweet ass Margaret, sailor boy.* He called his son, "Hey son, what you'd say to blowing this town early? I'll be home within the hour."

Before he left his office he put his Blackberry in his desk drawer. *Time to start using that old, personal cell that belonged to my dear, departed wife.*

Within two hours Ted and his son were headed to West Virginia in his son's Christmas present—a fully loaded, red, Jeep Cherokee. Ted's son was driving.

"Dad, do you have any news for me on the university issue? I sent in my application to GTU."

Think fast. "I will Monday night. Do you think you can wait that long?" *I guess I'll need to see Maggie one more time—assuming she is not in jail by then."*

"Dad, I'm glad we are coming back Christmas night so I can show everyone my new wheels. This car is awesome!

"Dad, I have a question for you. You're not a bigot, right?"

"Where are you going with a question like that?"

"Uh, I am dating a person of color—Bonnie Sabat."

Son of a bitch!

Chapter 36

Rich pulled his truck into a visitor's slot in the condo complex in southwest. He loved interviewing people. He thought he had the knack to get inside their heads. They just spilled their guts, and his medication kept him from getting too hyper.

Mrs. Dawson, in good shape but with bags under her eyes and an anxious look, opened the door to her condo for Rich. He looked around the spacious living room. Never in his life had he seen so many elephant knickknacks. "Mrs. Dawson, I appreciate your willingness to see me on such short notice."

"Young man, please come in, anyone who will help find my Donna, has my complete cooperation. My, you are tall, and I love your strawberry blond hair! Please sit down."

Rich took a chair across from the couch. He had a great view of the Potomac. Mrs. Dawson got right to it as she sat on the couch. "What do you want to know?"

"My job is to retrace Donna's steps before her disappearance and to learn about her plans for the holidays. Any people or places you know about will help us establish leads on which to follow up." Rich took out his pad.

"Donna was going to visit my sister in a nursing home in Williamsburg on December twenty-third and then spend the twenty-fourth and Christmas with me. She always called me at five P.M. on the dot EVERY DAY. I have not heard from her for days! When I called her number, a thousand times it seems like, I got the message This person is not available. Young man, do you think she is dead? She is such a good daughter! She would never go for one day much less five without talking to her mother!"

"Mrs. Dawson, I do not know what has happened to Donna. That's why I am here talking to you. I know you can help. What was she going to do on the first day she did not call you at five P.M.?"

"She had a luncheon at her church, near Chevy Chase Circle."

"Do you know the name of the church? If she was with anyone in particular?"

"No and no." Mrs. Dawson started to cry. "I know she is just dead, and I am no help!"

"Ma'am, we do not know yet, and you are being helpful. Can I get you some water?"

Regrouping Mrs. Dawson said, "Dr. Pepper, lots of ice, in the fridge, there. And, help yourself."

Rich was impressed. *She's a tough old lady. All business. I know she knows something I can use.* The contents of the refrigerator were impressive too—lots of veggies, fruits, and yogurt—all organized. *Electra would like that.*

Rich returned with the drinks. "Now, Mrs. Dawson, is there anything else Donna may have told you about what she was going to do on the day she went to the church luncheon? Think now—anything may help us."

"Young man, I am a retired history teacher and a Republican—see my elephants—don't you know that if I knew something, I would help you!" She threw up her hands and sat back on the couch, her velvet lavender hoodie bunching up around her well-toned neck. Suddenly, she had that lightbulb-going-off look. "Wait a minute. There is one more thing Donna told me about that day. She went for a manicure with her boss. It was her boss's treat before the luncheon."

"Who is her boss?"

"Margaret Sabat."

Bingo. Rich had a connection. He asked Mrs. Dawson for keys to Donna's place, which she provided without reservation. He was flying now. He popped a pill to slow him down and headed over to Crystal City in his truck.

After he negotiated his way passed the security guard/concierge in the lobby by flashing his ID, he headed to condo 1212. As he put the key in the door, he heard a blood-curdling scream from inside.

Chapter 37

About three hours after the scream, Rich was starving. He pulled into the drive thru and got his usual. He decided to just park and eat. He was not happy about how things played out at Donna Dawson's. Police can be so unfriendly to private investigators. Who knows how thorough they would be since poor George was not dead. He had to get a look at that condo when the police tape came off. His phone rang.

"Hi. About time you called me, Pip."

"I am sorry, Rich. I went to open my freezer, but was being careless about not holding on to a chair, and fell down. It took me an hour to get to a phone. I am okay. Can you come over and pick me up."

By this time Rich was heading to Alexandria. He owed Pip a lot—his life. He met her at one of her mental health clinics, under contract with the Veterans Administration to help vets transition to civilian life. She gave him a job when she started Forensic Specialists, LLP. "Are you sure you are okay? Where the hell is Suzy? You know you should have a phone with you ALWAYS."

"I KNOW. I KNOW. Don't lecture me. I screwed up. If you continue yelling at me, I'll start feeling sorry for myself and cry. Just get here and then we can talk about the case. What was so urgent anyway?"

"George Jones, a PSA security guard, was found alive but barely breathing by Rosa in Donna Dawson's condo, just as I put the key in the door."

Without missing a beat, Pip said, "Was Donna there?"

"No such luck. But I think if we can find Donna's car, we will find Donna. I think Sabat is working her way through a people-I-need-to-eliminate to-do list, but I don't fully understand her motives. Jones knew something about her, I suspect."

"Did you check her parking space at the condo?"

"No. I got an idea. One for Frank. See you in five minutes."

Rich dialed Frank's cell. "Hey, Frank, how'd you like to do some overtime? And some field work?"

Frank was checking out bike parts on eBay. "Rich, what do you want me to do?"

"Here's what I want you to do tonight. Find me every church within a three-mile radius of Chevy Chase Circle. Then, tomorrow comes the fieldwork. Oh, and one more thing—I'll e-mail you Donna Dawson's address. See if you can get the make, model, and color of her car. Try to get it by keeping hacking to a minimum. Pip will get pissed otherwise.

"Rich, we know all that. Remember Johnny found the MSRP sticker in her trash can?"

"You are so right, my man. But I need a plate number. And, find those churches. Thanks. Bye."

Just then he received a text message. "Police tape is down." *Another late night.* Rich belched.

Rich kept a key to Pip's condo in his car for emergencies like these. As he unlocked and pushed open Pip's door he said, "Hey, Pip, where art thou?"

"On the kitchen floor, wise ass."

I wish I had a camera. I could blackmail her. Pip sat in her red snowmen pajamas with her back to the wall, her cart next to her. She was using her iPhone. The kitchen TV was on *CNN*. No sign of dinner. Rich squatted and scooped her up and plopped Pip on a chair. "The mighty too shall occasionally fall on their asses."

Pip said, "Thanks—not for the comment, but the lift. I ordered pizza for two—Hawaiian. It should be here in fifteen. Start at the top."

"Nice to see you too. Here goes. I went to see Dawson's mom, a classy old lady. Only learned one interesting thing—Donna and Sabat did nails together before heading to church. I would like to talk to her again. I think I can learn more. After I got the key to Donna's place, I went there. That's went things got interesting.

"As I put the key in the door, a scream rang out. I rushed toward the sound and found a woman passed out on the floor near the door to a bedroom. A guy, looking kind of white for a man of color, lay motionless on the bed, a big bloody dent in his temple. I stepped over the lady and proceeded to the bed. I felt for a pulse. There was one. I dialed nine-one-one and then DCPD to get a number for Arlington PD. They said they would give them the address. By this time Rosa had come to. When she saw me, she screamed again. I was crouching over her about to wipe her face with a wet towel. I flashed my badge, it looks so real, she calmed down, and I helped her up and to the couch. I got her a glass of water. I told her to sit while I had a look around. I told her I called nine-one-one. I don't think she understood a word I said.

"I began in the kitchen. Spotless, but the dishes in the dishwasher were dirty. We need our own trace expert, you know. No trash in the trash can, except for one clear plastic glove. Being an honorable man, I did not take it. Yes, I had put gloves on." *Pip is amazing. She is just taking it all in. That's why I love her old bones. Anyone else would be crying about being cursed with cerebral palsy.*

"Next I went to the living room. Rosa, I said 'Como se lama?' and she spit it out. She had gathered up her things. I think she wanted to split. Suspect she was an illegal. I told her to sit with my most imposing six-foot-five frame, and of course she did. The living room, too, was cleaned up, no evidence of what had taken place. The bedroom was another story. The guy had Velcro on his wrists anchoring him to the bedposts. No evidence of a struggle. Smell of urine, bed soaked. Thirteen candles had burnt completely down, and an iPod player was on, but there was no iPod. Shiny sheets on the bed, with blood on the pillow from the wound.

"Before checking the bathroom I propped open the door for the EMTs and police. That was a mistake. Rosa took off and five minutes later everyone else came in. Since they did not have Rosa to grill, they grilled me. After they got my creds verified by Netherfield junior, they lightened up a lot. I assured them over and over that I had touched or took nothing. I told them about Rosa.

"The EMTs said George was in a coma and dehydrated and likely brain damaged. They said he was hit by someone strong with a heavy object.

"Oh yeah, there were more Velcro in the nightstand and a butcher knife, unused. AND George was blindfolded.

"So what do you think, Pip?"

"A woman seduced and then thought she killed George."

Rich said, "The sheet had stains, but from what? Who knows?"

"Many things remain unclear. What was the connection between Donna and George? Why would Donna or someone else—Sabat for example—want to kill him? What did he do to cause what happened to him? Seems like an overreaction. Was it planned or unplanned? But then again, life is sometimes stranger than fiction. If Sabat killed him in Dawson's apartment to implicate Dawson, can we assume Dawson is alive somewhere? Can the time between Donna's disappearance and your discovery of George tell us something? If Donna wanted to kill George, why would she do it in her apartment? Why didn't the murderer clean up thoroughly afterward? Did she have to leave in a hurry? For example, why didn't she turn on the dishwasher? I remain convinced Sabat is the perp, but like millions of us, she, too, watches CSI shows on television. We can only hope since she left in a hurry she left something for us that will link her to George and Donna. You need to get back into Donna's apartment."

Rich nodded. "The tape is off, so I'll go back tonight."

"How'd you learn that?"

"Do you really want to know?"

"No."

The pizza arrived. Rich retrieved some Coronas and limes from Pip's fridge. He made a great tossed salad with crumbled bleu cheese and made fresh dressing. For a single guy, who lived off junk food, he had great potential. He popped a pill.

Pip summarized her encounter with Ted Morton. "He is a little guy with piercing blue eyes. He revealed nothing, but I shook him up with the truth about Sabat. We can only hope he will warn her, and she will do something stupid. Boy, would I like to get my hands on her."

"The woman is dangerous, and if Morton tells her what we know, she could be desperate and dangerous. Don't you go near her old woman. Leave it to me!"

Pip resumed, "I talked to a PSA inspector general contact about the PSA credit card purchases. He said he would follow up with Morton. Sabat is not due back in the office till January second. If Morton tells her what's up, and she brings the loot back to "undo" the theft, I got the IG guy to agree to let us check the bar codes against the billing records."

Rich began pacing. The beer did not agree with his pills. Pip saw the signs, but did not want to make any comment for fear Rich's agitation would increase.

"I need to get my hands on that bitch, shake her up a little bit. Who knows what she will do between now and January second? I feel like going over to her place right now for a chat. There is no way she would get Velcro on me!" He went to the fridge and took another beer, no lime this time. "I need to go to the hospital and see George too and have a man-to-man talk."

"Those are interesting ideas, but think we should brainstorm about them tomorrow."

Rich turned red. "Don't be so patronizing P-a-m-e-l-a PhD. The difference between the two of us is I am a man of action, and you are a tortoise who thinks EVERYBODY needs to have input and buy-in. That's bullshit. You know it, and I know it."

"Let me propose an option. I'll throw some clothes on, and

we will go to Donna's together. Then we will go see George. What do you say to that?"

Rich came crashing down. He hugged Pip. "Oh Pip, I am sorry. I am a miserable shit. God bless you." Raising his arms, he said, "God thank you for my little friend." Sitting down, he closed his eyes. They just sat there. Finally Rich said, "If we go to Donna's first, we will miss visiting hours at the hospital. You need your rest, after all you are a lot older than me—I mean I."

Pip sensed the storm had passed with all its truth and fury. She could let her big little boy go, but oh how she feared she would not be there to calm the waters the next time, every time. Although, this episode, like others, came out of nowhere, it was very short, and that was good.

Rich kissed Pip on the cheek. He had a smashing idea. He left. When he got to his truck he called Johnny. "Johnny, what's up?"

"Hey, Rich. I am watching a *CSI* I recorded. My mom and dad gave me my Christmas presents early—cable and the basement as my *own* apartment. I have On Demand. I got a kitchen and food. Can come and go without telling them. I am set!"

"Awesome, man. You want to do some detective work with me?"

"Sure. When?"

"Now. Hit your mom up for some baggies. I got the gloves. And just to be nice, tell her you are going out with me and will be home around eleven P.M."

"Okay, Rich."

"See you in forty minutes."

Rich then called Frank. "Hey, Frankie, how many churches?"

"Twelve churches."

"License plate number?"

"VA twenty-four-five-six-seven-thirty-one."

"Great. Now go find that car." Rich laughed. "I am kidding—you understand that, right?"

"Don't insult my intelligence." Frank hung up.

Chapter 38

Rich pulled into the circular driveway at Johnny's parents' home. As he got out, Johnny came around from the side of the house.

"Rich get in. You do not need to talk to my mom. I told her we had to do some late night detective work. Besides, I am an adult now."

With that said, Rich got back in with his "partner" and off they went. Rich drove with one hand and texted the concierge at Donna's building with the other. Good, the condo numbers were on the garage spaces.

They pulled into the garage, Rich told Johnny to look for 1212. No car in that space. They parked out front and went in the front door to the lobby and then headed for the elevators. The concierge started walking toward them and said, "Who is he?"

"This is John Bond, my associate. Like me he is a forensic specialist. We are going to take a second look for evidence."

"Yeah, sure. And I am the coach of the Red Skins."

"No really. He is a trace man. You want to come watch him in action?"

"No way. Be quick."

Rich slipped the concierge a twenty—his second of the day. "Did a woman call to clear the guy in last night? Did it sound like Dawson?"

"Yes to your first question, and I am new so I don't know

Dawson's phone voice."

"Okay. Thanks. Remember, text me if Ms. Dawson or anyone else heads our way."

In the elevator Johnny said, "I like John. I want to be called John. Johnny is a kid's name.

"Okay, John it is."

Rich and Johnny went to Donna's condo. Rich turned on the lights. "Real investigators use flashlights, but we are in a hurry."

"I know. I am not stupid."

"Put on your gloves. Here're some baggies. You take the bedroom and master bath. Look for things out of place."

"I know what to do."

Johnny had watched detective shows his whole life, but this was the first time Rich had asked him to do field work. He was ready.

He went into the bathroom. He picked up camel threads from the rug and put them in a plastic bag. He opened the vanity drawer and saw one gold hoop earring. He put that in a bag. *Why would someone save one earring?* He went into the walk-in closet off the master bath. *Things out of place—a rake base, an air pump, size nine heels but all the others are size eight— DEFINITELY out of place!* He found a shopping bag and put them in it. Next he went to the bed. The sheet and mattress cover were gone. *Why not flip the mattress?* Johnny knew he was strong. He pumped iron with his dad. He flipped the mattress. He saw a small piece of red plastic fall to the carpet. He put the mattress back in place and picked up the red thing. *A piece of acrylic nail. A strange shape and so little.* Johnny bagged it. He took the stuff to the living room. Rich was sitting on the couch. He had several bags on the coffee table. "Let's debrief tomorrow. I have to get you home." Rich stood up.

Just then they heard it, a key in the door. In walked Margaret Sabat.

Chapter 39

Beamer went into the kitchen in his pajamas around 6:00 A.M. to fix some coffee. He lived in the office. To his surprise, someone had beaten him to it, but who? No one showed up until 9:00, and Pip was never in before 10:30. He fixed a cup and decided to take a look around.

He found Rich in his office staring at the wall. "Bro, what are you doing here at this hour?"

"Bud, it was one hell of a night." On Rich's desk and floor all kinds of stuff was in clear plastic bags and labeled—even a rake base and a pair of fine women's shoes.

"I came face-to-face with our suspect, and I had Johnny with me."

"What!" Beamer sat down across from Rich.

"Well, after I picked Pip off the floor and ate pizza with her, that of course is another story, I went back to work. I wanted to check out Donna Dawson's place. The police tape was down."

"What do you mean the police tape was down? Did they find her dead?" Beamer asked.

"No, not her. With a little help from an illegal alien, I found George Jones on Donna's bed in his own piss, alive but with his head bashed in."

"What! Go on."

"Getting back to last night, genius that I am, I decided to take Johnny with me on my return trip to Dawson's pad. You know how Pip is always saying how we have to make everyone around here feel included and give each one meaningful opportunities so they can reach their full potential? So, in the case of Johnny, I did. In spades! No offense intended."

"None taken. Get on with it."

"Johnny, to my utter amazement, did a great job." Reaching down on to his desk he picked up a baggie and thrusting it toward Beamer, "He even found this frickin' fingernail!

"Anyway, we had everything bagged and were ready to leave, when we heard a key in the door. Through the door came one gorgeous skirt—none other than Margaret Sabat."

"Shit! What did you do?"

"I think all three of us were shocked at first. She had a mask on! The kind they use in hospitals. Why—because she was coming back to check on a corpse? I flashed my badge and said, 'Rich Pritchard. We are with the FBI, investigating the assault on George Jones. Sabat fell back against the wall and pulled off the mask. Then she barfed marinara sauce all over the white carpet. Johnny brought her some wet paper towels from the kitchen.

"Raising her head between barfs, pointing to Johnny, she said 'Him too? I have seen you. I know you. I've seen him before. He's a janitor! I know you are a PI not an FBI agent!'"

"With the straightest face I have ever used I said with utmost seriousness, 'John Bond is in an apprentice program.' Johnny just stood there with his mouth open, clinging to his bags. After that he straightened up.

"Getting a second wind I said, 'What are you doing at this crime scene?' As far as I knew nothing had hit the news.

"The wheels in her brain turned a bit too long before she began lying with great abandon. You like that word, Beamer? Electra is trying to improve my vocabulary one word a day."

"Great. What did Sabat say?"

"Well, she said that she had visited Donna's mother and learned she was missing, got the key, and had come over to check things out. At eleven P.M. mind you. In a mask! I HAD DONNA'S MOTHER'S KEY! At that point I decided I'd heard enough. I told her she would have to leave and took Donna's key from her. She left. Johnny wet his pants. It had been a long night.

"I took Johnny to my place, put him in some of my sweats, told him to tell his mom and dad he had gone undercover. I said I would wash his clothes."

Reaching down he tossed a plastic bag to Beamer, "Here, put his pants in the dishwasher and run it. They'll be done and toasty dry before anyone gets here. I am exhausted. I have been up all night sorting this stuff. Pip is going to kill me."

Beamer left Rich's office with the bag heading for the dishwasher, still processing everything. *Rich was right about one thing. Pip was going to blow. She likes people to show initiative after she tells them what to do. Freelancing and creative thinking had to be channeled, directed by her. Well lady, two of your kids went off the reservation and graduated in the last few hours! Is that good or bad? Guess it depends on the results, which is Pip's other theme song.*

When Beamer got to the kitchen he saw the dishwasher was full of yesterday's dishes. *Shit. I'll just put the pants in and run them again!* As he turned to leave Pip was in the doorway, her cart full of bagels. He went over and retrieved the bagels.

He said hi. For lack of something else to do, he started toasting them.

Pip finally said, "Why did you put jeans in the dishwasher and turn it on with a full load of clean dishes?"

Beamer smiled, "Ask Rich."

Chapter 40

Pip had everyone except Electra and Sheila congregate in the main conference room. She managed to get a reluctant Bart there too.

"I appreciate everyone gathering. I think this is the best way to communicate on our unique case. I will begin by summarizing what I know, and then we will go around the room so everyone may contribute. Bart will be last. Suzy will take notes, prepare minutes, and give them to Johnny. He is keeping the files on this case.

"Okay, John. Let me continue. Administrator Swanson of the Public Services Administration has extended our contract to do three things. One, look at Medicare billing by one provider, Landmark Therapies of D.C. and talk to the operator. Two, talk to Donna Dawson's family because she seems to have vanished. And three, do preliminary work on the recent misuse of a PSA credit card. One individual is linked to each piece of this assignment—Margaret Sabat. She is the stepdaughter of the CEO of Landmark Therapies, Eloise Robinson, and sister of the medical director, David Sampson, also known by the name of David Windson. David Windson is the president's medical adviser. Margaret Sabat is Donna Dawson's supervisor. Using Sabat's authorization identification, someone, and we assume it was Sabat, used a PSA credit card to buy $1,300 worth of electronics in the last month.

"A very new development is a security guard at PSA,

George Jones, was found yesterday in Donna Dawson's condo with his head bashed in, but still alive. He is in Alexandria Hospital undergoing evaluation. That case is in the hands of the Arlington Police Department.

"Kit, I believe you, Suzy, and Frank have been pursuing the Landmark Therapies piece of our assignment. Please fill us in on what you've learned."

Kit began, "Landmark Therapies has billed Medicare for therapeutic socialization activities, physical therapy, speech therapy, and occupational therapy for eight people, some of whom have Alzheimer's disease and who reside in the Lake and Lawn nursing home in Alexandria, Virginia. So far, forty-seven thousand, five hundred and twenty-seven dollars have been billed to Medicare. All of it has been paid. There has been no billing by Landmark Therapies for the last three weeks according to Medicare employees in Philadelphia. Suzy, your turn."

"I tried to contact Eloise Robinson. When I called the contact number on the Medicare provider application, a recording said, 'Leave a message, please. We will return your call as soon as possible.'"

Bart said, "Male or female?"

Suzy smiled, "Female."

Pip interjected, "It may be useful to have access to the phone records for that number." She looked at Bart.

Bart ignored the look. "Did you check out the address for the provider?"

Suzy smiled again, "No. It's listed as a Twelfth Street address in southeast D.C. There is also a post office box number."

Bart said, "Well, you need to check those out."

Rich was losing patience with Bart. *I want to punch his lights out.Who does he think he is? Pip should rein in the SOB in, but I know why she doesn't.* "We can check out the address, but we would need authorization to check out the post office box. Can you get that for us, Bart?" Rich smiled. *Got him!*

"I'll check on it, but nothing is preventing you from checking out the address."

Pip took over. "Frank, what do you have for us?"

"The location of twelve churches and Dawson's license plate number."

"What's that have to do with Landmark Therapies," Bart asked.

"Nothing."

Having a passive-aggressive gene, Rich loved what was happening.

Pip said, "Do you have anything on Landmark Therapies?"

"I analyzed the patterns of schedules for therapies. Assuming the eight patients were old, because they were in a nursing home, it seems irregular they each had at least three therapy sessions each Tuesday until Thanksgiving. That's a lot of therapy in one day for an old person. And, it suggests the Twelfth Street facility must be big to accommodate eight patients at once. The scheduled times were the same for each patient. And, the facility, given where it is located, is violating zoning ordinances because the area is zoned as residential, period."

Rich thought, *That's my boy, Frank. Show that asshole. All he has to do is ask the right question.*

Pip said, "Thank you, Frank. Do you have any questions, Bart?"

"No ma'am."

"Okay, let's shift to Rich."

Rich summarized his visit with Dawson's mother, finding George Jones, and his second visit to Dawson's apartment with Johnny and their encounter with Margaret Sabat.

At that point Bart started to ask a question.

Rich held up his hand, "Hold that thought, agent. Johnny, talk about what you found."

"My name is John, not Johnny."

"Right. My mistake. Go ahead, John."

Johnny provided a detailed list of things he found that "did not belong." Two things were very much in the do-not-belong category—one pair of Ferragamo size nine shoes and one red acrylic nail. It was very small—not the normal size. My mom wears them. Her nails are bigger than that."

Bart decided to play along. "John, where did you find the nail?"

"Under Dawson's mattress. Sabat probably broke it off when she was making the bed to put Jones in it. When we saw Sabat, I wanted to take her gloves off and check her nails, but if I did, then she would have known we knew what she did. You have to think in these situations and do the right thing, or the perp will be on to you."

Bart was floored. "Right! But, maybe it is not a *size* thing, but a half of a normal nail."

Johnny didn't hesitate, "Bart you may be right, but we don't know, do we? If Sabat were missing a nail, a half a nail, or had other nails the same color as the one I found, we would have a connection wouldn't we?"

Beamer thought, *Score one for Johnny.*

Pip turned to Rich, "Can you elaborate on Margaret Sabat's demeanor when she walked in on you and Johnny—I mean John."

"She was clearly shocked. But, she recovered quickly. Then, when I told her we were investigating an assault, she lost it and vomited on the rug. I can only assume that when she entered Dawson's condo, she had thought Jones was dead. Is that you're your take too, John?" *Nice touch.*

"Yes, but we should have taken her gloves when we took the key and told her to leave. Then we could have checked for strange nails. Also we should have made her try on the shoes, size nine. Dawson's were size eight."

Pip intervened. "Thanks for the important details, Johnny—John."

"You're welcome."

Pip said, "Okay, let's finish up with the third item—the use of the PSA credit card."

Electra burst into the conference room.

"Who was the mother who put a pair of pants in my dishwasher? And, why in hell would he have a need to do that?"

Johnny turned bright red. Rich rose to the occasion. "Johnny—I mean John—and I were working late last night. I spilled coffee on them. I gave him my sweats."

Electra replied, "And then genius, you put them in my dishwasher?"

Rich meekly uttered, "Yes, ma'am."

Beamer was impressed because Rich never took the blame for anything, especially anything involving Beamer. At this point Pip introduced Electra to Bart and things calmed down—sort of.

Bart had to admit he was impressed with this motley crew. He took the floor, "I am sorry but I must leave shortly. What you have gathered suggests Margaret Sabat is the key person to watch. I will follow up at FBI headquarters on getting you authorization for access to credit card and bank records for Sabat, Dawson, and Landmark Therapies, and the post office box for Landmark Therapies. None of this will likely happen till December twenty-sixth at the earliest.

"I suggest you check out the Twelfth Street address and visit George Jones. I will take the evidence you found to Quantico."

As Bart got up, and Suzy said, "I'll show you out."

Bart said, "One more thing. What's with the twelve churches, Frank?"

Frank gave Bart an it's-about-time look and said, "Rich and I think Dawson's car is in a church parking lot somewhere near Chevy Chase Circle. I found twelve churches within a three-mile radius of the circle."

"I see. But if Dawson has left town, her car may not be in any parking lot."

Johnny said, "Let's check them out. If there is no car, then you can spend taxpayer's money on a nationwide search."

Rich loved his new partner. *Zing.*

"Okay. Check out the lots. One last thought on the credit card purchase—after Christmas find out what Santa brought Sabat's kids." Bart left.

Pip thought Bart was smart and confident. She didn't like him. He reminded her of his mother.

Sheila and Electra came into the conference room. Electra said, "There is romance in the air, ladies and gentlemen! Suzy took off with Bart to Quantico. My unbiased opinion is she is desperate, and he is in love."

Pip said, "Thanks for the update and analysis, Electra. Folks, Bart gave us some good suggestions. I would like Rich and Beamer to visit the Twelfth Street address for Landmark Therapies, and I will go to see the security guard in the hospital. Everybody else take off for the holidays. Let's reconvene the twenty-sixth at ten thirty. Merry Christmas!"

Everyone left to gather their things, except Pip and Rich. "Why do you always think I need a babysitter?"

Pip replied, "You watch TV, Rich. You did special ops. Every detective has a partner. That's what you have, so drop the chip on your shoulder. By now it must be getting heavy, I would think. Why don't you call that woman in New York and apologize. Maybe that would help you."

Where did that come from? Why? What happened to my nurturing old lady? Rich just stared. "See you Christmas Day, Pip."

"Okay. Now go do your job."

Pip went back to her office. Uneasiness was seeping into her bones, affecting her interaction with Rich, and tensing her muscles. She thought it would be good for everybody to have a few days off, including her.

Sam called. "Hi, cupcake, need to see you."

"Oh, Sam, why do you call me? Why did you make your son our liaison?"

"I called because I want to make you safe. I have present for you. As for Bart, it was the smartest thing I have ever done. I can trust him. He won't make a move without clearance from me. You don't like him because he reminds you of me and because he acts like his mother."

You have that right. "Sam, I am going to see the security

guard in the hospital. Do you want to meet at my place at seven?"

"Are you going alone?"

"Yes, what could possibly go wrong?"

"Pamela, I don't think it is a good idea. Take someone with you or let someone else do it. We do not have a clear picture of who is involved, and whoever it is, is capable of violence."

"Sam, you are paranoid." Pip hung up.

Rich stuck his head in the door, "Beamer and I are off. One thing I forgot to mention, I think Sabat knows who we are. When I saw her at Dawson's she said, 'You are not with the FBI. You are a private detective.' She could've gotten that from the White House, Morton, or the Web. Be careful Pip. She may be desperate. You sure you want to go alone to see the guard?"

"I can handle it. Call me when you've checked out Landmark Therapies."

Pip would not let herself be scared.

Chapter 41

Pip pushed her cart into George's hospital room. He was pretending to eat and drink. No food or drink was there. His movements were precise. He would smile between "sips" and babble or say, "Mama, I saw stars."

"Hi, George. I am Dr. Planter, but you can call me Pip, if you would like." He ignored Pip and continued his ritual.

"What are you drinking, George?" George continued his ritual.

"What are you eating, George? Candy?" George continued his ritual.

Pip sat there for a while, but knew she lacked a trigger to get George to interact with her. She knew these things take time.

She said good-bye to George and headed toward the elevator. In the lobby she saw the gift shop and decided on her next visit she would bring George some chocolates. She put her cart in her trunk and used her cane and the car for support to get to the driver's door. As she was about to start the engine, she saw a woman in a camel coat, holding flowers, staring at her. The woman turned and walked toward the hospital entrance. It was Sabat. Pip knew she did not have time to follow her. She did the only thing she could do. She called the hospital switchboard, identified herself as working with the FBI, and once she was connected to George's ward, said he was to have no visitors.

Pip just sat there. Sure enough the camel-coated woman, minus the flowers, came out ten minutes later. When Sabat entered the parking lot, she spotted Pip staring at her and stared back. *I wonder if she saw me loading the trunk?* She started her car and left the parking lot. Margaret followed her all the way to Pip's condo complex, and then she drove passed it.

That's not good. Pip went up to her place, changed into her swimming suit, and went down to the indoor pool to swim some laps. *If Sabat knows who I am, and her hard gaze suggested it, if she ever got me alone…God, don't think about it. White Volvo, Maryland plates ABG four-four-five.*

Later, Pip was happy to see Sam. Not because she loved him, but because he was big and strong. He was so pleased she cuddled in his arms and stayed very still for a long time. He felt her heart beat go from very rapid to just right. *What had happened?*

After sushi and Miramisou chardonnay at the coffee table, Sam pulled out his Christmas present for Pip. It was a sturdy square box in red satiny paper with a big bow. She opened it. It contained a Timex every day watch and an earpiece.

"Pamela, with this you can call me anytime, and I will answer. You need to wear it until this case is resolved. Promise me." He kissed her before she could respond. Sam showed her how to work it. Pip could do it. Being left handed, she wore her watches on her right wrist. It was easy for her to turn the device on and off.

"Cupcake, it works anywhere and has a GPS locator, which I have activated. The minute you say 'Sam' into that watch, I will come save you."

Pip kissed Sam. She gave him a copy of Lincoln's diaries of

the Civil War, a first edition. She then wanted to cuddle again. Sam wanted more. The doorbell rang. They both sat upright. Sam got up and went over and opened the front door. Rich and Beamer were standing there with their mouths open. Rich recovered first, "Director Netherfield, nice to see you again." Sam's cheek had lipstick on it, his shirttail was out, and he was shoeless. His fly was down, but his shirt covered it.

Sam nodded and let them in.

Unflappable Pip said, "Sam, you have met Rich. The other person, a colleague of ours, is Beamer Johnson." Sam and Beamer shook hands. Pip showed the guys her Christmas present.

Sam looked at Pip, "Pamela, you wear that thing all the time, you hear me?" Sam retrieved his shoes, tie, briefcase, and jacket, and motioned for Rich to follow him into the kitchen. He reached into his briefcase and handed Rich a box like Pip's without the wrapping paper.

"Son, here's yours." He showed him how it worked. I maybe out of the country between Christmas and New Year's, so you are my backup. You okay with that?"

"Yes, sir."

"Good. If you ever get a signal or hear her voice, go to a computer, establish Pamela's location, and get to her right away." Sam was tucking in his shirt and putting on his shoes.

"Yes, sir."

"I am depending on you."

"Does your son have one of these as well?"

"No."

Sam and Rich returned to the living room. Sam said goodbye and left.

Pip offered Beamer and Rich leftover sushi. They declined, ordered pizza, retrieved two beers from the fridge, and sat on the floor on the other side of the coffee table.

Beamer was shocked at what he surmised, but didn't show it.

Rich said, "What's with this *lite* shit? What happened to the Corona?"

"Lite is cheaper, fewer calories, and one can get use to it. So what happened?"

Rich began, "Landmark Therapies was shut tight. It is a row house at the end of the block. Beamer would not let me break in. In the backyard were a well-kept Honda and a dark blue van. The van looked like it at one time had had signs on its sides—the color was darker on the sides. No mail in the mail slot of the front door. We peaked in."

"Beamer, you want to add anything?"

Oh sure. So sorry we interrupted your tryst. This adds a whole new dimension to my perception of you, boss. Does anyone besides Rich know about your boyfriend? "Uh, we took the plate numbers, one Maryland and one D.C."

Pip reached into her pocket and pulled out Sabat's license number. "Here, Rich, when you get your contact in D.C. to run those plates, have him run this one as well. It's Sabat's."

"It's a she."

"Pardon me?"

"My contact is a she."

"Of course."

The pizza came. The guys killed three beers each. They talked about everything but Sam. Pip told them about her trip to see the security guard and about Sabat following her. Pip fixed coffee. Then they left.

Walking down the condo hall Beamer said, "You never know, do you, Rich?"

"Got that right, bro." He patted his pocket with his new watch.

Chapter 42

Margaret could not stop throwing up. After she ran into the intern/PI/FBI and the other kid, she knew her days were numbered. She had to get out of town, but first she had to make a nice Christmas for her girls and find out what Ted knew. The first was easy. The second was proving to be a problem. Ted would not answer his phone. She was sitting on the bathroom floor, having barfed most of the night.

By mid-afternoon Margaret was feeling weak. She still could not eat. She had ordered groceries online earlier, had wrapped presents, and had paid $1,000 for a decorated live tree that had been delivered. The girls were coming the next day, so Margaret found a bottle of Pinot Noir and took it and a toasted bagel to her bedroom. When she reached the doorway, Don Pelham was standing in the middle of her room naked. She fainted.

When she came to, she was on her bed, and Don was bathing her body with a cool sponge.

"Seems like I am always washing you down, Margaret. I came back to wish you a Merry Christmas and bury Eloise." She jumped as he slid into her. Somehow she thought she was dreaming. *This can't be real.*

As he moved back and forth, he kissed her and stroked her breasts. She stared at the ceiling. She was too weak to feel anything. Realizing his efforts were having no effect, he rolled over. "Margaret, what's wrong?"

"How did you find this house?"

"Margaret, I know everything about you."

Margaret had dry heaves over the side of the bed. *Not EVERYTHING, lover boy.*

Don decided Margaret was ill and dehydrated. He got up, put on his jeans and sweater, and went down to the kitchen. He came back with chamomile tea and dry toast. He lifted her up and put all the pillows behind her. Over the next thirty minutes he fed her the toast and short sips of tea. He waited to see if she could keep it down. He put coffee grinds on the vomit on the carpet.

He gave her a bath and changed her sheets. She sat up in bed but did not talk for a while. Then, she told him her life story and what had transpired since he had vanished, although nothing about George Jones or Ted. She knew men couldn't handle competition. Even in her weak state she remembered that.

He went to his backpack and pulled out an envelope. She looked at the contents—a one-way ticket to Mexico, a passport with her picture and the name Dawn Pelham, cash, a credit card, and a gold wedding band. They kissed. She thanked God. They fell asleep in each other's arms. In the morning when Margaret awoke, Don was gone.

She was no longer sick. She finished preparing for the arrival of her girls. She packed her suitcase, ticket, and passport, and placed them in the back of her walk-in closet. Getting through Christmas and taking care of few loose ends were the only things between Margaret and a new life.

The girls arrived early in the afternoon loaded down with presents and wine. Margaret hugged them. They saw a special joy in her eyes. That made them happy since they thought their mom loved them and cherished the time they had together.

After about two hours Margaret suggested the girls make a quick run over to see their dad and his family. The girls were surprised, but pleased with their mother's suggestion. After they had departed, Margaret put on black sweats and a hoodie. She founded a roll of electric tape, black plastic trash bags, her pink-with-crimson-streaks ten-pound dumbbell, and headed for D.C.

She lucked out. Pamela Planter had decided to work on Christmas Eve. Margaret waited in her car sipping a Diet Coke. Around 4:30 Pip entered the garage. Margaret walked up behind her and banged her hard on the head. Pip went down. Margaret put tape on her mouth and taped her left arm to her side. *From what I could see in the hospital parking lot, her right arm is useless.*

She put Pip on a trash bag and dragged her under her car. She pushed Pip in so she was centered under the car. She put additional trash bags around the body. *No one will be looking for a body. No one will see a body. No one will smell or discover a body until I am on my way to Mexico.* Margaret took Pip's cash, and put her cart and its contents in a dumpster in the garage. *Didn't hear a crack. Didn't see any blood. Oh well, too late now. I have to get out of here. Don't want to push my luck.* Margaret went home. The girls would be back at 7:30. She took a shower with the dumbbell and fixed a roast duck with green-bean casserole dinner for her girls. Margaret, Shane, Shawna, and Bonnie enjoyed a great dinner together, told stories, drank too much wine, opened presents around midnight, and after lots of hugs and kisses, fell asleep in front of the fire in the living room.

Chapter 43

Pip regained consciousness and banged her left knee and head on the underside of her car. She could not move her left arm. It was pitch black. She lay still and tried not to panic. *What happened? There is tape on my mouth. My head hurts. I entered the garage and...? Can I roll over?* She did. She tried to bring her right fingers together around the tape on her mouth. It took an hour, but between saliva and using her fist she rubbed it off. Her face was raw. Her eyes had adjusted. She knew where she was—in the garage. She then concentrated on rolling out from under the car. She could not get the tape off her left side. She could not sit up. She had to urinate. She looked at the watch. It glowed in the dark. It was 12:30 A.M. Then she remembered. She could feel the earpiece. She held the watch up and hit the on switch against her nose.

"Sam, it's Pip. I need help. I am in the garage at work, next to my car. I was mugged, I think."

Sam was in bed. Edith had given him a hard time about keeping his dumb new watch on in bed. She had said it looked cheap and would bruise her. When he wouldn't take it off, she turned away from him and feigned sleep. He got out of bed and went to the bathroom and shut the door. He called Pip. "I am on my way, cupcake." Edith heard him. She cried.

In Arlington, Rich got the same call. He was in his truck in twelve minutes. Rich would be in the garage in fifteen minutes. He had heard Sam's reply to Pip. It would take Sam at least forty-five.

As soon as he entered the garage, he called. "Pip, it's Rich. I am here." He walked toward Pip's car. He looked down. Pip was lying on her back. Her eyes were closed.

Rich slid Pip out from under car. "Pip, wake up!" He patted her cheek.

She didn't. He called 911 and the D.C. PD. He squatted and checked her breathing. It seemed regular. He went into the building for water and towels. He wondered if had been wise to move her.

He borrowed a bucket from the night cleaning crew. He rinsed it as best he could. He tore the towel dispenser off the wall and returned to the garage with the bucket, an arm full of towels, and a paper cup full of tap water. Sam was cradling Pip in his arms talking to her. Her eyes were open. Sam was sitting in a puddle. Rich smelled urine. Rich squatted and handed Sam a dampened towel. Sam wiped Pip's face. Then Rich handed Sam a cup of water. Pip took a sip. "Don't talk, darlin'. The medics have to check you out. Son, give me another towel."

Rich did. Sam wiped Pip's head wound. The blood around it had clotted. Pip winced. Sam stopped. He leaned in and kissed Pip. "I am going to kill whoever did this to you."

"No you're not."

Rich thought, *She has that right. I am going to get to her first.* Rich started walking around. He put on gloves. He retrieved the cart and its contents from the dumpster. By then the EMTs and police were there. Rich walked up the ramp with his friend, a police detective, Sara. "Let me have that video, girl. I swear I'll get it back to you before eight A.M. She handed it to him.

Pip was taken out by ambulance. Sam went with her. Rich

followed in his truck. He called Frank. "Frank, listen carefully. Meet me at GTU hospital's emergency entrance as soon as you can. Pip's been hurt. I need you to take a video to the office and copy it now. Do you understand?"

"Yes. I will be there in twenty-three minutes."

He was. Rich said, "Call me when your done, Frank, and I'll come pick it up and give you a ride home." As they walked toward the door Frank said, "That guy sitting next to you looks like Netherfield."

"He's his father."

"His pants are wet."

"Yeah."

After Frank left, Rich went back and again sat next to Sam. Sam walked outside twice to make some calls. When he came back the last time he looked at Rich and said, "Thanks for getting there so quickly, son. At first, I thought you hadn't come."

"Pip was unconscious when I got there. I called nine-one-one and the PD. Checked her breathing and went to look for water to wake her up. How'd you get her to wake up?"

"I kissed her. I put surveillance on Sabat, Christmas Day or no Christmas Day."

"Good. Thanks."

"You'll have all the stuff you need to nail the bitch by Monday, I promise."

"Thanks again. If the "stuff" you are referring to includes warrants, that would be a help."

"It will."

The doctor said they could go see Pip. Except for a shaved crown and some stitches, she seemed okay. They could take her home. The doctor assumed Sam and Rich were her family.

The looked like father and son. They went in smiling. They came out with Pip in hospital pajamas and winter coat, and a bag with her clothes.

"One of you guys will have to stay with me. I have no extra cart at home."

"I was invited over for Christmas, so I guess it will be me—I mean I," Rich said.

Sam added, "Sounds like a plan, darlin'. I'll come over later in the day and bring you a new cart." He handed Rich the instructions about how to care for and monitor a person with a head injury.

Back in the office garage Rich said he had to go in the building for a minute. He wanted to give Pip and Sam some time alone. He called Suzy. "Get your ass back here, sister. Pip's been hurt and needs a female companion. I'll be damned if I'll help her shower and believe me she needs it." *Her boyfriend needs one too.*

"I haven't left yet. Bart is here."

"Are you crazy?"

"Yes, in love."

"Well put some clothes on, walk over to Pip's, make some coffee, and meet me in the lobby with a wheelchair. I fill you in then."

When Rich went back to the garage, Sam shook his hand. "Do not let her out of your sight. Got that? And don't let her sleep for a while."

"Yes, sir."

"I need to get home and fill Bart in."

How about if I do it, Dad? I'll be closer to him. "Yes, sir." *I need a drink!*

Chapter 44

Pip was lying in her bed. *I am drained. I think I have been up for twenty-four hours. It's safe to go to sleep now, I suspect. It was a good day. Everyone came to see me and cut his or her Christmas holiday short. I am blessed to have so many people who care about me. Even Edith came! And the police! If I were honest with myself, I would have to admit, I'm no longer brave. I feel vulnerable. Whoever that mugger was, she or he knew me. She only taped my left arm. The unknown is whether she had planned to give me a slow death or just to slow down the investigation.*

Suzy said, "Pip what are you thinking?"

"Suzy, go get some sleep. What time is it anyway? We have a lot to do tomorrow."

"I will get some sleep. It is only eight P.M. You've been awake all day, and you must be very tired. How is your head?"

"It hurts. But I'm afraid to take the painkillers they gave me. I am antimedication. Go now. I'm going to go to sleep."

In McLean the Netherfields were sitting at the kitchen counter eating pumpkin pie.

Edith said, "Thank God Pip is okay. She has enough to deal with, with cerebral palsy. Her staff are devoted to her. I guess it's like an extended family rather than a firm. You want another piece, Bart?"

"No, Mom. I'm going to bed. I need some serious sleep. One thing. Dad—who did you get to stake out Sabat's place in Bethesda?"

"Nobody. I got Bob to put a tracking device on her Volvo. If she leaves, we'll know it."

"Okay. I will go over to Forensic Specialists, LLP in the morning. According to Rich, they will be prepared to continue the investigation even while Aunt Pamela is recuperating. He told me you were going to get some warrants. How are you going to do that between Christmas and New Year's?"

"Go to a Republican judge."

Bart left the kitchen. Edith poured Sam a cup of decaf. "Why do you call Pamela cupcake?"

Sam took too long to answer. "In our senior year in high school Pam learned to bake. Her grandparents raised her. Her parents died in a car crash when she was an infant. She could not pour the cake batter into the cake pan with one hand without losing half the batter. So she made cupcakes. She was so excited. She made cupcakes for everybody's birthday all year long."

It's the truth. But of course, it is also a term of endearment. I know you know that, Edith.

Sam's cell rang. "Yes. Okay. Just keep an eye on it. See where it goes on the grid. If it takes an interstate, let me know. If it stops, also let me know that."

"Sam, why don't you let the underlings handle things. Why do you need to be involved? You are the third highest-ranking official in the FBI for God's sake."

"You know the answer to that, Edith. This is a sensitive case. And, I'm in charge of it. Just go to bed and dream about your water projects!"

Edith was stunned. She put the pie plates and coffee cups

in the sink and left the kitchen without saying a word.

Sam thought, *Sometimes Sam, you are an idiot. That was unnecessary. Are you trying to subconsciously bring things to a head? Think long and hard about that.*

Back on Pip's couch Suzy and Rich were the only two left in the condo with Pip. They were drinking milk. They both had had too much alcohol during the day. Sheila lived with her brother, his wife, and two kids. Sheila had brought chocolate chip cookies, so Suzy and Rich were finishing them up, dropping crumbs all over the cream-colored carpet and couch.

"I do not mind staying with Pip tomorrow, but I think the other women in the office should take turns if she's going to be out all week. Also, she will get antsy. We both know she will want to start directing the traffic again very soon. Maybe we could move the office here, at least the staff meetings, beginning midweek. What do you think?"

"Look, Suz, Pip feels more comfortable with you over anybody else. So as far as I'm concerned you are stuck with that job. As for moving staff meetings here, let's wait and see how things evolve. The way I see it, we have about a week and then the big boys will take over and take this whole thing away from us. So we can't waste time just to make Pip feel good."

"What are you going to do tomorrow?"

"Figure out how to get to Sabat's kids. Start looking for Dawson's car. Interview some of George Jones's colleagues. Hopefully Netherfield will nail down those warrants."

"What are you talking about? Bart is getting your warrants? To do what?"

"I'm talking about the old man. He's the third-ranking

dude in the FBI. We want search warrants for Sabat's house, her car, Landmark Therapies, the townhouse, and the vehicles."

"How did you and him become such fast friends? I've thought Bart was our liaison with the FBI?"

"It is complicated, Suz. Just take my word for it. Speaking about Bart, I can't believe you're sleeping with the guy."

"It's complicated, Rich. Just take my word for it."

"Touché. I need to go get some sleep. You are going to stay here, right?"

As Rich started to get up, Suzy put her hand on his arm. "I know Pip loves Netherfield. I saw it in her eyes, his eyes, and his wife's eyes."

Rich removed Suzy's arm, stood, and looked down at her. "I'm not going to unpack that one for you. If you want affirmation, you'll have to get it from one of them, not me."

"You will tell me nothing?"

"I did tell you something. I used affirmation not verification."

Rich left.

Chapter 45

Staples opened at 8:00 A.M. on December twenty-sixth. Margaret purchased the same tech stuff she had ordered on the PSA credit card. Fortunately George Jones had a copy of the receipt in his sports jacket, so she knew what to buy. She paid cash, with the help of cash advance from a new Visa card. She had saved money with the after-Christmas sales, so she bought some CDs to make the order come out to $1,365. Now the challenge was to get the stuff up to her bedroom, undetected by Bonnie, who had spent Christmas night with her. She let the twins take the Volvo back to their apartment.

After establishing Bonnie was not home, Margaret lugged the bags up to her room. Just then she heard the front door open.

"Mom, are you here? I am starving."

Margaret said, "Yes, I am. I'll come right down and will make us some lunch."

As Margaret entered the big, bright yellow and amber-accented kitchen, petite Bonnie, in a chocolate running suit was opening a water bottle. The room had windows across the wall that held the sink. The backyard, about a quarter of an acre, had a stone wall around the perimeter, a rusted swing set, a weather-beaten tree house, and a matching doghouse. Although it was winter, the trees and shrubs suggested neglect. The great room opened to the kitchen and had windows on three sides, which illuminated the kitchen as well. Bonnie jumped on a kitchen stool, took a swig of water, and sat it on the chocolate-speckled granite counter top of the island in the center of the room. "Mom, we got to talk. You have been pretty scarce and mysterious. What have you been up to?"

Margaret put the crab soup in the microwave, trying to decide how to respond. "Babe, I have had a lot going on."

"At night, I mean. You KNOW how I hate staying in this place by myself. It is so BIG."

"You have been staying with your sisters and have more freedom, so what is the problem?"

"I want a parent who comes home at night!"

"Whoa! What are you talking about?"

"You know, Mom. You are not senile. You and I were to go Christmas shopping on December nineteenth. I came home, and you were not here. I ordered a pizza and watched TV. At midnight I tried to go to sleep, but I couldn't. I called you, but your cell was off. I was scared. I wandered around the house until around three A.M., checking the doors and windows. I set my alarm for ten A.M. and fell asleep around four A.M. MOM, YOU DID NOT COME HOME. Where the frickin' were you? Shane and Shawna have each other. Dad has Angela and the babies. ALL I HAVE IS YOU!" Bonnie started to cry.

Margaret was spreading mayo on the toast trying to think. "Don't cry and don't use *frickin'* in my presence.

"I was with a sick friend, a very sick friend. I had to stay with her."

Wiping her tears, Bonnie knew her mom was lying. *What was the point? Oh what the hell.* "Look, if you are seeing someone just tell me. I can take it. I know you are human."

Ah, a way to bring this to an end. "You are correct. I am seeing someone, but at this point I would rather not discuss it. I'm still trying to sort out how I feel about the guy and whether or when and how to introduce him to my baby."

Bonnie smiled. "It's okay, Mom."

After that they talked school, and Margaret learned Bonnie was going to babysit for Jeremy on New Year's Eve and spend the rest of the week with her sisters. *That would be good.*

"So, Mom, I'm going to gather up my stuff and head out. You'll have this place to yourself." Bonnie turned on the stairway leading to her bedroom and, "You can do a lot of 'sorting out'—like deciding if you are in love!"

When Bonnie reached the upstairs she went to the laundry room off her mom's room to retrieve the jeans she had washed. She saw the Staple's bags on her mom's bed. She could not help herself. She went into her mom's room and took a look. *Strange. The SAME stuff Mom had given us for Christmas.* She sat on the bed. *Oh God, Mom's a shoplifter! No, no. She couldn't have lifted this much stuff without being caught.* Bonnie looked for the receipt. She found it and was relieved. Margaret came into the room.

She shouted, "What do you think you are doing?" Bonnie jumped. Her mom looked like a pissed coach after someone had missed an easy jump shot.

"Mom, I am sorry! I was just curious. Who's this stuff for anyway? It's exactly what you gave us for Christmas."

"Bonnie, you must respect my privacy! This room is off limits unless I am in it. Do you understand?"

Bonnie was shocked. Something was wrong. She pushed, "Mom, why did you buy this stuff AGAIN? You always say we are poor!"

"Get out of here! Go back to your sisters! When you can respect my space, you can come back!"

Bonnie flew out of the room crying. She threw her stuff in a tote bag and left the house. When she got into her Civic, she was still crying. She couldn't even see. She willed herself to stop. She wiped her nose on her hoodie sleeve. She started to back down the driveway, but stopped. She recalled the purse she had seen on the floor next to the low dresser in her mom's room was black. Her mom never used a black purse. It looked full, yet her mom's camel bag had been on the bed. If there was a simple explanation to all this, her mom would not have exploded. *It's NOT a man. It is something else. I have to figure it out and help my mom.*

Margaret sat on her bed, her head in her hands. *You handled that poorly, Margaret. Now she will blab it to her sisters, and God forbid, to Jeremy.* Margaret decided she needed to focus. She had much to do. For the next two hours she took the technology she had bought that morning out of its original boxes and placed it in the boxes in which the Christmas stuff had come. She was banking on the staff in the PSA inspector general's office checking only bar codes on the boxes. *Bureaucrats are so lazy.* Margaret planned to give it to Ted and tell him she had retrieved it from Donna's apartment. He could turn it in.

Margaret knew she should have called Bonnie and tried to make up, but she didn't have time. Margaret had too much to do between when Bonnie left and Ted was to arrive for dinner. First she went to the local recycle center and got rid of the technology boxes she didn't need. She then went to three different dumpsters and disposed of most of the contents of Donna Dawson's purse. She regretted not bringing the ten-pound dumbbell. It was still in her gym bag in her walk-in closet. Finally, she threw the purse in a ditch along a jogging path. Then she went to have her nails done.

When she got back home, she put the eye of round in the oven, washed two potatoes to bake, clipped the asparagus and put them upright in a small glass pitcher of cool water to chill, and made a pear and walnut salad and a raspberry vinaigrette dressing. She put on her favorite music, Rod Stewart singing oldies from the '40s, and opened a bottle of very good cabernet to let it breathe.

Ted arrived on time. He was strongly attracted to Margaret, but he knew she was a liability. He was curious— would his good sense or Viagra win out? Would he have the discipline to make this the last time? As was their routine, he brought the hors d'oeuvres—crab balls, some sharp Vermont cheddar cheese, olives, and crackers. He had a copy of his son's application to GTU. *Business first.*

Ted walked into her house carrying roses and the hors d'oeuvres, "Hi, there, Maggie. Flowers and food for the lady of the mansion! I have been looking forward to this all day long. You look so edible in your camel silk PJs, sort of like a caramel sauce."

"Oh, ho, ho, what have you been smoking—a Viagra cigarette?"

Ted walked over to Margaret, looking at her not eyeball to eyeball, but on an angle. He was a half a head shorter. He kissed her gently on the cheek. He put a hand under her shirt and one on her backside. "What do you care?"

Margaret backed away and smiled. "Let's take everything into great room and sit down so we can get comfy, okay?"

"Your wish is my command, madam. I sense this is going to be a good night, a long night, a night worth remembering." He had dressed in camel flannel slacks and a black cashmere V-neck. A few chest hairs were in evidence. He had given his Cole Haan black loafers a navy shine.

"You got that right, Teddy."

The great room was huge. It was the last thing Margaret and Jeremy had agreed on and decorated before their divorce. It was done in burgundy and navy with lots of antique pieces. The large burgundy couches formed an L in front of the fifty-two-inch-flat screen that hung over the gas fireplace. The room had navy vertical blinds and two identical Persian rugs covering most of the white big-tiled floor. The throw pillows, chair, and ottoman were blends of burgundy and navy geometric patterns.

Ted poured some wine for both of them. Margaret fixed two crackers. They held hands and put their heads back on the sofa. Ted said, "This is the life. For a brief moment in time, we don't have to worry about a thing."

Margaret kissed him hard and went for his inner seam.

"Ah, ah, honey let's take it slowly." He sat up and took her hand in his hand. It was once again a beautiful hand, no broken or deformed nails in evidence. He patted her hand.

She unbuttoned her shirt. He kissed and caressed her chest. A timer went off in the kitchen. Margaret got up, buttoning her shirt, and said, "I'll be right back."

Ted put his head back on the sofa again. He had to get his son into GTU. *But, I want sex tonight so I think I'll address it in the morning.* Ted had always been successful in life because he played things out in his mind, laying out the pros and cons. But then again, he had never met anyone like Margaret before—she was strong, driven, self-centered, a manipulator, gorgeous, and sexually precocious. *What is it? Do I like danger? I know she's going to jail!*

Margaret had checked everything in the kitchen. She poured herself another glass of wine. She sat on Ted's lap.

"Margaret, I'm going to ask you a question. If I get the right answer, I will arouse you."

"If I give the wrong answer?"

"I will do even a better job."

"Sort of a win,-win. What's the question?"

"Can you get my son into GTU?"

"Yes, I can. Now what?"

Margaret couldn't believe it. Ted did everything right and slowly. She had no idea he knew or could demonstrate the fine points of lovemaking. After about thirty minutes, he was still dressed and pressed, and she gathered her pajamas and walked to the kitchen.

Dinner went smoothly and included a lot of handholding and wine sipping. Toward the end of the meal, Ted began to cut back; he was beginning to become concerned about his "ability to perform" if his consumption of cabernet continued. Margaret, on the other hand, drank freely.

She went upstairs before Ted. She lit candles, put on soft music (*Gary Lamb*), put the champagne on ice, and put chocolate-covered strawberries on the nightstand. *Perfect.* The room had the same view as the great room. It was done in teal and white. The Louis XVI imitation white furniture was a gift to herself when Jeremy left.

Ted came upstairs with a commitment to continue to pace

things. It seemed like every other time he and Margaret got together they were always rushed. *I am going to show her sailors know how to make love to a woman. His dead wife could attest to that fact, but I know she's up there in heaven not approving of what I am doing. But then again, after tonight Maggie may not have an opportunity to make love for a long, long time. It is my civic duty to make her happy this one last time.*

Ted put his clothes neatly on the chair, and tossed his Blackberry, change, and wallet on the edge of Margaret's dresser. Margaret came out a bathroom with a silk, gold, see-through robe on and sat down next to Ted, now under the white satin sheet. She began feeding him strawberries and guzzling champagne at the same time. "Teddy, this is going to be a fantastic night for us—no rushing, no worry about kids, just lots and lots and lots of lovemaking."

She stood up and slipped off her robe. His eyes absorbed the bronze, shimmering, perfectly shaped, firm body standing over him. Margaret pulled back the sheet, leaned over to kiss Ted and hopped in bed on top of him. Unfortunately, her unsteady feet became tangled in the robe as it hit the floor. She fell sideways, bashing her head on the side of the nightstand. Blood was seeping on to the white carpet. She fell to the floor unconscious. Ted leapt out of bed. He leaned his naked body over her. He patted her cheeks. He poured champagne on her face. She smelled like cocoa butter. He could not revive her, but he knew she was not dead. And, since she was bigger than he was, he could not lift her up. *Shit now, what? Better get dressed.*

After he dressed he still could not revive Margaret. The bleeding had stopped. He went downstairs and got ice and put it in a plastic bag. He wrapped it in a towel and placed it on the side of her head. He knew he would have to call 911, but he had to get her dressed first. When the towel started turning red, he knew he could not delay calling 911. In a hurry he reached for his Blackberry and knocked it under the dresser. He got down on his hands and knees, put his head down on the carpet, and looked under the dresser. He saw his Blackberry. He reached in and pulled it out. He also saw a pill bottle. He pulled that out too. He leaned against the dresser and read it. It was a prescription for Zoloft made out to Donna Dawson. *Oh my God!* He put it in his pocket, dialed 911, and went downstairs to wait for the EMTs. He left Margaret naked, a pretty shade of pink seeping into her carpet all around her head. Ted wanted desperately to flee, but that was not the navy thing to do. So he sat on the couch with the Zoloft bottle in his hand staring down at it.

Chapter 46

Forensic Specialists, LLP, with Pip and Suzy tucked away in Pip's condo, was without a calming influence the twenty-sixth. Everyone was motivated but not sure what to do. Rich "took charge," but he was not a manager. Bart showed up at 9:00 A.M. with a consulting contract to be signed, authorization codes, and badges, but no warrants. When he learned Suzy wasn't in and where she was, he said he would take the contract to Pip to be signed. He warned Kit and Frank to not look at any records, till he called and said he had the signed contract. Electra said she could sign for Pip, but Bart wasn't buying it.

Johnny said he was no longer a clerk and would not help Electra. His name was John, and he was a detective. There was no going back. He gave his skimpy files on the case to Sheila and told her she was in charge of them. Frank was frustrated because no one seemed to care about his twelve churches. Kit was reading her boyfriend's online newspaper, indifferent to the tension around her. Sheila was helping Electra. Beamer was in Rich's office. He figured his job was to keep Rich calm.

"Beam, you and I need to divide things up till Pip recovers. If we ever get those damn warrants, we will be busy. I am going over to D.C. PD to hang with my friend Sara and see if they have any leads on who mugged Pip. There was zilch on the videotape. All it had was the front and rear views of cars, no Volvo, or anything else. The perp must have walked in and out undetected. You hold down the fort, okay?"

Beamer made a quick calculation. It seemed safe and harmless to let Rich go to a police station. "Okay, bro. But what if junior comes back?"

"You can handle him. He won't be back for a while. He went to see his girlfriend, remember?"

"What about Papa Bear?"

"He's out of pocket or soon will be. He told me yesterday he was heading to Geneva today. He'll be back Friday. Relax. Nothing is going to happen. And, I am a mere phone call away. You are creative. You will think of something for the troops to do.

"After I finish at the station, I am going to give Suzy a breather and stay with Pip. If I work it right, you may not see junior today because he will be 'otherwise occupied.'"

Later Beamer was pumped. Because of a cancellation he was able to arrange a gig for his band, the First Light, at a bar near GTU. He knew he needed some help from others in the office in order to pull off his plan to get to know Margaret Sabat's twins. He tended to think on a grand scale, so he convinced Electra to fix lasagna. Beamer considered Big E and himself as the parents of the outfit. It did not seem to matter he was thirty, and Big E was around sixty. They took care of everybody else, while Pip and Rich got all the glory.

It took some convincing on his part to convince Big E to fix lasagna for everyone. She agreed when he indicated he would buy the groceries, and make the salad and garlic bread. He also had to track down everybody he wanted included. He thought about including Johnny but decided that would be too complicated.

So there they were sitting around the conference table with a four-star meal, looking at Beamer with great anticipation.

"You guys know we have to find out what the Sabat kids got for Christmas. I got a plan. The truth is, I cannot do it alone. I need your help to establish a good cover. So this is a working dinner. We're going to a bar in Georgetown and look for the twins. Our job is to engage them. We need to find out as much as we can about their family, but especially their mother, Margaret Sabat. Since I have to be with the band part of the time, I will be able to join you at breaks. Sheila, if Suzy can't join us, your primary job is to take notes on my Blackberry and pretend like you're sending a text message to Kit, although in fact, you will also be letting Kit know what the hell is going on since it probably will be dark in the place and not so easy to read lips. Kit your job is to save all the text messages you get from Sheila or Suzy if she shows up. Of course, anybody else can also send Kit text messages. The basic task of the evening is to ask lots of questions and get lots of answers we can sift through tomorrow to share in the morning at the staff meeting."

Beamer continued, looking at Kit, but spoke to Electra, "This food is fantastic!" Everyone applauded. Big E smiled broadly. Then Beamer added, "And, Sheila is going to help you clean up the kitchen!" There was another round of applause.

Beamer was pleased with himself. He did think creatively. He did not regret bringing in three bottles of Chianti. Everybody was happy. Big E was talking to Sheila. That was also good. Hanging out with Big E in the kitchen will teach Sheila a few things about how amazing Big E was. She could not see, but that did not stop her from doing anything. She did not even use a white cane in the office, although that meant everything had to be put in its place, a place selected by Electra. Now the questions started flying.

Sheila said, "I really get to come with you and send messages to Kit?"

Without blinking, Beamer said, "Sure. Ole Frank will look like he has a harem when I am playing! Do you think you can handle them, Frank?"

Frank said, "I can handle anything as long as I have a beer in my hand." He raised his Chianti glass. Everyone laughed. He was very pleased with himself. He could not recall ever having made such a spontaneous funny comment in his entire life. He had remembered the line from a beer commercial.

Kit took the floor. "Look, you guys, you gotta remember I can't see in the dark. I wanna know what's being said at all times! You got that? You're all pretty good at texting me when you want something in the office, but you forget when we are out. You never share jokes or side remarks with me, unless we're sitting around this damn conference table!"

Suzy, who had just walked in and had caught the plan, said, "Don't worry, Kit. You will be in a loop tonight. You will not miss a thing. That's a promise. Beamer did you clear all this with Pip. You know, all of us going with you?"

Beamer replied, "I couldn't get her on the phone. But there is no way I can play in a band and talk to the twins at the same time, got it? Besides, Pip is into results. She trusts this grand orchestrator!" He expanded his arms over his head. Everyone but Suzy laughed again. Suzy wasn't so sure. *Head injury or no head injury, Pip should know what is going on.*

Beamer then said, "We rendezvous in ninety minutes. Go

back to your desks and brainstorm about questions to ask."

Everyone took dishes to the designer kitchen. There were some advantages to being on the top floor, "the penthouse." Beamer listened to Big E directing Sheila where to put things. *So far so good. I only hope the rest of the night goes as well.* He tapped Big E on the shoulder. They went into the hall. "Do you have a ride home, Mama?"

Big E smiled, "Of course. Joe's picking me up after he finishes with his last stiff at the funeral home. Don't worry 'Big Daddy.' You take care of the rest of the brood. In the morning Pip's going to kill you for taking those kids with you. And if she doesn't, I will for the bar bill. Either way you're screwed. But have a good time." Electra marched back into the kitchen.

On schedule the band of detectives trooped toward the First Light's van, their transportation to *Never-Never Land*, the bar where they would do their detecting on the twins. Beamer thought they made a fine cover; Frank, now that he was spruced up with Beamer's other leather jacket and Big E's Burberry scarf, hair moussed by Kit; Kit, with her four-inch platform boots, two-inch long, black skirt, black-and-white checked coat with matching hat, and twenty-foot-long yellow scarf to match her goldilocks; Sheila, in jeans that looked painted on, a short red jacket, and a Gucci knock-off bag; Suzy, super sweet in pink cords and a ski jacket.

Beamer had arranged with Pip to live at the office while he was putting his younger brothers through community college. That had ended two years ago. Moving out never came up, so he never moved out. He was stashing his money now to some day make a demo video and go on tour as someone's backup. His band all had day jobs like him, but unlike him, they wanted to be famous.

Once in the van, he looked his crew over one more time. They had been greeted warmly by Jake, Al, Harry, and Pete, and then shoved in between the drums, guitars, and Beamer's sax. Beamer was concerned about Frank, the makeover, Chin and Sheila Ramirez. *God only knows how they would do. The ladies—Ms. Suzy and Ms. Kit—were take-charge women. They would do just fine.* "Now look fans, remember we are working, so control the alcohol intake and thereby control the final bar bill. Got it?" Suzy had texted Kit the complete thought before Beamer finished it. Kit smiled.

Never-Never Land, better known as NNL, catered to poor graduate students with cheap booze, a basic menu of popular food, hot three-course dinners on Thursdays, a Wi-Fi corner with some extra soundproofing, and live music Fridays and Saturdays. Any real money was made off tourists, who were easy to spot and were given a 'special' menu and drink price list.

Frank spotted an empty booth and made a beeline for it. He had many talents, including a photographic memory and being keenly observant; he also loved research, understood technology, craved searching for patterns in anything, and quoted statistics at every opportunity (until Rich told him it was uncool). Pip discovered him at a self-advocates' meeting for people with autism. Over snacks and soda she offered him a job, and he accepted. He told her straight out he had a degree in criminology, but no social skills. She had told him not to worry about it. She said, "Frank, just watch others and do what they do. Also, watch a lot of chick flicks." So far that worked.

Beamer and his band were well into their first set when

he thought he was seeing double. Through the door came two of the most beautiful girls he had ever seen—the twins. They joined a group of friends off to his left. His pals were two booths further down. *Perfect.* The neodetectives spotted them too. Beamer's iPhone vibrated. He finished the number, talked to Pete, and looked at his iPhone message. Suzy had texted, Wat now. Beamer replied, relax, i'll fix it so they com 2 u.

Suzy showed Kit and everyone else. They nodded in unison. Beamer rolled his eyes. *Jesus, nothing like being inconspicuous!*

The band played three oldies and the crowd sang along. Beamer looked at the twins and then said into the mike, "Great voices, although I got to tell you guys, the ladies know how to harmonize, you don't." There was a chorus of boos and simultaneous laughter and clapping. "The final number in this set is for those two angels to my left—tell me am I seeing double from too much beer or have I died and gone to heaven?" With that the band struck up the Double Mint Chewing Gum jingle from the '60s and Beamer belted out "Double your pleasure, double your fun…." and jumped off the stage. Everyone laughed, clapped, and cheered him on as he headed straight for the twins.

Still with the mike in his hand, he said, "Ladies, ladies, may I introduce myself? Beamer Johnson, aspiring musician and sax man—that's sax not sex, for the First Light. Pointing in the direction of his dumbstruck compatriots, he said, "The fan club of my band, the First Light." The crowd roared. "Will you join us and share a pitcher?" The crowd shouted, "Beamer, Beamer, Beamer."

The twins were amused and got up and went to Beamer's booth. The crowd roared again. At this point Pete thought everyone needed a diversion so Beamer could get down to "business." So Pete and the rest of the band launched into a danceable medley. That did the trick, especially for Frank.

As soon as the twins arrived at the table, Frank said to the one smiling, "May I have the pleasure of this dance?" Shane was surprised, but accepted. Beamer, shocked, leaned over to Kit and said, "Can Frank dance with someone other than you?" She shrugged. "We all know he can dance."

To everyone's amazement Frank and Shane took over the dance floor. Their moves were graceful, perfectly synchronized, and creative. The crowd loved it. Frank was smiling and Shane was beaming. *Who would have thought Frank could be cool with a stranger!* Beamer pondered how to get the colts back into the corral. He walked over to Frank and cut in, "Rich is on Suzy's cell for you." Frank looked confused but let go of Shane's hand. Beamer said, "Thirsty?" Shane nodded, and they head back to the booth. Frank seemed okay. He winked at Beamer. Shane thought he was winking at her and winked back. Frank winked again.

When two new pitchers arrived, Beamer said, "How about if we begin with introductions? Ladies, how about if you go first."

Frank took in the details, filing them away. Shane and Shawna Sabat, although identical, had very different styles. Shane was all smiles and bubbly, out going, into shabby chic, and the real-deal in a bag—Coach. Shawna was reserved, cautious, suede camel skirt, camel cashmere V-neck, and Ferragamo black boots with a matching bag. Her nails were acrylic, black. Shane's nails were unpolished, but neatly filed. Hair fell in soft waves on their shoulders and makeup, on either, could not be detected, except for some clear lipgloss. Frank was in love, or so he thought. He had heard many times women love the tall, strong, silent type. That was him, or so he thought.

When the twins were finished, Beamer introduced his pals. *Let the questions begin.*

Suzy turned to Shane, sitting next to Kit, and said, "You have an interesting last name."

Shane said, "It's more of pain. It sounds too much like Sadam. Long-story-short, our dad is Egyptian American, and Mom is African American Native American."

Beamer thought, *One for Suzy.*

Frank, feeling a new strength in interpersonal prowess, "I am Cambodian American. Want to dance again?" Shane smiled.

Beamer intervened, "Ah, Frank, my man, let's chat for a while first."

Something registered with Frank. He gave a thumbs up. Suzy texted Kit.

Kit said to Shawna, "Do you live at home?"

Shane answered, "No way! Anyway our parents are divorced."

Shawna frowned at her sister, who was across from her. Feeling obligated to say something Shawna said, "Our family situation is complicated, but fortunately we all get along. Moreover, we are twenty-three, so we should have our own place."

Shane piped in, "What she means is, our dad, being the handsome dog he is, married a blond number ten type, fifteen years younger than him, and bam, they had twins. No room in the inn so to speak, at least one inn."

After a pause Kit said, "Wow, how'd your mom take that?"

Shane again, "She started going to the gym, period. You should see her body. It is curved, but hard as a rock."

Shawna frowned again. She asked Suzy, "Why are you texting? It's kind of rude." Suzy stopped texting and looked at Kit.

Beamer intervened, "Kit graduated from the University of Rochester. Suzy is working on her master's in organizational development, whatever that is. Yeah, they are rude. Can't believe they are members of my fan club."

Frank interrupted, "Kit's deaf. She is a good lip-reader, but not in the dark. Suzy let's her know what is being said."

Suzy texted Kit.

Kit was relieved. Beamer was curious.

Shawna seemed to open up, "Oh, I am so sorry for my comment. I had no idea."

Kit said, "Yeah, I look just like anyone else."

Shawna replied, "Your speech is perfect."

Kit said, "I was born with hearing but lost it at seven. My parents were aggressive. They threw everything at the schools and me so I would have a 'normal' life. They made me learn to lip-read and American Sign Language. It was not easy or fun growing up, but I am glad I am an adult now, I can make my own choices."

Shane said, "I am impressed. Text away girls! God knows we talk fast! You'll get carpal tunnel after one night with us!" Everyone laughed. Kit did too, though three seconds after everyone else.

Out of the blue Frank said, "What did you get for Christmas?"

Shawna said, "More than we should have."

Shane added, "We each got a DVD player and recorder to share, new cell phones, and things lawyers like, digital recorders. Oh yeah, we each got new cameras too."

Sheila said, "Boy, that is a lot! Your parents must be loaded."

Shane replied, "Oh contraire. Our dad has NO MONEY. His new wife bought us cashmere sweaters from Nordstrom's on sale. I know because the woman has NO TASTE and left the sale tags on the sweaters! Our mom is responsible for all the tech stuff. She just maxes out her credit cards because she loves us and reminds us of that fact repeatedly!"

Shawna looked resigned. She took a sip of beer.

Beamer thought they had enough, so leaving the troops to their on devices, he went back to join the band for the last set. After a while, he saw Frank dancing with Shane again. After the last set, Beamer ordered coffee for everyone. And, he offered the twins a lift. He wanted to know where they lived.

Before the twins left the van, everyone exchanged contact information and gave each other hugs. After that Beamer drove everybody else home too. His head hit the pillow at 3:30 A.M. He was satisfied.

Rich was not. Around 9:00 P.M. he had received a call from Johnny.

"Rich, you want to come over to my place for a beer?"

"No can do. I am babysitting Pip. Suzy's out with Beamer."

"I know. Beamer didn't invite me. Why didn't he?"

Like I need this. Help me here, God. "Look, Johnny—I mean John—those guys see us as the serious investigators. They do the easy stuff. Whatever they learn, you and I will do the follow-up detective work."

"Okay. I get it. Thanks Rich. See you tomorrow. We'll grill

them tomorrow, right?"

"You bet. We'll have plenty of follow-up. Don't you worry. You could have woman problems."

"I don't any more. Good night, Rich."

With that last comment, Rich clicked off and went searching for hard liquor. He found some Blue Sky vodka. He fixed a bucket of ice, found a glass, and took the vodka to Pip's den. He flipped on ESPN and reclined in Pip's favorite chair. He had fed her, but he had not eaten.

His cell rang about an hour later. H had killed a third of the fifth. "Yeah."

"Netherfield here. Sabat is in Bethesda hospital. A guy named Morton called 911. She fell and hit her head. No word on her condition. Morton found pills that belonged to Dawson and bags of technology from Staples at Sabat's. Do you know Morton?"

"Yeah. Remember he is her boyfriend and boss. Where are you?'

"At Sabat's."

"How did you end up there?"

"Put a tracker on her Volvo. She lent her Volvo to her kids. Now we have trackers on three cars."

"Good for you, junior. Do you have any warrants yet?"

"No. But the stuff you collected will pay off. I'm going to the hospital to get some Sabat fluids to get DNA."

"Thanks for calling. Assume I'll see you tomorrow."

"Yes."

"Bye, man."

Wow. No food. No medication, and I acted like an adult.

Pip walked into the den with one of her three new carts.

Thanks to Christmas presents and manual labor, she now had three assembled carts of three sizes. She looked at Rich concerned. He looked at her and smiled.

"I got a tell you, Pip, you look like Friar Tuck with blond curls. I guess that makes me Robin Hood, huh? Let's go to the kitchen, and you can watch me make and eat some bacon and eggs and junior's mom's cake. Suzy organized your fridge. You have enough food for a month thanks to all the people who came through here yesterday." They walked to the kitchen.

"I see you found my vodka."

"How do you feel?"

"My head still hurts."

Pip's cell rang. She reached into her robe pocket and sat down on as kitchen chair.

"Hi, Sam."

Pip hoped Rich would take a walk. He did not. She was too tired to leave the kitchen.

"How are you feeling, darlin'?"

"My head hurts. Why are you calling me at two A.M.?"

"I am in Geneva. I thought I would take a chance and wake you up."

"Geneva? When are you coming back?"

"Friday. I'll come straight to you, I promise. The White House knows what we are doing."

"What you and I are up to or the case?"

"I know they know the latter, and I suspect they also know the former."

"Rich is here. He's eating eggs."

"Good. Let me talk to him."

She handed the phone to Rich. "Sam wants to talk to you."

"Director."

"How is Pamela doing?"

"Okay. Sabat is in the hospital. She fell and hit her head. Bart is on it."

"I know. Son, I am sorry, but no warrants till I get back to work things out. I suspect our involvement may be cut off soon. Concentrate on finding Dawson. That will give us leverage. I'll be back Friday night. Thanks for looking after Pamela. Bye."

Chapter 47

As Rich walked out of Pip's condo, Suzy and Bart were locked in a kiss by her front door. She saw him and pulled away.

"Morning, folks. Have a good night?"

Bart spoke first. "Is Dr. Planter up?"

"She hasn't made it to the kitchen yet, but I heard her moving around. Go on in. I have made a big pot of coffee. I'm headed to the office to get the troops mobilized. I'll fill you in when you get there, Netherfield. Suzy, you are staying with Pip today, right?"

"Yes."

"Good. See you guys later."

Pip was in the kitchen when Bart and Suzy came in. Suzy kissed Pip on the cheek.

"Good morning, Aunt Pamela. Hope you are feeling better."

Aunt Pamela? Suzy was surprised.

"I am, thank you, Bart."

"I thought I should give you an update."

"I appreciate that. Please have some coffee and a bagel."

While Suzy was fixing coffee and bagels, Bart sat and brought Pip up to speed. "Well, I put a guy on Margaret Sabat at her house around seven o'clock last night. And it's good thing I did. Morton showed up at her house around that time. At ten thirty P.M. an ambulance arrived. Sabat was taken out on a stretcher. She is in the hospital with a head injury. The agent confirmed that with the hospital. It appears to have been accident. It's too early to tell how she was affected. I've arranged for us to get an update later this morning."

Pip sat back in her chair and put her coffee cup down. "Anything else?"

"Yes. Morton has decided to cooperate with us. He did not go with Sabat to the hospital. He stayed at her place for about another hour and then left. I think he came to his senses. He found tech stuff in Sabat's bedroom. What possessed him to go looking for that I don't know? He delivered it to the inspector general this morning. They're looking at it now. They indicated everything appears to be in order according to the bar codes on the boxes. They will send the stuff over to us later this morning so we can take a look at it as well. There's more—he found a pill bottle belonging to Donna Dawson under Sabat's dresser. He gave it to the PSA director of security. He called me, and I went over and picked up. I'll get it to Quantico."

"What do we do now?" Pip asked.

"We have a ton of circumstantial evidence, most of which we cannot use in court because of a lack of an official chain of custody. The higher-ups still want to maintain a low profile. I think we need to go by the book from now on. This case is now considered an FBI case exclusively because of the missing person, Donna Dawson. Your office will continue to be involved, but we cannot tolerate any freelancing by people who have not been designated as investigators. Only two people in your office have been cleared—Kit to continue handling financial information and Rich to do interviewing and investigating. However, I will interview Margaret Sabat.

We cannot have any screwups. Suzy told me Rich could be unpredictable and blow up."

Pip thought, *but not in an interview situation. He is a professional.* Pip did not like that last comment, but she understood what was at risk.

Meanwhile at Forensic Specialists, LLP, Rich was convening with Beamer in Rich's office.

Rich took a bite of a bagel, "Beamer, four things need to happen today. First, find Dawson. Second, find Dawson. Third, find Dawson. Fourth, anything else."

Beamer filled Rich in on events at the bar. He said that Kit, Frank, and Johnny were going to have lunch with the Sabat twins and check out bar codes on their electronics. Rich thought, *Good, that will keep them busy.*

Beamer also said Kit and Frank were starting to look at bank and credit card records. Then Beamer dropped a bombshell.

"Last night after I took everyone home, I was wide a wake. So, I swung by Landmark Therapies. The van was gone."

"What!"

"I swung around the back of the property. The Honda was there, but not the van."

Rich pulled out his cell and a piece of paper from his right pants pocket.

"Hey, Sara, run this plate number for me, Doll. Call me back. I have FBI credentials now, so you are not breaking any laws. Yeah, I know I owe you big time. Thanks."

"Beam, get everyone in the conference room. We need to divide things up."

Rich's phone rang. "That was fast, Sara. What 'ya got for me?"

"When you said FBI, that greased the wheels. Van is a leased vehicle. Owned by Hamilton Leasing in Bethesda. Turned in yesterday."

"Give me the address of the leasing company." He wrote it down. "Lease was held by Landmark Therapies, right?"

"Yep."

"Thanks, babe."

He signed off and headed to the conference room.

As soon as he hit the door, he started barking out orders and asking questions.

"Beamer, if we have authorization, go check out the P.O. box. Do we?" Beamer nodded.

"Well get going. You and I are going to Bethesda when you get back."

Bart walked in with technology Morton had turned in.

Rich continued, "Kit, Frank, and Johnny—John—go have an early lunch with your new friends and get back here so we can decide how too deal with the churches."

Bart said, "What are you going to do, Rich?"

Asshole. "Make a short trip to PSA to interview some of George Jones's pals. What are your immediate plans?"

Kit interrupted. "Frank and I have been looking at Landmark Therapies accounts. There is a lot of traffic between them and Dew Point Graphics. Can you get us access to Dew Point's account, so I can work on it when we get back?"

"Ugh, sure. I'll work on it now."

"Okay. We will reconvene at two P.M." Everyone but Bart took off.

Bart looked at Rich and said, "Isn't the priority finding Dawson?"

"Yes, it is. But don't you know groundwork is important. George's cronies could give me some leads, and I had to keep the kids busy. It's good management."

Bart said, "George has been transferred to a veterans hospital at Robin's Bay."

"I'll file that fact. Sabat can't go after him. She has joined the same club."

"What club?"

"Head injury, genius."

Chapter 48

Frank, Kit, and Johnny were standing by Kit's car in the garage. Frank said before they took off, "Do you think we can get the barcodes off their electronics while we are with Shane and Shawna?"

Johnny said, "They will think we are nerds, but we can try."

Frank replied, "I am not a nerd. I have a photographic memory."

Kit said they could try, but thought bar codes were only on boxes. She put the car in gear. "Now keep quiet you guys while I drive. Remember the rule—we only talk at red lights."

Johnny was once again enjoying his new life. It certainly beats reading to Electra, helping her with invoices and filing, and listening to her complain. He hoped Pip would not stop his fieldwork. *I am good! If Frank can get barcodes, I bet I can too!*

They rode in silence the whole way. Kit was a good driver, and they had all green lights. When they arrived at the twins' neighborhood, it took a while to find a parking space. Everybody was home, so there were no available parking spaces. They had picked up some beer and Diet Coke so the twins would not consider them total moochers.

When they got to the twins' apartment, they were introduced to Bonnie, their little sister, who had puffy eyes like someone who had just cried a lot. The Sabats were introduced to Johnny.

Kit said, "Let's go to the kitchen and let Frank and John

hook up your stuff."

Shane said, "John, you know how to hook up electronics?"

Johnny replied, "You would be surprised at what I can do. Don't worry—I will not mess up your stuff. I can even read and write. You wanna see?"

Johnny went over to the pile of electronics in the corner of the small living room. He said, "Give me a piece of paper."

Shauna brought him a piece of paper without questioning his request.

Johnny held up the DVD player. "See this barcode? I can copy it on a piece of paper." And, he proceeded to do just that. After he did three in a row, the girls went to the kitchen. Johnny slapped Frank five.

Frank said, "That was good, John." Out of view of the girls they copied down all the bar codes in no time.

In the kitchen Kit, Shauna, and Shane were fixing plates. Bonnie had never met a person who could not hear, although they had some students that looked like John in her school. Bonnie said to Kit, "I guess because you can't hear we shouldn't watch a video while we eat. You wouldn't enjoy that, right?"

Kit, not usually diplomatic, was gentle in her response. "That is very thoughtful of you, Bonnie. However, most DVDs nowadays have closed captioning. So I can watch along with everyone else and enjoy a video just as much. Also, I am a wicked lip-reader. As long as I can see a face, I can usually figure out what somebody saying."

Bonnie continued, "How did you meet John, being he is retarded and all?"

Kit said, "John, Frank, and I worked together. John has his own apartment, and he is learning to drive. He has an intellectual impairment, called Down Syndrome. FYI the term *retarded* is out."

Bonnie blushed. "I'm so sorry. I did not mean to be offensive."

Kit said, "It's not complicated, just treat everybody with respect, and the right words will come to you naturally."

Before anything else was said John came into the kitchen. "Everything is hooked up now." Bonnie smiled at John.

Everybody carried plates and drinks into the living room. They sat on bright yellow faux leather beanbag chairs, the chocolate microfiber couch, or the cream-colored carpet. The living room was decorated in an African theme with leopard and zebra throws. Shauna started the movie *The Duchess*. Frank thought, *Good, a chick flick*. Johnny thought, *Cheez, a chick flick*.

After the movie Frank explained to the twins how to use all the new electronics. He wrote directions for Bonnie so she would know what to do with her new electronics when she got home.

Shauna said to Frank, "What do you all do?"

Frank replied, "Forensics."

Shane chimed in, "What kind? "

Kit, getting worried, thought she better take over, "We do research to help federal agencies solve problems. It could be on any topic. We are generalists."

Shauna then said, "What are you working on now?"

Before Kit could stop him, Johnny said, "Three things— fraud, an assault case, and a missing person."

Shane said, "That sounds like detective work to me."

At this point, Kit was worried. She explained their role was more background. They could not share details because it was confidential. Much of their work was computer based and surfing the Web. The twins let the topic drop. Kit was surprised and relieved at that, given they were law students. But the next topic didn't prove to be easier.

Shauna said, "How did you meet Beamer?"

Kit said, "We heard his band one night, and became 'groupies' I guess. His band is good. It just hasn't been discovered. I know it is just a matter of time."

Johnny wanting to get back into the conversation said, "We are more than groupies. We are Beamer's friends. We see him every day," and he smiled at Kit.

Frank was bored. He was worried about the time. He stood up and said, "Let's go." And so they did.

In the car Kit said to Frank and Johnny, "Guys, loose lips sink ships. We told them too much, now I have to decide how much we should tell Rich and Pip. When I tell them, I suspect Pip's going to tell us to stay in the office and not help with fieldwork. I don't think we screwed up, but we almost did. If there is a next time, when they start asking questions, you let me answer them."

Neither Frank nor Johnny said anything because they were not at a red light.

Frank thought, *Kit always has the advantage. She can talk any time.*

Johnny thought, *Got to ask my dad about "loose lips sink ships." I can't ask Kit because she'll think I am dumb.*

Chapter 49

Margaret sat up in bed. She had a headache, but other than that she felt okay. *How do I use this turn of events to my advantage? I know! I'll have amnesia! I won't remember anything from December fifteenth till now. That would solve multiple problems. Whatever it takes. I need to be on that plane to Mexico on Friday.*

A tall, emaciated man in a white coat entered her room. "Good morning, Mrs. Sabat. I am Dr. Ramirez. You had a nasty fall last night. How do you feel?"

"What do you think? I have a headache." *Genius.*

"Mrs. Sabat, do you remember the fall?"

"No I do not, but I could use some Advil."

"Could you tell me what you do remember?"

"Well, I was sitting at my desk thinking how cold it was outside, wishing I did not have to walk to the Metro. My car was in for a tune up."

"Mrs. Sabat, what day is it?"

"Look I know my name, I know my birthday, I know who's president, and I know today is December fifteenth. Just trying to save you and me some time, Doctor, so I can go home and get ready for Christmas."

"Mrs. Sabat, it is Tuesday, December twenty-seventh."

"Great sense of humor, Doc, but my daughters will not appreciate it if there are no wrapped presents under the tree."

"It is Tuesday, December twenty-seventh, Mrs. Sabat. He flipped on an all-news TV station that had the date and time in the lower corner of the screen.

"Oh my, God! I have amnesia!" She looked at Ramirez as if it was his fault, trying to project rage, anger, fear, and confusion. Margaret then put her head in her hands and attempted to cry. That was easier said then done. *Ramirez is a stoic, unsympathetic son of a gun.* Ramirez stood silent while Margaret tried to sob. She put her head up and stared at him.

"Mrs. Sabat, the brain is a complicated organ. We need to run some tests to determine the nature of your brain injury. Some wiring has been jolted. It appears you have lost memory for some days."

"What does that mean? Am I going to get them back?"

"That's hard to predict. There is a high probability you will with time and the right clues, cues, and therapy. We can also use your family, friends, and contacts to help create a new memory of the missing days if your actual memory of those days fails to return. Consider yourself lucky. Some people experience much worse consequences from a severe head trauma."

Such a comforting bastard. "Can I see my children?"

"Yes, after we run some tests. It is important to not to delay putting together an assessment of the extent of damage and to monitor things for a few days."

"When did I get here?"

Ramirez looked at his PDA and punched in something. "Around eleven thirty last night."

"What time is it now?"

"Two thirty P.M."

"You have done no tests in the last fifteen hours?"

Ramirez punched more information into his PDA. "You

came to in the ambulance when smelling salts were placed under your nose. You knew your name, date of birth, and the president. Your head wound was cleaned and sutured. We did a scan. We checked for broken bones. We took a blood sample and checked your vital signs. We kept you awake until seven thirty A.M., and then let you sleep.

Margaret thought she had dreamed all that. *Maybe some of my wires did get crossed after all.*

"With head trauma, monitoring and interacting with the patient is a sound, conservative way to chart a course of action. All the indicators we have so far suggest no damage. Only what you have just shared with me about no recollection of many days indicates there may be damage we have not detected."

"What will happen next?"

"Multiple things. Targeted scans, more blood work, additional interviews, memory tests, and time with a physical therapist. You should be out of here by tomorrow, if there are no contraindications. What we learn may suggest the need to spend time in a rehabilitation center."

"A rehab center?"

"Yes, Mrs. Sabat. Such a center may help you recapture those lost days, if they do not return spontaneously. But, I see no reason why you cannot spend time with your family first."

Margaret smiled. She couldn't help herself. She just thought of how she could improve Jeremy's finances so he could pay spring tuition for the girls.

"I would like to go to Lake and Lawn Rehabilitation and Nursing Center in Alexandria so I can be with my mother-in-law and father-in-law."

Ramirez almost showed his surprise but kept his facial

expression in neutral. *This is one strange woman. Why would she say this at this point?* "Well, let's not get ahead of the situation. We need to see if your memory will come back by itself in the next few days. Being with your family may help."

Ramirez decided to try something and see how Sabat reacted. "I have to admit Mrs. Sabat yours is an intriguing case. I have never seen a case where someone lost days as you have. Usually people have total amnesia or amnesia for the time immediately around the event following head trauma."

Sabat's eyes widened, but she repressed any further reaction. Ramirez thought perhaps he had a faker.

Margaret, reading his mind, decided she needed to proceed carefully. She just stared at Ramirez her mind racing. She needed to get a laptop and read up on head trauma so she could exhibit credible symptoms. *Where the heck is Ted? I am inclined to put a pillow over his head too, just like I plan to do for my in-laws—put them out of their misery and free up some cash!* She laughed out loud. She could not help it.

Ramirez decided he had something more or other than head trauma with Mrs. Sabat. He made a note to add a psych evaluation on his PDA.

"Well, Mrs. Sabat, we will try to get the first round of tests done by mid-afternoon so you can visit with your husband and children."

"Thank you. I am divorced. It's Ms. Sabat. Put that in your PDA, Doc."

"Okay. See you later." *Why does she want to spend time with her mother-in-law and father-in-law if she is divorced?*

Margaret leaned back and closed her eyes. She was tired. *I have lost control of things. I need my phone, my BlackBerry. Why hasn't anyone called? Why hasn't Ted called? I need to have him turn in that tech stuff to the IG. I need to check my finances. I am handicapped. I can't write any of this down. Who knows who will see it? Moving to Lake and Lawn for a few days may work. I wonder how George is doing? I wonder where George is? Boy, would it be convenient if he were in Lake and Lawn too? Ah, that's too much to wish for!*

She picked up the bedside landline and dialed Shauna's cell. "Hi, there."

Shawna said, "Mom, some guy named Ted called and said you were in Bethesda Hospital. What happened? I called but they would not put me through to you and said we could not come to visit till after four P.M. today. Mom, what happened?" Shawna was cool and reserved, so she asked the questions calmly.

"I fell and bumped my head, or so they tell me. I have partial amnesia—lost some time. They are running tests."

"Mom, who is Ted?"

"Look, you are my smart, cool-headed girl. Your mother needs your help. I need my phone, BlackBerry, and laptop. Can you go and get them and bring them to me? I'll see you and your sisters later this afternoon. Don't worry. Bye."

Shawna stretched out on her living room floor, still full from lunch, and put a gold pillow under her head. MTV, muted, was on the thirty-seven-inch flat screen in front of her. Shane and Bonnie were out for a run, trying to channel their concern about their mother. *She is amazing. So detached. So focused. What kind of mother is that? Oh well, she seems okay. I'll go take a shower.*

Just then there was a knock at the door. Shawna looked at herself in the floor-length mirror by the apartment door.

She wore a navy hoodie and gray sweat pants. Even with no makeup and greasy hair, she thought her five-foot-eleven frame looked very good. She peeked through the peephole. A short white guy in gray flannels, pale blue turtleneck, and a destressed leather bomber jacket was standing there with her mom's camel tote in his hand. *Ted?????????????*

Chapter 50

About the time the trio had taken off for lunch with the Sabat kids, Rich walked over to PSA. It was a clear, but cold day. Rich wanted to find out how warm his new black cashmere overcoat was. He wanted to try and connect with George Jones's work buddies before hooking up with Bart to go to Bethesda. He had agreed to go with Rich to the leasing company and then go see Sabat in the hospital.

He got in and was directed to the break room for the guards. Only two guys were there. Rich flashed his badge, said FBI, and pulled up a chair between the guards and the wide-screen TV.

I am here to talk to you about George Jones. "Did you know him?" Both men nodded yes.

"Do you know someone tried to kill him?" They nodded yes.

"What can you tell me about George? Something that might help us to find the person who assaulted him."

The short chubby guard with acne whose name badge read Haines volunteered, "I don't know anything. Jones was a loner with an attitude."

"What do you mean?"

"Well, he was a vet. Did the Gulf War. He was constantly reminding us of that fact. It got old real fast, man."

"How about you, Johnston, what can you add about Jones?"

"He did keep to himself except when he was bragging and

not just about the war."

Haines snickered. Johnston was almost pretty. He had gentle features and a perfectly shaped nose. The same could be said for his body on a six-foot frame, the right proportions, but not too hard, yet not flabby. Rich thought may be he was a swimmer and possibly gay.

Rich said, "Come on, enlighten me here. Let's stop dancing around. What do you know?"

Johnston smiled, "He was a ladies' man. He fucked someone different every night, or so he claimed."

"Did he talk about anyone chick more than others?"

"No. There were many, many conquests—married and unmarried."

"Did he talk about anyone he wanted to bang, but hadn't yet?"

Haines couldn't resist, "Yeah, a golden-brown honey named Sabat. He called her PMS—pretty mighty Sabat, who he said, and I am quoting, 'needed to be laid out, bored into, and rung out.' Then she wouldn't have PMS anymore." Haines laughed.

"Did you know if he ever scored with Sabat?"

Haines said, "I don't know. But he suggested once he had recently acquired leverage, but never gave details. You'll never find out now that his brain is mush."

"Can you recall when he made the remark about having leverage?"

"No."

Rich tried a shot in the dark, "Did Jones ever talk about Donna Dawson?" He showed them a picture he had taken from her apartment—short brown hair, medium frame, a little plump, in a navy suit, white sweater, and pearls.

Haines and Johnston laughed in union. Haines then said, "Jones may have been a prick, but he dated 'sweet meat'. Dawson was an old maid who took care of her mama. Jones wouldn't waste his time with the likes of her."

"What about on a dare?"

Johnston reentered the exchange, "Jones took his lovemaking very seriously. It was, as he said, 'his gift from God'. There is no way he would use it on the vulnerable."

"Yeah, but your buddy there gave us a pretty strong quote about Sabat."

Johnston pondered then replied, "Jones saw himself as God's avenger and/or messenger. He had a mission—bring the ice princesses of the world down a few pegs and/or comfort the distraught, but don't get caught!"

The guards laughed in unison again.

"Can you think of anyone who would want to harm Jones?"

Haines said, "Sure, any jilted bitch, her husband, or boyfriend."

Rich decided he had wrung these idiots dry and left.

Chapter 51

Rich had the troops back in the conference room by 2:15. "You are going back into the field but let's keep it to ourselves. That is, don't tell Pip while she is recuperating. We won't tell Pip until we have the evidence. You are going out to find Donna Dawson's car. I think it is on a church parking lot. Frank found twelve churches. So you are going to twelve church parking lots and look for a gold Honda. And you are going to do it this afternoon."

Beamer knew he was to be the chauffer and babysitter for this adventure, but he couldn't do that or go with Rich either. *What happened to his morning plan?* Beamer needed to book his band for New Year's. He wasn't going anywhere. "No can do, Rich. I need to stay close to home base and set up some gigs. You'll have to go with Johnny and Frank."

Rich frowned. He had not planned on this, now that Bart and he were going to Bethesda together.

"My name is John, remember. All Frank and I need is transportation. We can do the legwork."

Frank said, "There is no subway line out there, and a bus would take forever—eighty-seven and a half minutes from here to Chevy Chase. Taxis for twelve stops would cost between eighty-five and two hundred and twenty dollars, depending on the number of red lights you hit, and that doesn't include time for a meter to run while we are looking for Dawson's car."

The sun was out and up high projecting bright light on the

mahogany conference table. Rich was stumped. He knew he had to focus on interviewing and convincing Bart to not spend Friday night at Suzy's. He might run into his old man. This was a perfect job for Frank and *John*, but they needed wheels.

Johnny slapped the table. Everyone else jumped. "I have a plan. Sheila has a driver's license. She can drive Frank and me. Now, all we need is a car!"

Rich thought, *Not bad. I'll give them Pip's car.* And so he did. Beamer agreed to cover the phones. Sheila was ecstatic about doing "fieldwork." A win-win situation for everybody. They were to call Beamer or Rich every thirty minutes and report in. The office kept a set of Pip's keys, so she didn't need to know her car was in use. They were to return to the office no later than seven.

Frank went back to his office to get his laptop and jacket. He came back to Rich. "You know there is no way we can check twelve parking lots in five hours, right?"

Rich replied, "I feel you are going to hit the jackpot early in your search."

Sheila in her long red down coat, black ski cap, matching twenty-foot long scarf and gloves, Johnny in his North Slope vest and Ralph Lauren jeans, and Frank in his baggy cords and distressed leather jacket marched out of the office with great confidence. They had an important mission and a deadline. Sheila thought, *This is easy, and it could be fun, as long as I don't have to parallel park the Lexus.* Her depth perception was not great, and nonexistent in the dark.

They headed up the Rock Creek Parkway. Sheila was a good driver. The Lexus was easy to drive. Frank noticed she kept two car lengths behind the car in front of her.

Sheila said to Frank, "Okay fill me in. What are we to do?"

Frank had a map of the sites they were to visit on his laptop screen. "We are going to visit twelve church parking lots looking for a gold Honda belonging to a woman who has been missing since mid-December. First stop is St. Barbara of the Vine. Next exit. I'll direct you."

As they pulled into the church lot, they saw few cars. There was one champagne-colored. Frank told Sheila to pull up next to it. Johnny said, "Forget it. It's a Lexus."

Sheila said, "You are so smart, John"

Johnny replied flatly, "You know why Sheila—raised on cars."

Sheila asked if she should drive behind the church. Frank said, "Yeah, good idea."

They found nothing.

Johnny said, "I am starving. Can we eat?"

Frank looked at his watch, "Time to check in."

Sheila said, "I'll look for a Starbucks."

Johnny said, "I want food, not coffee."

Frank replied, "That's where you can meet chicks."

Johnny, "I want food, not sex."

Sheila thought, *Amazing*. She pulled into a McDonald's.

Before they left the car, Frank talked to Beamer. "We finished one lot."

"Damn man, you better pick up the pace."

"Johnny wants to eat. He's not interested in picking up chicks."

Beamer processed that one and decided not to seek a clarification. "Okay. Call me in thirty minutes. Don't call Rich because he may be interviewing. Hold on a second. I'll be right back to you."

Kit came up to the reception desk. "Beamer, where the hell is everyone?"

"Fieldwork. What can I do for you?"

"I found something interesting. Seems like I have no one to share it with."

Beamer said, "Try Bart."

Another line rang before he could ask Kit what was interesting. It was Suzy. "Beamer the church where Dawson and Sabat both went to a luncheon on December nineteenth was St. Joseph's of the Sad Willow. Tell Rich to get on it."

"Sure, Babe. How'd you manage to do that?"

"I called Bart and told him Pip was driving me crazy. He got us remote access to Dawson's and Sabat's Outlook calendars."

"Creative guy. Great."

Beamer switched back to Frank. "You still there, Frank?"

"Yeah, for the last seventy-nine seconds."

"Sorry. Get carryout and head over to St. Joseph's of the Sad Willow. Is that one of your twelve?"

Frank looked at his list. "Yeah. Why do people have to eat?"

"Because they are hungry. Call me back real soon."

"In thirty minutes, right?"

"Yes. Good luck. Be careful. Adios."

Frank recounted what they had to do. If St. Joseph's was it, they had plenty of time.

Sheila said, "Look Frank, Johnny—John—and I can get the food. You get us directions. What do you want? We'll be back in a flash."

"A number five, no mayo, no catsup, and no pickle."

Johnny got out and said, "Look, Frank, why not just say

cheeseburger straight up?"

Frank, "Because then I would get no drink or large fries."

When Sheila and Johnny returned with the food, they ate without talking. St. Joe's was right on Connecticut, five minutes away.

As they pulled into the lot, it was packed. Frank and Johnnie split up. They told Sheila to stay with the car. In about twenty minutes she needed to empty her bladder. She went into the back of the church, read the signs, and went down to the lower level where the restrooms were. She saw a guy in jeans and a black hoodie heading for a rear door. He had two white plastic bags that looked heavy and were jingling. *Shit. He's ripping off the collection boxes!* He saw Sheila. She went into the restroom and put her body against the door. She texted Kit. "What's Frank's cell? NEED IT NOW." She did not wait long. Kit sent it. She was relieved the robber didn't come after her. She texted Frank. "Robber went out back door, lower level. Meet me by door NOW! *Please dear God let us catch the SOB. Forgive me. Also, please do not let me wet my pants.*

She opened the restroom door very slowly and peeked out—no robber. She sprinted to the back door and looked out. She could not believe her eyes. The robber was sitting on a brick wall counting and organizing paper bills. He had four stacks to his left. *What if there had been wind? I almost feel sorry for him.* Sheila stayed inside, but kept her eye on the robber. She heard feet on the stairs. To her relief it was Frank and Johnny. By now the robber was putting coins in wrappers. *I can't believe it. The guy must be OCD!*

Sheila pointed him out to the guys. Johnny said, "There are three of us. We can nail him and then call nine-one-one."

It sounded good. Sheila said, "Okay, but I got to pee first. You keep watching him, in case he takes off before I get back. *Guys never have to go. Why?*

When Sheila was coming out of the restroom, she saw Johnny and Frank running out the back door. She did the same. At the door she tore off her coat. It hindered her speed. She was five-one but fast. She ran track in high school. She caught up with Johnny and Frank without trouble. The robber had taken off with one bag when he saw the guys peering out the door. He was about twenty yards in front of them running at a steady clip. He was fast. Johnny spotted paper money on the robber's path of running. The robber was heading for some woods. Sheila and Johnny were running at the same speed, but Frank was slowing down. He wondered about his computer and if Sheila had locked the car. Frank decided he better stay with Johnny and Sheila. He picked up his pace, but they were about forty yards ahead of him. He saw them enter a wooded area.

The robber was behind a fern tree catching his breath and watching Sheila and Johnny approach. They spotted the robber, so he took off running again. He saw a gulley and dropped into it expecting that they would not see him and run past. He crouched and backed up slowly watching for them. His foot hit something, and he tumbled down backward on to something hard. He started to get up and looked behind him. He screamed. Sheila and Johnny saw the robber in the gulley. He was standing straight up looking down. His eyes looked like they would pop out of his head. They approached the gulley. Sheila shouted, "FBI. Freeze." She had wanted to do that all day. The robber didn't move. Frank was running in the direction of the scream, the money on the path helped too. Frank got to his pals, and they all saw what the robber was looking at. Everyone was frozen. Johnny said, "I'll be right back."

He walked into the woods and took a leak. His dad had taught him that when they went jogging on Christmas. It was okay to do it in private outside. Besides his mom would kill him if he wet his jeans. He also thought Rich would be proud of him. He marched out of the woods. Somehow Sheila and Frank had tied the robber's hands with Sheila's scarf. Frank was on his cell phone.

"Beamer, it's Frank."

"Man, you are thirty minutes late. This better be good. Did you find the car?"

"Not yet. We caught a robber. We found a body—a woman's body. What do we do now?"

Chapter 52

As Rich was approaching the front door of their office building after a nice brisk walk to organize his thoughts, Bart came pealing out of the garage and rolled down the front passenger window of his current-year black Beemer, and yelled at Rich. "Get in. We need to get our asses to Bethesda pronto. Your freelancers found a body, and we need to get to them now!"

Rich figured they found the car, and Dawson's body was in the trunk. *God I should not have let them go alone. I bet Johnny wet his pants, and Frank is now catatonic. Pip is going to kill me.*

"Do you think it is Dawson?" Rich said.

Bart replied, "God I hope so. Kit is working on Sabat's financials. It looks like she bought the same items on an Eloise Robinson credit card she purchased on the PSA credit card, and threw in some CDs to round things out to the exact amount. Kit also tracked down where Sabat bought the stuff. I got a guy going over now to show the clerk at the checkout Sabat's picture. Since it was yesterday, I think he'll remember. It was a large and unique purchase. The clerk probably had an exchange with her. If we get an ID, the U.S. attorney will get us a search warrant so we can search Sabat's house. If the body is Dawson and there are any forensics at the scene linking Dawson to Sabat, we can go to a grand jury."

"Did you contact the local police about the body? We don't want our undeputized scout troop guarding a body and a church robber by themselves for very long."

"Of course I did. I am not an idiot."

"Anything else happen while I was out."

"Yes. Beamer got videotape from the post office. A guy came in and emptied and then closed out the post office box for Landmark Therapies."

"A guy? Was it Morton?"

"No, a tall, light-skinned guy."

"Was it George Jones?"

"It couldn't be him. He was in the hospital."

Rich thought, *Shit. Another player! And Netherfield is calm. So organized. So much authority. So young. He makes me sick.* "How old are you Netherfield?"

"Twenty-nine. Why? You think I am an asshole, and if I am younger than you that would explain everything, right? Give you a strong justification to feel as you do."

"Whoa, bro. Don't pull that on me. I am the expert on anger management in this posse."

"Well, what does my age have to do with anything?"

"Look, you are so perfect. I was just trying to find out if you are for real, you know, human. If you and I are going to be hanging together, I want to know if you are an alien. I thought starting with age was simple enough, and you would volunteer other details."

Rich rambled on, "You see I was in Afghanistan. I have killed people. I am bipolar. And, I consider myself Suzy's big brother. You get my drift? Nobody can be as 'straight' as you pretend to be. Do you drink, smoke weed, look at porn, eat junk food, or watch ESPN? Come on man, give me something so I have a reason to trust you, to know you care about my little sister."

Bart thought, *I don't need this right now. Maybe Pritchard needs to eat and takes some medication.* He abruptly took the next exit off the parkway, and pulled into a White Castle parking lot. "Let's get something to eat."

Rich replied, "Now that's human. Aliens probably don't eat."

When they took off again, munching burgers, Rich said, "I am sorry man. How about you and Suzy take off early Friday for the weekend. I'll cover Pip."

"You are a piece of work, but thanks. Kit suggested we go to the Poconos for New Year's. I'll ask Suzy."

Meanwhile, three miles away, Sheila, Johnny, and Frank were standing guard over the corpse and the robber and freezing. They made the robber sit on a tree stump.

Johnny said, "My dad won't believe this one. You guys need to back me up when I tell him. He always says jogging is important. Now I know why."

Frank was like a fish out of water. He was not on mission any more. He had been diverted to guard duty, nothing to count or scan. They caught the robber. That was not part of the plan. They found a body that may or may not be linked to their case. They had not found the gold Honda yet.

Sheila seeing his distress said, "Frank, what's the matter?"

"We haven't found the gold Honda yet, and we must be back by seven."

"We may not need to. If that body here in the ditch is Dawson, that's better than finding her car. "

Johnny said, "Yeah. Forget the car, Frank."

Just then two police cruisers stopped at the curb. Four

policemen walked toward them. Johnny turned to Sheila and said, "You summarize for them, and Frank and I will fill in."

The cops turned to Frank. The oldest one said, "Okay. Start at the top."

Frank just stood there. Sheila walked over to Frank and did as Johnny told her—a clear summary.

The cops could not believe what was in front of them. A short Latina chick with no coat, who looked like a high school chick. A retarded kid dressed like he had just dropped out of a Polo ad. A speechless dude in wrinkled, worn clothes who kept flicking his fingers. And, at the end of her story the chick said they worked for the FBI! Two facts were certain. They had caught the notorious poor-box robber whom the cops had been looking for six months, and they had found a body.

Johnny walked way from the gathering for a minute and called Kit using the relay operator number. *Someone at that number hears what you say and then texts it to Kit. Then Kit texts what she has to say, and the voice tells you.* Kit had put the number as Kit two on Johnny's call list. *It was cool. It just took more time than a real conversation. Kit said that if a relay operator ever repeats a private conversation, the government would cut out the operator's tongue.* Johnny didn't believe that. Kit had laughed when she said it.

"Hi, Kit. Johnny here. You got a digital picture of Dawson?"

"Yeah, Rich got some from her apartment. I think there on our shared drive. Just a minute." In about two minutes she came back on the line. "I have it and will send it to your phone. Why do you need it?"

"I think we found her body."

"Are you kidding? Who's we?"

"Sheila, Frank, and me. Rich sent us out to find her car. We chased a robber and found a body in a ditch instead. We are with the cops now."

"Holy shit! Does Rich know?"

"Yeah. He and Suzy's FBI boyfriend are on their way. You better tell Pip in case Beamer hasn't yet. You know how she likes to know what is going on. Bye."

Johnny walked back over to the others. He flipped open his phone. "Here's a picture of the missing person Donna Dawson." The mouths of all four cops dropped open. The oldest cop said, "Thank you, young man. The body is face down but as soon as the CSI and ME say it's okay to turn her over, we will compare. So stay close by."

Johnny said, "Okay."

Sheila was impressed with Johnny, but continued to be concerned about Frank. The only thing he would talk about was the need to find the gold Honda.

Just then Rich and Bart hopped in and out of the ditch and joined the group. Two of the cops took the robber to the first cruiser and stuck him in the back of it. The youngest cop brought Sheila her scarf, she wrapped around her shoulders. She was shivering. The CSI team arrived. Everyone got filled in. Bart told Sheila, Johnny, and Frank they could leave. Rich told them to get something to eat and gave Sheila two twenties. Johnny forwarded the picture of Dawson to Rich's Blackberry.

They started into the woods toward the church and their car. Johnny stopped and made an about face. Sheila and Frank followed him. Bart and Rich were on the edge of the ditch conferring with a member of the CSI team. Johnny went up to them, "Excuse me. Make sure you guys keep an eye out for a bright red acrylic nail that goes on a pinky, okay?" He then turned and walked off with his two companions.

As they approached the church parking lot after retrieving Sheila's coat, Sheila said, "Let's take a swing around the parking lot to see if we can spot the gold Honda. It won't take much time since most of the cars have left. Frank got in the back and pulled up the license number on his laptop. The parking lot was well lit. Sheila drove slowly. They found the car. Frank was happy about the car but not the time.

Sheila said, "We need to let the others know we found the car." Johnny flipped open his phone and speed-dialed Rich."

Rich picked up instantly, "What's wrong, John?"

"Nothing, Rich. We found the car. It's on the edge of the parking lot by a lamppost. It's easy to see. I'll send you a picture now. He took a picture and sent it to Rich. "Did they turn Dawson over yet?"

"Yes. It's her—I mean, it's she. You guys did great work today. Drive carefully."

They were now getting ready to enter rush hour traffic on Connecticut Avenue. Sheila stopped the car. "Guys, I got a confession to make. I cannot see well enough to drive after dark."

Frank said, "Pip will be mad if she doesn't get her car back."

Johnny said, "I can drive. Sheila can sit in the back. Frank you ride shotgun and give me directions."

Somehow Sheila knew John could do it, but to be safe, she asked him to take a turn around the front and back parking lots. He passed her test, and off they went.

As they drove by the CSI crew, Frank rolled down his window, and Johnny yelled to Rich, "See you later, dude!"

Rich looked up, as they flew by. He could swear Johnny was driving, but no way.

The happy trio made a detour to Georgetown, Johnny parallel parked in an end slot, and they went into Clyde's to celebrate over burgers, fries, and nonalcoholic beer since they were all contributing to "driving" Pip's car. Sheila was pleased to be out with her two friends. They got some strange looks. Sheila kept thinking each time they got a stare, *You have no idea how brave and smart these guys are. No idea at all. In fact, until I took this job, neither did I!*

Chapter 53

All the girls were together in Margaret Sabat's hospital room. They were eating pizza and drinking Diet Pepsi. It was a reunion of sorts. Bonnie and her mom had made up. Shane and Shawna were relieved their mom was okay and happy she was not bossing them around.

Margaret was pleased Shawna had brought her all she asked for and a change of clothes. She had things to do—research, check accounts, send e-mails, rent a car. She was furious with Ted that he had not stayed with her through this ordeal. She was also afraid she would slip and recount something that had occurred that she should not remember because of her "amnesia." She was, if she were to admit it, drained and hung over. She wondered why God had screwed her. She realized she could not wallow in self-pity. She was distracted from her reflection by Shawna.

"Come on, Mom, tell us who Ted is?"

"A friend from work."

Shawna would not drop it. "You got to do better than that. He had your purse! He came to our apartment! He's the one who called us!"

"All right, all right. I had him over for dinner last night. I drank too much, fell, and hit my head."

Bonnie was sitting on the floor Indian style. She turned pale. *I thought Mom couldn't remember anything.*

Shawna jumped up, "Mom do you realize you

REMEMBERED what happen last night? You are making SERIOUS progress."

Oops. "Ugh, I wish. The hospital staff told me." *That's the SECOND time I have done that!*

Bonnie frowned.

The relationship among these four women was complicated. Margaret expressed love through presents. The more presents one of the daughters received, the more costly a present, the more evidence of Margaret's love. She was not into hugging or kissing. It was their dad who provided that when they were small and even now. Margaret did the best she could by making sure the girls had what they needed. In fact, with help from their dad, the girls pretty much raised themselves. Mom provided the clothes, toys, and extras—swimming, riding, tennis, and music lessons. The girls and their dad did the cooking, laundry, and cleaning. He didn't move out till the girls had well-developed domestic skills.

Out of the blue Bonnie asked, "Mom, why did you buy a black tote? You hate black."

Margaret knew what Bonnie was talking about Donna's purse, but this time she would not slip up. "I didn't buy a black purse. Or at least, I do not remember buying one."

"Before I left the house I saw it next to your dresser. Because it was black, I thought it was strange."

"Well, I have no idea how it got there. Why don't you bring it here, and that may refresh my memory."

Bonnie nodded and seemed satisfied.

"What did Ted say when he gave you my purse? Did you invite him in? You have a cute place when you keep it straight."

Shawna said, "Sure I invited him in, but he declined. He

seemed sad. He just handed me your purse and said, "I think your mom may need this. I hope she turns out to be okay. Then he turned on his heels and left. He's short, Mom."

Yes, a short bastard.

Margaret's cell phone rang. She took it out of her purse and flipped it on.

"Hi, Margaret. It's Ted. My son got drunk. Crashed into tree and killed himself early this morning. He's with his mom now in heaven. I don't need your help with getting him into GTU. I gave your purse to one of your daughters. I gave the IT stuff in your trunk you said Dawson bought to the IG. I also gave her pill bottle I found under your dresser to the IG. Good luck with the FBI investigation. I think it's better if we don't see each other anymore. Bye."

Margaret heard a click on the other end of the line. Margaret flipped the phone shut. She laid it in her lap.

She looked at her girls—her trophies—they were indeed beautiful she thought. Then her mind turned to more practical matters.

"Ladies, your mother needs some rest. Thanks for coming. I'll call you when they are ready to let me out of here."

Shane said, "Good, okay, who was on the phone, Mom?"

"The short guy." She forced a laugh.

The girls laughed too and in union gave her a thumbs up. Bonnie said, "Guess you want to call him back without an audience! Shane and I haven't seen him yet. So, when he is next in your presence snap a picture on your cell phone and send it to us, will you?"

Margaret thought, *That girl is cute but so dumb, dumb, dumb. Men only disappoint you. They are not dependable. They are liars. All*

they want to do is satisfy their sexual urges. She'll learn soon enough.
"Will do. Now you girls get out of here."

Shane said, "Okay. Okay. When you come home, you want to do a just-us-girls New Year's Eve party?"

"Maybe. Let's see how I feel when I get home. I am sure you girls can pull a party together quickly." She faked a smile.

Bonnie, Shane, and Shawna, dressed in pastel turtlenecks and ski vests to match, straight-legged jeans, and Ugg boots, kissed their mom and departed. On the way out the door, Bonnie said, "Let's invite Mom's boyfriend."

Margaret put her head back and closed her eyes. Her head throbbed where she had hit it. In about five minutes, when she was sure the girls were gone, she flipped open her phone and rented a car for tomorrow morning. Then Margaret ordered a taxi pick up for midnight, after the shift change.

Chapter 54

It was about 7:00 P.M. Beamer had his sock-clad feet on the reception desk drinking a Corona, eating chips and salsa, reading the morning *Post* sports section. He hadn't heard from anyone in over two and a half hours. Kit had left. Pip walked in. Beamer sat up.

"I came to get my car."

"Should you drive?"

"I have a hard head."

What should he tell her? *Ah ma'am maybe you should reconsider because your car is involved in a murder investigation. No, he would need to devise something more mundane.* Then he had it—*I'll order Chinese. She'll take pity on me and stay and eat and keep me company. If I can get her drunk, she can have my bed. I'll sleep on the couch in the conference room. That's a plan.*

The private line rang. Beamer picked up, "It's about time one of you folks called."

"Beamer, I need a break. It's Suzy. I am in the garage. I want to go home. Can you ride with Pip or keep her company or both?"

"As a matter of fact yes. I was getting ready to order Chinese. Why don't you join us?"

Suzy thought *why me?* "Okay."

The phone rang again. It was Electra's husband asking to speak to her. *Where the hell was she? Not at home, that's for sure.*

He ordered Chinese—sweet and sour shrimp, beef and

broccoli, chicken chow mien, fried rice, and egg rolls. He took a bottle of white and a bottle of red from the "wine cellar," the closet next to the HVAC closet. He carried plates, napkins, and the rest to Pip's office.

Beamer was a very calm guy. Nothing flustered him. With both his hands full, it was a challenge to open the door to Pip's office. She kept it open unless she was concentrating. Evidently she was concentrating. He opened the door without losing anything and pushed the door fully open with his right foot. Pip was on the floor. Her cart, minus the right back wheel, was on its back about five feet from her. Her cell phone was on the floor, too, but out of her reach. Pip was sitting up against the side of her mahogany desk with her eyes closed.

She opened her eyes when she heard him come in. "You can see what happened. I crossed the room to close the blinds. The rest is obvious." She had a corner office with a great view of the fish market and the Potomac.

"Pip, you should have stayed home. You are not recovered yet. And besides, you know you are suppose to get that cart serviced every six months." He sensed that something was bothering her.

He put everything on the small circular conference table. Then, although not as muscular as Rich, he lifted Pip to a standing position and lending his arm for support, helped her to her desk chair. He retrieved the spare cart from Pip's coat closet, loaded the stuff —eight and one-half pounds in two canvas bags from the fallen cart into the spare cart and hung Pip's cane on the left side of the cart. Pip was back in business. She had learned over the years that eight and one-half pounds positioned toward the front of a cart was enough to prevent her from tipping the cart when she leaned on it to walk. She could easily unload the two canvas bags into her car trunk, fold the cart, put it in the trunk, and use her cane and the side of the car to get to the driver's car door. That was the good news. Without a cart with at least eight and one-half pounds in it, she could not walk anywhere. She was not stable enough to walk with just her cane. She did, however, do fine with an arm from someone for short distances. She could walk extended distances with someone's arm and her cane. She preferred to use her cart because that made her totally independent. And, when she walked with someone, using her cane with her left hand, she knew she put great weight on the other person's left arm.

Beamer sat himself on the floor and was looking at the broken wheel. "Pip, it broke right off. You need a new axel. Think we should order a new one online for a backup. I'll take care of it. Oh, yeah, are you okay?

"Yes. I am just tired. When I fell I did nothing to cause the fall. I think God is pissed at me. The wheel just flew off, no warning! All I want to do is go home and go to bed. But first I need to know what has been going on today. Do you have any news for me?"

Beamer thought fast. "Well, Suzy and Chinese food will be here momentarily. Then you can go home, or you can have my bed, and I'll sleep on that bright red leather couch in the conference room."

Pip looked disappointed, like she was expecting some other answer. "Look at me—black slacks, black turtleneck, black clogs, no makeup, no jewelry, bald around my crown, and my hair needs to be washed. I look like an overweight, short ninja, with hair plastered to its head like a helmet."

"Well, now that you mention it."

"Oh shut up. I have to go home at some point." Kit had texted to Pip what Johnny had told Kit. Pip decided to give Beamer one more chance, "By the way where is everyone?"

"Kit went home. Everybody else should be checking in sooner, rather than later. Although one is AWOL—Electra. Her husband called and asked if she was here."

"Oh jeez. I can't get into the details, but she's all right. She spends the last Tuesday of every month with her blind lover."

"No kidding!" Beamer got off the floor.

Suzy walked in carrying the bags of Chinese food. "Somebody owes me twenty-nine dollars and thirty cents." She put the food on the table and retrieved a wine opener from the credenza drawer.

The three of them sat at the table eating but not talking.

Pip finally said, "I have been reading forensic reports from Quantico all day. Sabat was in Dawson's apartment with George Jones. What we cannot pin down is whether Dawson was there too at the SAME time. Where the hell is everybody?"

As if on cue, Sheila, Johnny, and Frank walked in. They were all smiles.

Sheila said, "Johnny drove all the way here from Chevy Chase and took a detour to Georgetown so we could get something to eat!"

Johnny added, "Yep. And, Pip I did not get a nick in your car!"

Pip's face went from shock to double shock. Suzy and Beamer were beyond surprised as well.

"What the hell were you three doing in Chevy Chase and

Georgetown in my car?" Pip said.

Frank, oblivious to the impact their adventure would have, said, "We caught a robber stealing from a church, we found Dawson's body in a ditch near the same church, and we found Dawson's car in the same church's parking lot."

Pip dropped her wineglass, and wine spilled over the table and on to the oriental rug. Suzy knew she should go get towels, but she did not want to miss anything. Beamer was glued to his chair as well.

Johnny said, "Yep. It was quite a day. Sheila can't drive at night. Frank doesn't have a license, so that left me to get us back here."

Pip leaned back in her chair. The room was silent. Pip wanted all the details to force Beamer to acknowledge his role in the don't-tell-Pip plan.

"Who told you to go to Chevy Chase in my car?"

Sheila decided she had to put things in context. "Dr. Planter, Rich asked us to go to Maryland to visit churches and attempt to find Dawson's car. Frank had the addresses for the churches on his laptop. Rich said to call Beamer every thirty minutes and check in and be back here by seven P.M. Catching the robber and finding the body were fortunate accidents."

Pip looked at Beamer. "You were in on this plan?" she said.

Beamer did not answer. He figured he looked guilty—why add an answer?

Pip then told Johnny, Sheila, and Frank to take off there coats and sit on the couch. They did so. She turned around her chair to face them. Methodically she walked them through their day. To Sheila, it seemed like every second. At first their eyes looked like deer in headlights, sitting stiffly in a row, not taking their eyes off Pip. Gradually they relaxed and sat back. Beamer brought them water. Suzy by instinct started taking notes. Pip's office had the smell of a Chinese kitchen. The clock on Pip's desk emitted nine chimes.

When Pip was satisfied she understood what happened, she got up and took two twenties out of her purse, giving one to Sheila and one to Frank. "Take a taxi home. I'll see you in the morning." Although exhausted they both leaped up and hurried out of Pip's office. But Frank turned back, "Pip, your gas gauge is on empty."

"Thanks, Frank."

Pip next turned to Suzy, "Would you mind taking Johnny home? You can use my car, assuming you can get gas. Then take the car home. I will take a taxi when I am finished here. Please leave your notes. I can decipher them regardless of what shape they are in."

So Johnny and Suzy left.

Beamer felt exposed and vulnerable. Pip never showed anger, but he sensed she was very upset. He had taken "the troops" to the bar with the Sabat twins. He knew she didn't like that. What happened today was a hell of a lot worse. Frank, Johnny, and Sheila had no direct supervision. Beamer knew what was going on, and he did not tell Pip. Why hadn't he? Simple— he didn't want to rat on Rich. He never wanted to be on the "wrong" side of Rich. That guy is a volcano waiting to blow. It is only a matter of time.

Pip looked up at Beamer who was stacking plates because he didn't know what else to do. He couldn't bear to look at her eye to eye. "That can wait. Sit down. We need to talk."

"Beamer, you and I have known each other for ten years.

There is a lot I liked about you. You never tell people what other people say if the information is harmful, hurtful, or confidential. You have quiet confidence. You have big dreams. You are trustworthy. You have common sense. So I thought I was making a smart move when I asked you to come here three years ago. I must tell you I did not like it one bit when you dragged Kit, Frank, Sheila, and Suzy into your makeshift undercover venture at a bar. I did not say anything because you were THERE with them. You usually never make the same mistake twice. So I thought you would not be part of a second episode.

"What happened today and your role in it are very unsettling. What if something happened to those young people? You know and I know they will do whatever anybody, but especially Rich, asks them to do. You are my brakes. You are my voice of reason. Why didn't you stop it? Why didn't you tell me? Why didn't you at the very least go with them?"

Pip put up her hand. "Don't give me an answer now. Think about what I said. Go clean up the kitchen, then come back, and we will talk about it. A lot is riding on your answer. Now take the Chinese leftovers and dishes and get the hell out of here!"

Beamer couldn't tell Pip he was a safe-ass chicken shit, scared of countering Rich and more focused on his band then the case. No way he would give those as his reasons. He carried everything to the kitchen in one trip using a filing cart. He did not want to go back into Pip's office for a while. In fact he needed time to think, maybe confer with Rich. He put the dishes in the dishwasher. Pip had never told him to do dishes. Jesus, she wanted to hurt him, suggest he was nothing but a butler. He put the Chinese leftovers in the fridge. He leaned against the sink and dialed Rich.

"Hey, Beamer, that FBI ass wipe dropped me at a Metro stop. He went to the morgue. Got anything to eat at the ranch? I am about fifteen minutes away."

"Rich, Pip is pissed. Sheila, Johnny, and Frank told her EVERYTHING in minute detail, including your role as the instigator and mine as fucking collaborator. I wouldn't be surprised if she fired our sad asses. We need to talk."

"Fuck. I told those twits to go home—not go to the office."

"Well, genius, they had to bring the fucking car back, with a gas gauge on empty I would like to add!"

"Where's everyone now?"

"Suzy is taking Johnny home on the gas fumes left in Pip's car. Pip gave Sheila and Frank money out of her Brighton purse, not the office petty cash, to take taxis. Kit went home before any of this happened."

"Did Pip talk to you alone after she learned everything?"

"Yes."

"What did you say?"

"Nothing. She did all the talking. When she finished she told me to go clean up the kitchen and come back with answers. A lot was riding on them."

"Fuck. What did she say?"

"That she was very upset. She posed a fucking shitload of questions. Quote—You know and I know they will do whatever anybody, but especially Rich, asks them to do. You are my brakes. You are my voice of reason. Why didn't you stop it? Why didn't you tell me? Why didn't you at the very least go with them? Unquote. She didn't want answers just then.

She said think about what answers to give. As I said, she said a lot is riding on them. May be we should meet somewhere and strategize. She doesn't know you are on your way back."

Beamer heard a sound. He turned and looked at the kitchen door. Pip and her spare cart were standing there listening to him on the phone. He said to Rich, "I stand corrected."

Rich said, "I'll be there in five."

Pip just looked at Beamer. Her pupils were pinpricks. If there was an expression for feeling betrayed, it was all over her face. She stared at him for an eternity, then without saying anything, got a Deer Park water out of the fridge, threw it in her cart, and left the kitchen.

Beamer had thought there was a high probability that, after being reamed by Pip, he would be looking for a new job and a place to live. Now, after she'd overheard who knows how much of his phone conversation with Rich, it was a certainty.

Rich came into the kitchen ten minutes later, when Beamer was sitting at the kitchen table nursing a beer. Rich went to the fridge and took out the food cartons and a beer. He went to the sink and put three pills in his mouth and took some water from the tap with his hands to wash them down. He dumped all the leftovers on a plate and put it in the microwave. He set it on three minutes and pushed the start button. He opened the beer. "I need to eat before I talk to Pip. My pills won't work without food."

"You may need to eat man, but you better do some quick thinking too. She's a smart lady, but she is also a control freak. Right now she may feel like she has lost control. Right now, bro, you better pray to Jesus that her smart self wins out over her control freak self, or you, like me, will be toast tomorrow without peanut butter or jelly!"

By this time Rich was inhaling the Chinese leftovers, wishing there was more, and heading for a second beer.

"Is it okay to drink with those mothers?"

"Within moderation." Rich had never 'strategized' with Beamer before, but this was a perilous situation. At least his new best friend could be a sounding board. Let's face it: he had discovered several amazing things about his colleagues in the last few months, but especially in the last few days—all positive. And, if God is around, help him with Pip. Rich sensed he was losing his biases and prejudices. *That was a good thing, right?*

"Beam, tell me exactly what our trio of vigilantes told her, starting at the top."

Beamer thought about Pip back there fuming in her office. He thought they should go back there and grovel at her feet, promising never to screw up again. But, he gave Rich what he wanted as fast as he could.

Rich got another beer, sat down, kicked off his Gucci loafers, and put his sock-clad feet on the table, tilting his chair back.

"How's this. We have had this case for a very short time. We have dealt with a gazillion jurisdictions. We have brought about every break in the case. As an organization we are known for results. We deliver. Today the angels were on our side. Yes, it would have been better if the kids had had supervision, but they did just fine. They were professional. They used sound judgment. Nothing bad happened. Because of our 'team,' everything worked out. The FBI dude hopefully is on his way to get the necessary warrants. So get over it, Mama, everything worked out."

For the second time that night Beamer heard a sound in the doorway. They were sitting with their backs to it. They turned. Suzy was standing there. She came in and sat down. Rich got her a beer. "So what do you think, Suz? Will it work?"

Suzy took a sip of her beer. She couldn't believe she was sitting with these guys drinking beer. For two years, she had been loyal to Pip. Everyone knew she was. Yet spending so much time with Pip since the mugging, she saw Pip as human, vulnerable. Suzy saw the organization, not Pip, as her focus of loyalty. She wanted Forensic Specialists, LLP to succeed. Pip saw staff as children and herself as Mom. That didn't work. In an organization, people collaborate, people grow, people make mistakes, people play to their strengths, people step up to the plate in a crunch, and people form teams to get things done. Suzy shared these thoughts with the guys.

Suzy then said, "Let's go see her together. We will blend what Rich said with my thoughts and make the case for continuing as a team—all of us. I think all we need to add is some reliable communication strategies and supervision of junior staff—say a daily staff meeting and/or an end-of-day debriefing. And most important, someone designated daily to keep Pip fully informed. Guys, it's not she wants to control everything. She just wants to know what is going on."

They agreed. With new confidence, a restored purpose, and a great deal of anticipation, the three marched down the hall to Pip's office. Beamer had the ice cream, Suzy the hot fudge, and Beamer the bowls and spoons from his less-than-spotless kitchen that smelled like a Chinese kitchen.

Pip's door was closed. Suzy knocked. No answer. They

looked at each other. Rich turned the handle and opened the door. The lights were off. Because of the hall light they could see Pip was not there. Rich and the others proceeded into the room and put the ice cream stuff on Pip's round table. Beamer turned on the light. They each dropped into a chair. The air had gone out of their enthusiasm, determination, and conviction that they could make things right. The test of their newly formed alliance would have to wait. And, uncharacteristically for her, Pip had left without saying good-bye.

Suzy scooped out ice cream for everyone and passed the hot fudge around.

Beamer said, "If Pip heard us talking, we are up shit's creek without a paddle!"

Rich said, "Man, after Suzy came in, I shifted my chair so I was facing the door. Neither Pip nor her cart came near us."

Suzy said, "Let's assume she didn't hear us. Maybe it's better if we sleep on our plan. Maybe Pip will feel less dissed in the morning and have more of an open mind. And, I've been thinking—"

Rich cut her off, "That could be dangerous."

"Hear me out. Where we find ourselves is not tied solely to Pip's perception of us. Our problem is we view her as a mom more than a boss. We do what we think needs to be done, often letting her know after the fact. The mugging just reinforced these tendencies. Since we see her as our mom, we assume she will forgive us. So we need to add recognition of our flaws into what we tell her tomorrow. It will show maturity and our willingness to own up to past actions, and accept responsibility for changing. What do you think?"

Beamer said, "You have my vote."

Rich added, "You may be right, but tomorrow could be hectic given what was learned today. When are we going to have our mea culpa gathering?"

Suzy said, "I suggest we do it first thing, as soon as Pip comes in."

Rich said, "Well, you know and I know your pal, Bart, will pounce on her as soon as she gets in, and may derail our best intentions."

Suzy looked at Rich, "Don't worry. I'll wear him out so he comes in late." She winked but couldn't believe what she had just said and done. Rich looked surprised. His eyes widened and his jaw dropped. He tried to think of a G-rated, clever retort. His cell rang.

"Hi, Rich. Bart here." Rich put his phone's speaker option on. "No warrants. It seems like everyone in the legal system is 'on holiday.' Maybe we can use the time to read and update reports. Dawson had no fingertips. Squirrels or raccoons must have gotten to them. No purse. No acrylic fingernails. Tell Johnny I am sorry. Dawson was hit by a blunt heavy object. I am going home. See you tomorrow." Bart clicked off.

"That son of a bitch now thinks I am his sidekick."

Suzy said, "Well, what's wrong with that? You gotta get over your Lone Ranger and holier than thou attitudes. Bart wants to solve this as much as you do. Don't worry, Rich. You'll get your precious credit!"

She stood up and stomped out. Beamer and Rich looked at each other. Beamer said, "Let's toss to see who cleans up the kitchen. Heads for me."

Rich lost. Beamer went to bed, and Rich went to the kitchen. Rich had a lot to digest. He needed to be mellower, more mature. There was more to Beamer and Suzy than he had thought. Maybe he could work with them to turn things around or at least make things better. He needed to pay more attention to what people said and not shoot from the hip. I am thirty-five. I am not a kid anymore. He stood surveying his clean-up job. He had even gotten the coffee ready. Everything was where Electra would expect it to be. He couldn't believe he had lost the coin toss. He couldn't believe the dude had the nerve to suggest it. He couldn't believe he complied. The times they were a changing.

Chapter 55

What a day. Kit had spent the whole day in front of her computer. Margaret Sabat had some serious debt. Kit had tracked about $42,000 thus far. The most fascinating piece was a cash advance she had drawn off a new credit card. A strange amount, down to cents. Then apparently she used the cash at Staples to buy the exact same things that were on the government credit card. Except for some CDs, Kit guessed they were needed to bring things out even, given after Christmas discounts.

Then when Johnny called and Kit relayed his story to Pip, Pip just listened and then said thank you. That was unnerving. God, they found a body! On the Metro, Kit texted her boyfriend, Jack Danielson, to see if he was free and wanted to eat out. He agreed to meet her at Tapas Hughmungus off of DuPont Circle.

Jack worked for the *DC Rag*, an independent online newspaper that nipped at the big boys' heels on bureaucratic scandals and also covered weddings, deaths, and/or murders associated with bureaucrats. Kit was dying to tell him about their case, but she wouldn't. She had a very strong sense of right and wrong, not to mention self-preservation.

Kit got to the restaurant first. She ordered a beer. She looked like shit, and she felt worse. Maybe the beer and Jack would help. The current case was stressing her out. What if she missed something? Should she raise the question of Donna

Dawson's financial records? Someone should be looking at them, if the body they found is hers, and the murderer took her wallet. She kicked her Uggs off under the table and rubbed her thick socks together. Her feet never sweat. She needed a massage.

She saw Jack. "Hi, gorgeous." He signed in American Sign Language. Both his parents were deaf, but he was not. Kit had met him on the street coming off Gallaudet's campus where she had gone to get her graduate school transcripts. Pip wanted to see them before she hired her four years ago. Jack and Kit did not live together. It cost them a fortune to maintain two places. It was out-of-concern-for-parents thing. Jack lived alone. Kit had two roommates. So most of the time they spent together was at his place.

Jack was tall, had dark curly hair he wore shaggy, and most often was sweet; he was a man of few words, mostly of questions.

Kit signed back as he sat down. "Hi, is that the suit your parents gave you for Christmas? I almost didn't recognize you. Did you do something special today?"

"Things are slow at the paper. I had to go interview a guy named Ted Morton about the death of his son. It was a bummer. Nothing I wanted to do. He is some big shot at the Public Services Administration—PSA for short. I think it is the central processing office for a lot of government grants and contracts. He may be a valuable future source for information if I ever get a big contract scandal to look into."

Kit thought, *I can't believe it!* She was curious. "What's he like?"

"Short. Sharp, traditional dresser. Had pictures of his

son all over his corner office. Lots of navy stuff too. Stacked papers everywhere. His office was a mess. Since his son was killed TODAY, I thought it was strange he was in his office. I asked him why. He said his wife had died of cancer some time ago, and his son was now with her in heaven. Then he said the coroner had the body, so why not come to work? I can tell you, if I were killed, my dad wouldn't go to work. He would stay home, get drunk, and let my mom do everything."

"What else did he say?"

"You know—where his son was going to go to college, what varsity teams he had been on, that he liked a chick of color, that he will never see his son graduate from high school or college or get married."

"Did you push on anything he said?"

"Yeah, I asked him how he would feel if his son dated a non-white chick. His answer was amazing. He said his son didn't know it, but Morton was dating his girlfriend's mother! Then I said, 'Is it a serious relationship?' He said, 'Not any more. She is under investigation by the FBI. I told her too.' Then he shut down and showed me out. I am going to do some digging. I know I can get the woman's name.

"How was your day?"

Kit's stomach was churning, and her heart was about to push her boobs out of her sweater, but she forced herself to be calm. "Tedious. Just reviewing financials for a fraud case."

They ordered tapas and ate without talking.

Kit finally said, "I am going home tonight, Jack. You can come with me. Both my roommates are out of town for the holidays." Jack agreed. He had his Jeep so they swung by his place so he could pick up a change of clothes.

Kit lived in Ballston in a new condo she had bought. Her roommates' rent covered most of the mortgage, but not the hefty condo fee. She and Jack stripped between her front door and the shower. Later, lying in bed with the light on, Jack signed, "Why did you give me the third degree on the interview I did today?"

"Oh, I don't know. Maybe I was trying to act like I give a shit about what you do for a living!" She punched him in the stomach and smiled. Jack turned out the light.

Two hours later while Jack was sleeping, Kit slipped out of bed. She picked up their clothes, folded Jack's, and put them on the green leather loveseat in her bedroom. She put the clothes she had taken off into the three-part hamper next to the washer-dryer combo off the kitchen. She went to the kitchen and took bagels out to thaw for breakfast and fixed the coffee for the morning. Then, she texted Rich. "My boyfriend interviewed Morton today. His son died in a car crash last night. Morton told Jack (my boyfriend) that he'd told Margaret Sabat she's under investigation."

Kit jumped. Jack had entered her kitchen. The kitchen was decorated in chocolate, teal, and white, with spanking new white appliances. He signed, "Couldn't sleep, Kitty Kat?"

Kit got up. She signed, "Right, I'm too wound up."

"Why are you wound up about a fraud case?"

"Let's have bacon and eggs now." Jack gave her the okay sign. He turned on the coffee and sat down at the table. While Kit was at the stove breaking eggs with her back to him, he glanced at her text message. He zoned in on *Margaret Sabat*. Then he pushed send. He thought to himself, I do love my Kitty Kat. She is so helpful without knowing it!

Kit turned abruptly, looked at her iPhone, and sighed. Then smiled and put it in her pajama shirt pocket.

Jack watched, but didn't say anything. While they were eating he signed, "Want to get married?"

Chapter 56

Rich was dazed on the drive to his apartment off of Wilson. He had so much to process. Johnny and Frank doing things no one thought they could do; Pip getting totally pissed; Suzy being wise, reasonable, and not an ass kisser; Beamer, being an okay dude; and Rich, himself being fairly calm, with and without medication.

By the time he opened his fridge his mind was in overdrive. "Shit. There is nothing worth eating!" He smelled the eggs. They seemed okay. He cut the mold off a bagel. He opened a beer, fried two eggs, and toasted the bagel. The butter was rancid, so he put olive oil on his bagel. He craved some meat, but all he had was frozen ground beef—too much trouble to thaw, even in the microwave. Besides he had bought it last March according to the date stamp.

He plopped on his black leather sofa in front of his flat screen and devoured his "breakfast." "My fridge is a metaphor of my life. It sucks. I gotta shape up." He changed into some sweats and over the next three hours cleaned his refrigerator, threw away everything in it, wiped everything in his kitchen with Windex, the only cleaner he had, made a wholesome grocery list, went to an all-night grocery store, bought the stuff on his list, came home, and put everything away. He fell asleep on the sofa, satisfied with his unmedicated self, watching *Law and Order* reruns. His bliss was short-lived. His iPhone vibrated on the hardwood floor.

He sat up and read Kit's text message. "Shit." He texted her back he was on it. Thanking her for the heads up. He thought about calling Pip, but decided to go to his alter ego, Bart.

"Hey, Netherfield, where are you?"

"Just left the morgue. Donna Dawson's mother identified her body."

"Sorry man. Why did you have to be there? I thought you were going home to sleep."

"I volunteered to pick her up. I didn't want to bother you."

"Where you headed now?"

"The office. I got paperwork to do."

"Kit just texted me that Margaret Sabat knows she is under investigation."

"How'd Kit find that out?"

"Her boyfriend interviewed Morton, and he told the guy. I think you better put one of your minions on stakeout by the hospital to keep an eye on her."

"She has a HEAD INJURY. She won't be going anywhere."

"I don't know. I have a sinking feeling we are underestimating Sabat."

"I got an idea, why don't you check it out first? We are spread pretty thin at the Bureau till Monday."

"Of course, why didn't I think of that? Thank you so much for the suggestion. It would be a nice drive. Traffic will be light. I'll let you know if we need an all points, pal." He clicked off his phone before Bart could answer. He wanted to throw his phone across the room at his balcony glass doors and shatter them, but he didn't. He went into the kitchen, made coffee, and then took a hot shower. He was out the front door and heading to the hospital in thirty minutes. He had taken his medication. He needed an insurance policy.

As he was walking down the silent, dimly lit corridor toward Margaret's room, he fantasized about waking her up and shaking the truth out of her. No one stopped him or seemed to care that a guy in jeans, black leather jacket, looking like a halfback charging had invaded the nighttime quiet of the hospital. When he got to her room he checked the name, *not Sabat*; he opened the door slowly. It creaked. He looked in. His eyes had to adjust to the darkness. The body in the bed was the wrong age, the wrong color, and the wrong sex. "Shit."

He went to the nurses' station. "Margaret Sabat is not in three fifteen B. Where is she?"

The nurse checked her records. "We discovered she was not in her room at one A.M. We did not have a number to call, so after checking in the hospital, using our security staff, we called the police. Because she has a head injury, they put out an alert."

Rich dialed the Montgomery County Police Department. An officer confirmed the alert and no news as to Margaret's whereabouts. He then called Bart. "Hey, bro, we got a problem. Margaret has left for parts unknown. Think you need to get your vacationing compadres to put out an APB and to get those warrants BEFORE Monday. At least put out something on the frickin' car. Got it?"

"Oh God! Okay. Cut the sarcasm—we are on the same side. This is not a contest. Go home and get some sleep. Take some of your drugs. I'll call you when I am heading to Suzy's. Later today you and I need to start interviewing people who know Sabat. Maybe get a lead as to where she went. If you utter one more wisecrack, I will punch out your lights the next time I see you! Got it?"

Rich just hung up. He didn't head toward home. He headed toward Alexandria and Pip's condo. He needed a hug. He suspected she did too. Beside, he had to brainstorm with her about the unknown man who was involved—Sabat's brother, her ex-husband, or someone else. Sabat had a partner.

Chapter 57

Margaret had no trouble leaving the hospital undetected at around midnight. She had the taxi drop her off two houses down from her house in Bethesda. She walked home in a cold drizzle, thankful for her trench coat and its hood. She made coffee and after two cups went upstairs. She retrieved her packed suitcase and her "gift" from Don from the back of her closet. She took a shower, put on a lavender turtleneck, jeans, and sneakers. After loading everything in her car she headed for Alexandria. She wanted to make one last trip to see her in-laws before any shift change.

Getting into Lake and Lawn Rehabilitation and Nursing Center was a snap. She had the code for the staff entrance in her wallet from years ago. The code had not changed. She slipped in and went to Mrs. Sabat's room. She was asleep. Margaret locked the door. She picked up the cushion from the chair, put it on Mrs. Sabat's face, and sat on it, counting to 360. Mrs. Sabat was fragile, so she did not put up much of a fight. Margaret made sure there was no pulse. She put the cushion back, unlocked the door and left. Mr. Sabat's room was the next door. Margaret pushed her glove down to look at her watch—2:45 A.M. She went into Mr. Sabat's room. He, too, was sleeping, so she killed him as she had his wife. As she walked out of the facility she had a satisfying thought, *Now Jeremy could more easily cover some of the girls' tuition. I will send him more money from Mexico.*

Margaret drove to Eloise's row house. She was hoping Don would be there. He was.

Don met Margaret at the back door. He smiled at her, took her hand, and gave her a cup of coffee. She had dried vomit across the front of her coat. He took it, and left it on the back railing.

"I have been waiting for you. What happened?" Don looked at her bandaged head. "You better wear a hat when you board the plane on Friday."

Margaret stared at Don. She was bordering on being catatonic. *I just killed two people who loved me before they acquired Alzheimer's.* She sipped the coffee.

Don was alarmed. "Sit here, Margaret. I'll make you some breakfast." She did.

Don prepared breakfast in silence. He put scrambled eggs, toast, and bacon in front of Margaret. He fixed a plate for himself and sat across from her. He shouted, "Margaret eat!" *What am I dealing with, a complete meltdown?*

Margaret began eating. She looked at Don. "Have you taken care of Eloise, yet?"

Definitely a meltdown. "Margaret, what has happened to upset you? Please tell me."

"I am under investigation by the FBI. I used a federal credit card to buy a few Christmas presents."

God! Why did you do that?"

"Because I thought Dew Point Graphics might drain my other accounts."

Margaret's back! "Touché. Good point. For the record, I have not and would not take money for my own use, just to help you."

"Don, is the five thousand dollars you gave me in cash from one of my accounts?"

"No."

"I am so exhausted. I need some sleep. I have a rental car picking me up at seven thirty A.M. I need to lay down for a while."

"Margaret, cancel the car. I'll drive you to a hotel near Dulles, after you take a nap. I suggest you stay there until you are ready to get on the plane to Mexico at four P.M. on Friday."

I don't have the strength to argue with him. "Okay, are we flying together?"

"Yes, I will meet you at the gate. Now cancel that car rental." She did.

Chapter 58

Pip could not sleep. When she got home, she drank a beer and ate leftover pizza. She didn't even bother to heat it up. She took a shower, put on her red flannel pajamas, and fell into bed. She was good at self-analysis. *I have to get a grip on what everyone is doing. I have to nip this freelancing in the bud. Yeah, sure. What about empowerment? Don't you wanna help them grow? Reach their potential? Don't you want them to love you? Don't you want them to hang on your every word and do what you say? What were they suppose to do while you recuperated?* Tonight Pip did not have the answers. *Maybe this case is too big. Maybe it's too visible, too risky. Maybe we're not ready. Maybe I am not ready? Maybe we should make it quick, graceful, quiet exit and let the FBI do everything from now on? I'm angry. I'm hurt. Everyone thinks they can do anything without checking with me first and that there will be no consequences. I have to fix that. I am in charge. I am responsible!*

Well, some of this could be explained or justified on the basis of the fact that this is Christmas week. We've had opportunities to do things we wouldn't necessarily do, if there were more real live bureaucrats available to do this stuff. Right? You know you love being in the thick of things. Your problem is, everybody but you has been in the thick of things. You just sit at your desk reading files or stay home nursing your head. You are jealous! You wanna find dead bodies. You wanna do interviews. Well then, get off your ass. Pip laughed out loud.

She got up and went into the kitchen and made a pot of coffee. She heard the *Post* hit her condo door. She had a morbid habit. The first thing she looked at every single day was the obituaries. She did not know why she did this. She could remember when she started doing it, when her granddad died. But today it paid off.

The *Post* had added a feature where it just listed deaths reported from official sources. Pip almost dropped her coffee cup. There third from the bottom were two names: Raha Sabat and Lizt Sabat, parents of Jeremy Sabat of Silver Spring. Pip said aloud, "There are no coincidences" She looked at the clock. It was 5:30 A.M. She dialed Bart's number.

"Aunt Pamela, you are up quite early this morning. What can I do for you?"

"Bart, I have some unsettling news. The *Post* reports Sabat's parents are dead."

"You mean Eloise Robinson and Margaret Sabat's father?"

"No. Margaret Sabat's ex-husband's parents."

"Are you sure?"

"I googled him and read his biography. It had their names."

"Margaret Sabat left the hospital undetected last night. I put an alert out on her car."

"Oh my God. I hope you find her.

"On the other, I'm not sure, but I think people in the Middle East bury their deceased relatives quickly. I think autopsies are in order."

"Aunt Pamela, find my dad. Get him on this. I'm swamped. If we are looking at a worst-case scenario, we may be dealing with multiple homicides, and it's increasingly apparent that Margaret Sabat is the common thread. This is way beyond coincidence. I'm coming to your place. Get a hold of Rich and Suzy. We need to a shitload of interviews today! Somebody connected to Sabat must know where she is."

"Okay."

Pip was wired now. Margaret Sabat has spiraled downward. She would be linked to all these deaths and George Jones's injuries.

The guard gate called her condo. "Dr. Planter, you have a visitor. Rich."

"Please let him in, thank you."

There was a knock at her door as she hung up the phone. Suzy let herself in, in zebra PJs.

"I could not sleep. God knows when Bart will be back. I will fix us some breakfast. Do you have anything worth eating in your refrigerator?"

Pip laughed. "As a matter of fact, I do. Bagels, bacon, orange juice, and eggs. None of which has expired. Coffee is made. Sweetie, make breakfast for three. Rich will be here any minute. Did Bart fill you in on what is going on?"

"Yep. This holiday is turning out to be a real nightmare."

"Look at this. Jeremy Sabat's parents are dead." Pip passed Suzy the paper.

"What!"

Suzy sat down. She did not feel like cooking. Part of her wanted to run away. The other part wanted to get to the office and start plotting all the facts they had, all the things they did not know, and all the things they needed to do. She took a legal pad off the counter and started her to-do list for today. When Pip let Rich in the condo, Suzy looked up and said, "Rich, you cook. I have to work on my to do list."

Rich laughed. "Yes, sir, general, sir. You and Sabat must have the same to-do gene pool!" He rolled his eyes and winked at Pip. She raised her hands, "Whatever. We need to eat since we've had no sleep."

Pip left Suzy with her three-page list, and Rich with the dishes. She went into her den; there were floor-to-ceiling bookshelves on two sides and a desk in front of a huge three-panel window. She pulled back the steel blue drapes. With dawn breaking, she could just make out the ice on the barren tree limbs. She sat down at her weather-beaten, but finely polished, big oak desk and turned on her laptop. For the first time in about twelve hours, she was going to do something that made sense, something that restored her need for purpose.

Rich interrupted her. "The dishes can wait. We need to talk. Sabat has a partner—taller than Morton and a non-white guy but not necessarily black."

"What? Let's go to the kitchen."

"I am frustrated," Pip said. "Kids, we have two major challenges—guessing where Margaret will go and getting authorizations and autopsies on the Sabats. Any suggestions?"

Suzy said, "On our to-do list I have Rich interviewing Jeremy Sabat and the three girls— Bonnie, Shane, and Shawna. Also, he should return to Morton. Someone needs to talk to David Windson, aka Sampson. And how about Sabat's doctor?"

Pip said, "I agree those are key interviews. Bart has asked me to go with him to see Sabat's brother.

"Another thing, how do we find out where the Sabats' bodies are and secure autopsies?"

Suzy replied, "I'll leave that last one to you, Aunt Pip. It is going to be hard to talk to the Sabats on multiple counts— Margaret being a fugitive, the parents/grandparents being dead, us possibly being responsible for delaying burial, and

Margaret possibly being involved in their deaths. You want me to go with Rich to add a feminine touch?"

"Yes. That makes sense. Can you live with that, Rich?"

Rich leaned forward and put his hands palms down on the table. "Shit yes. I get no pleasure out of breaking bad news to anyone. It would be good to have Suzy's cute ass with me."

Suzy said, "You have had too much coffee, Rich. I think what you meant to say was—It would be beneficial to have Suzy on the interview. She has sound judgment, solid analytical skills, and tact—all things I lack."

"Whoa. That was below the belt. True, but below the belt." Rich smiled at Suzy.

Pip was amazed at how calm and agreeable Rich was. Why? Perhaps Suzy was having a good impact on him or maybe he was taking his medication on the prescribed schedule or maybe both.

"Okay. You two make a list of potential, tactful questions. I am going to get dressed and try to track down where the Sabats' bodies are."

Chapter 59

Rich was sitting at Pip's kitchen table. Suzy had gone back to her place to get dressed, but she had lent Rich her laptop. He wanted to google Jeremy Sabat and David Windson. He knew Pip and Bart were to interview Windson. Rich's plan was to finish the Sabat interviews quickly and then volunteer to go with Bart to the White House to see Windson. *Fat chance.*

Rich ran his hand over his beard. "Shit, I need a shave."

He got up and walked to the den and peeked in; Pip was busy writing on a notepad. He did not interrupt her. He headed straight for her personal bathroom. He opened her medicine chest and found what he wanted. "I am going to smell like flowers, but this lady's shave cream and Venus razor will do the trick! Ah, I will also take a few swipes of this cucumber deodorant!"

As he was shaving, looking in the mirror, he said, "Dr. Windson it is an honor to be here in the White House, I promise…" He hadn't heard Pip's cart. The old ones squeaked, so you knew when she was headed your way.

Pip said, "What the hell are you doing in my bathroom, Rich?"

Rich jumped. "Lady, it is obvious, isn't it?"

Pip rolled her eyes. "Finish in the other bathroom, but bring the damn razor back here. I need to take a shower and get to the office."

Rich did as he was told. He finished up, but had no intention of taking the razor back to Pip. *I don't want to see her naked.*

He went to the kitchen and waited for Suzy. He returned to his Google research. Both Windson and Sabat had impressive bios. Both went to GTU. Sabat and Windson were both medical doctors. Sabat had worked at the State Department his whole career. All his overseas assignments were tied to short-term visits, no postings at embassies. "I wonder if Windson and Jeremy knew each other before Sabat married Margaret? David Windson has no family?"

Suzy came in, dressed in a black skirt, white blouse, pearls, and killer boots.

"We haven't been invited to the funeral, Suzy."

"It's a matter of respect, Rich."

Pip came in the kitchen from the other doorway. "I am trying to find the Sabats' bodies, but you could help. When you interview Sabat, without giving away the store, see what his plans are for burying his parents."

Rich stood up. "Will do, boss."

Pip said, "When you know, please call me right a way, okay? And Suzy, take good notes. Include your observations of body language and facial expressions."

"Okay, Aunt Pip. Do you think we should call first, before we go?"

"No. I think showing up unannounced suggests urgency. And remember, as far as the Sabats are concerned, this is a missing person case, not multiple homicides. The homicides will surface soon enough, but we do not want to control how and when. Thank God there have been no media leaks."

Rich said, "Maybe that would help us."

Chapter 60

After Rich knocked on the Sabats' door, he started to straighten his tie then realized all he had on was a charcoal sweater and his leather jacket. Bonnie Sabat let Rich and Suzy in. She hardly looked at their credentials. She took them to the living room. Toys were everywhere and a scrawny Christmas tree was in front of the window.

Bonnie said, "I can't understand my mom. She was to come home to have a party with us. Why would she leave town? Something is terribly wrong."

Rich thought, "*You can bet your sweet little, suede-covered, tight ass on that, Bonnie.*"

Jeremy, Shawna, and Shane were sitting on the couch, staring at *CNN*. Shawna recognized Suzy, but she could not place her. Jeremy stood up and then the twins. Before Rich could introduce Suzy and himself, Sabat said, "Are you here about my ex-wife?"

Rich said, "Yes, sir. We are working with the FBI on her disappearance."

Rich and Suzy quickly showed him identification. He didn't even look at it.

He continued, "This is very unsettling on top of everything else. Early this morning I received word BOTH my parents had died. How strange is that?"

Suzy said, "Dr. Sabat what are your plans for your parents?"

"What do you think Ms.——I forgot your name."

"You may call me Suzy, sir."

"Well, Suzy, I have demanded autopsies. I don't believe in coincidences."

Rich breathed a sigh of relief.

"Then the hospital called to say that damn Margaret had disappeared from the hospital grounds. How could that happen? She had a head injury for God's sake! Then this morning I received a cryptic e-mail from Margaret saying she was on a business trip! What the hell is going on?"

Rich saw Sabat's frustration. He was in an agitated state. "May I suggest, Dr. Sabat, that we go somewhere to talk? Suzy will see if the girls have any helpful information."

Without missing a beat Suzy said, "Where are your parents bodies right now Mr. Sabat? I might be able to make a call to expedite the autopsy process."

"Alexandria City morgue. There is no way in hell they died of natural causes, neglect maybe, but not natural causes or at the same time!"

Suzy went into the hall and called Pip.

After the call, Suzy heard the girls down a hall. So she followed the sound to the kitchen.

Shawna said, "We're making hot chocolate and cinnamon toast."

Shane smiled and looked at Suzy, "Dark chocolate, of course."

Soon they all had mugs and toast and were sitting around the cozy round table.

Suzy said "I know you are concerned about your mom. We are too. I suspect you do not know how you can help us find her. But sometimes the smallest detail can make all the difference. So let's start with some questions. Let's start with the last time you visited her in the hospital. Was your mom in good spirits?"

Shane said quickly, "Yes, although something about her memory was not so good. What was the black purse thing, Bonnie?"

"Oh yeah. Mom NEVER wears black or uses a black purse. I saw a black purse next to her dresser and asked her about it. She had no recollection of it. When we went home and started cleaning for the party, the purse was gone. So from the time I saw it, around one thirty P.M. the day she banged her head, and when we went back to clean, Mom did something with it. The question is why?"

"Good. Details like that matter." Suzy looked at Shane. "Did your mom say if anyone was with her when she hit her head?"

"Yes. We assume a guy name Ted. But Mom said she knew this because the hospital staff told her. She said she had lost her memory."

Shawna said, "Yeah. Remember that guy...ah...Ted Morton brought us her tote. He was probably with her. He is so short."

"Was your mom specific about anything she wanted you to bring her?"

Shawna said, "Yes. She wanted her computer and personal cell phone, and a change of clothes. When we brought the stuff we threw in her professional nail kit. She is very sensitive about her nails. Because she has only a shred of a nail on her pinky fingers, she is always losing and replacing the acrylic nails on those fingers."

"I see. She had her BlackBerry? Her BlackBerry doesn't have a phone in it?"

Bonnie answered "Of course, but Mom uses her personal cell phone for personal calls. Her BlackBerry belongs to the government."

"I see. Did you know she had a business trip scheduled for now?"

Bonnie said, "She didn't. She wasn't due back in the office till January second."

"Why do you think she has disappeared?"

They all shrugged their shoulders.

"Do you have any idea where she might have gone?"

There were three headshakes indicating no.

"Is there anything else you would like to share?"

Shana said, "Yeah. She received one phone call on the BlackBerry. She answered, listened, didn't say anything, then hung up, and put it in her lap. After that she told us to leave. She was tired."

Everyone heard the doorbell ring.

Shawna went to answer it.

Chapter 61

While Suzy was in the kitchen with the girls, Sabat took Rich to his office. Papers and books were everywhere, piled three feet high on his desk, as well as on the floor, the window ledge, and on bookshelves. The piles were very neat, precise. Sabat took a pile off the only chair, other than the desk chair, so Rich could sit. Sabat sat in the desk chair.

"Where do you want to start?" he said.

"The most important time period is," Rich hesitated. He almost said right before Christmas. That would make no sense to Sabat and raise his suspicions.

"Uh, the last few days."

"I am at a loss to help you there. My ex-wife and I communicate through the girls. Everything I know is through them. I'll tell you one thing. Bonnie thought her mother's behavior has been off since before Christmas. Bonnie said she bought the same tech stuff twice! Bonnie told me her mom was seeing some bureaucrat. Shawna confirmed it. She met the short little twit. But I think it is more than a boyfriend issue. Let's face it, when we did communicate, we fought over money, or the lack of it, if you get my drift."

Rich recognized he needed to give this guy some structure or he would just meander. "Okay, Dr. Sabat. That's helpful. Do you have any idea how Margaret left the hospital?

"No, I don't. Neither the girls nor I gave her a ride."

"Dr. Sabat, did the girls know if Margaret was on any

medication?"

"That never came up, so I do not know."

"Do you know if Margaret went back to her house?"

"No."

Rich thought a minute. Sabat wasn't much help. "Let's try another approach. How about telling me about Margaret. What's she like? What's she like to do?"

"How much time do you have, man? She is a piece of work. For starters she is gorgeous. Her number-one priority is her appearance. Every other human being is an accessory to make Maggie look good. If that cannot be accomplished, then they are discarded. You are looking at one."

"I am sorry, sir. How about your girls? Does she treat them okay?"

"If you mean by 'treat them okay' she buys them stuff, the answer is yes. If you mean loves them, I don't know. You see Margaret is a master manipulator, so it took me eons to discover her true character. Having the right house in the right neighborhood, letting the girls go to the right schools and have all the right extra curricular activities were all things I bought into. When I would challenge anything that would seem excessive, she'd cut me off. You know what I mean? She was an excellent lover. And, if there were something she wanted that she had not planned for, she would soften me up so I would agree with it. She was a logistical genius. She made sure we went where we needed to go in the right outfits. She made the money work, at least for a while. Finally, as the girls got older, the costs escalated, and there was not enough money. I was stressed all the time. I was tired of being pussy whipped. I bailed out. She didn't seem to mind. I guess to her divorce was in. She was not happy when I remarried. She went ballistic when Angela and I had twins. You see she had no control over those two events. Margaret needs to be in control."

"Dr. Sabat, how does she feel about money?"

"Money to her is an abstraction. What is important to her is credit and lots of it. She believes and practices, pay the bastards enough to protect your credit."

"Dr. Sabat, what would stop Margaret from doing something, she shouldn't?"

"Getting caught."

Shawna knocked on the door and came in, "Dad, Uncle David is here. He wants to know if he can do anything."

After introductions and man-to-man bear hugs between Sabat and Margaret's brother, David, Suzy, and Rich were about to begin the interview. Rich couldn't believe his luck. *Sorry Bart! Better luck next time chump.*

Suzy called Pip quickly to tell her there was no need to go to the White House, as Suzy, Rich, and David Windson headed to the dining room for the interview.

Rich sat up straight in the dining room chair. Suzy sat next to him. The doors to the kitchen and living room had been closed. David Windson, the president's chief medical adviser, sat across from them.

Rich said, "We appreciate your willingness to let us interview you here and now. We recognize these are trying times for your family."

David leaned forward, "Call me David. How can I help?"

Rich liked the guy. *How could he have such a messed up sister?* "Do you know where Ms. Sabat is or do you have any idea where she might be?"

David had the saddest eyes. "Not a clue. I wish I did."

Rich began to think this might be a very short interview. "When was the last time you heard from her?"

David pulled out his BlackBerry. "This morning around eleven thirty. She sent me this e-mail." He scrolled down on his BlackBerry and then read aloud "Dave, just read about the deaths of Jeremy's parents. It is sad, but perhaps a blessing, given their conditions and the nursing home costs. I am out of town on business. I know you will support him and the girls. Love, Maggie"

Rich said, "Did you know she had been in the hospital?"

David put his BlackBerry back in his pocket. "Yes. Jeremy told me. He had learned it from the girls. I was planning on sending her flowers. Too late for that obviously."

Rich decided to try again. "Look, David, we need to find your sister, for her well-being and your peace of mind. If you were to speculate, where do you think she would go—maybe some place for comfort, some place safe?"

"I am going to be candid with you, Rich. My sister is not one to seek comfort. However, she might seek some place safe."

A glimmer of hope. "Where is safe for your sister, David?"

David sat back and thought, "You are assuming safe for Maggie is some place I know. We are not now nor ever have been close. I cut off the tips of her little fingers playing doctor when we were kids. With that I think our relationship became one driven by practicalities that held no real feelings, and my sister's emotional development took a nosedive."

"Do you think she would go visit anyone in particular?"

David leaned back, balancing on two chair legs. "My

mother is dead. She died when Maggie was born. My dad is dead. I don't think Maggie was close to my dad's second wife, Eloise. I just don't know."

Rich did not want to push David, so he decided to wrap things up. "Thanks for your time. If you give us a contact number, we will keep you in the loop as things develop."

David said, "I'll give you my personal e-mail address. I do not want your updates going through another party. I hope we can keep a lid on this."

Suzy handed David her notepad, and he wrote down his e-mail address.

Suzy said to David as he handed her pad back, "Thank you, David. Is there anything else you care to share with us that might help us find your sister?"

Suzy looked at her iPhone. She had a message from Bart. "Babe, they found Sabat's Volvo, in Herndon. Burnt to a crisp. On my way there, with Sabat's dental records."

Chapter 62

As Rich walked into the Bethesda Hospital cafeteria with Suzy, he saw Ramirez right away. He was inside the entrance along the right wall, drinking a large coffee and staring at his PDA. Rich could read his name tag on his less-than-white lab coat. He looked like he hadn't slept for days. He had a plate of something that would pass for scrambled eggs in front of him untouched. The toast was burnt, and the bacon looked like it had died rather than been fried.

Rich thought, *If that's what you look like and that's how you live in order to make big bucks, I'd rather not.*

As Susie and Rich approached the table, Ramirez looked up. Rich said, "My name is Rich Prichard and this is Suzy Simon. We are with the FBI, and we have a few questions for you regarding Margaret Sabat." Rich flashed his badge.

"Sit down. I only have about twenty minutes. There's not much I can tell you. First, there's patient-doctor privilege and second, we hadn't finished tests when she bolted. I'll say this much, her problems weren't related to a recent head injury. She is a strange person. When I was explaining to her the possibility she might have to go to a rehabilitation center as part of the therapy for getting her memory back, she had one all picked out. She wanted to be in the same one as her in-laws, and she was divorced! That's about all I feel comfortable in telling you right now so you probably have to come back in a couple of days with the right kind of legal paper to get what you need. Now I got to go. Here's my number. Do you have a card?" Ramirez stood up.

"Not so fast, Doc. What tests were you going to run?"

"Well, my plan was to conduct a few tests today, and then let her go home to be with her daughters. Then, have her comeback on an outpatient basis for any subsequent tests I feel are necessary and arrange for counseling/therapy sessions if I think they're warranted."

Rich stood and handed Ramirez his card. He looked at it. Ramirez said, "I thought you said you were with the FBI?"

"Under contract. One last question—why did you say 'therapy sessions if I think they are warranted'? Do you think Sabat is recovered already?"

"More than that, old boy. I think she's faking it. The question is why? See you. By the way, my sister, Sheila, works for your firm. She likes it." Ramirez walked off.

Rich thought, *Well, well, talk about small world.*

Chapter 63

Jack Danielson sat up straight in his chair. He could not believe his good fortune to be on television. He was sitting across from Harold Wolf on the Daily Take.

"Thanks for joining us, Jack. Let's get right to it."

"Glad to be here, Mr. Wolf."

"About an hour ago on the *DC Rag* you broke a story concerning the sister of the president's medical adviser, Dr. David Windson. So why don't you fill our viewers in."

"I will be glad to. It's important to remember, however, this is an evolving story, and what I've learned so far is preliminary and requires additional work. With that caveat, I can say this much. Yesterday I interviewed Ted Morton. He is the assistant administrator for management in the Public Services Administration. I was interviewing him about the car crash that caused the death of his only child, a son. He volunteered in the course of the interview he had been dating someone in the Public Services Administration and that this woman was under investigation by the FBI. He did not disclose her name. Of course that piqued my curiosity."

"And you learned that this woman was the sister of the president's medical adviser?"

"Yes I did. But I'm not at liberty to disclose how I find out."

"I understand. What else can you share with us, Jack?"

"The woman's name is Margaret Sabat. She suffered a brain injury and then mysteriously disappeared without being discharged from Bethesda Hospital."

"Well, this looks like a missing person's case rather than an investigation. An investigation that includes the FBI would seem to imply criminal activity, right?"

"You are right about that, since it has been less than forty-eight hours. As I said this is an evolving story and what I know so far is preliminary. So you're right—part of this case could be characterized as a missing person's case. But I have learned some interesting facts in the last several hours suggesting to me this case is broader than a missing person's case."

"Well, Jack, what can you tell us at this point?"

"I pieced together the following facts from doing research through public records and from interviewing people in PSA, excuse me, the Public Services Administration." Three people who knew Margaret Sabat have died recently."

"Can you tell us who they are and indicate why you think there is connection to Sabat?"

"On the day Margaret Sabat disappeared from Bethesda Hospital the mother and father of her ex-husband, Jeremy Sabat, were found dead in the nursing home in which they resided. Also, the night before, Donna Dawson, an employee under the supervision of Margaret Sabat, was found dead in the ditch near Chevy Chase Circle."

"Interesting, so what is the connection?"

"At this point it may be just coincidence, but I plan to keep looking into things, to look for a connection."

"Have you interviewed Margaret Sabat's brother?"

"I have a request for an interview with him into his office."

"Does the FBI have any idea where Margaret Sabat is?"

"Not that it's sharing with the likes of me."

"Do you have anything else you'd like to share with us at this point, Jack?"

"No, I think I have shared as much as I can at this point, but I think there will be more to come."

Chapter 64

Jack's television interview changed everything. Milking the limited facts, television analysts were suggesting a cover-up and incompetence.

The FBI director ordered Sam back from Geneva on the next available plane. Also, the director created a multijurisdictional task force and included the Forensic Specialists, LLP staff and Bart. It was tasked with pulling things together and finding Sabat. It would start operating at 2:00 A.M. Sam was put in charge.

David Windson resigned.

Jeremy Sabat left town with his family.

Don Pelham had a ticket on a plane for Mexico City that would leave at midnight.

Margaret Sabat had taken the hotel shuttle to the airport and rented a car. She went to Tysons Corner and bought a pageboy wig.

The Herndon coroner confirmed the body in the Volvo was not Sabat. He did not know who it was.

The members of FBI task force started coming into the headquarters building around 1:00 A.M.

As Pip came into the conference room Sam walked toward her. His eyes were sunken. His suit was wrinkled and hung on his large frame. His tie was loosened and had grease stains on it. He smelled like a stale plane. Pip had a red beret and scarf, strawberry blond waves, and a navy suit with gold buttons.

Suzy had done her makeup.

"Hi, cupcake. I missed you. You look good enough to eat."

"Sorry, but you don't."

They shook hands. Sam explained to Pip what he would like her to do.

Sam explained what was going to happen to the forty people around the conference table. Then he turned things over to Pip.

She said, "Ladies and gentlemen, this is not an investigation of a cover-up. It is a task force responsible for finding Margaret Sabat. Sabat is the person who can most likely tell us who killed Donna Dawson, who injured George Jones, why Jeremy Sabat's parents died, where Eloise Robinson Sampson is, who burned up in the Volvo, who hit me on the head, and who else may know something about these events.

"We have great expertise in this room. We each have done what we were expected to do. We were not organized so we could share what we learned. Now we are and we will share.

"I will begin by giving a profile of Margaret Sampson Sabat."

Pip did. Sam then went around the room. Everyone had something to add. What became clear was Margaret Sabat had the motive, opportunity, and ability to inflict harm or murder.

Sara from D.C. PD reported on finding a white nightgown in Eloise's freezer with blood on it. She gave a contact number to the Herndon police for follow up.

At about 3:30 A.M. they took a break. Rich approached Bart with two coffees. He handed one to Bart. "Looks like the cavalry arrived from Geneva, but I think he's a tad late. That bitch could be anywhere by now. And, as Kit said, there has been no activity on her credit cards for two days and all her bank accounts have been closed. She has assumed an alternative identity on top of everything else. You should have kept surveillance on her."

"Shut up, Pritchard. The one good thing is WHEN THIS IS OVER I won't have to listen to your fucking commentary. What a relief!"

Rich threw his still-steaming coffee at Bart with his right hand and punched him in jaw with his left, knocking Bart off balance and into three Montgomery County detectives.

Bart recovered, hooked his left leg around Rich's right heel. Rich fell hard on his back. Bart intended to get on top of and choke Rich, but Sam pulled him back.

Rich got up. Sam was between Rich and Bart. Sam smiled and said in a whisper.

"Stop. Shake hands. If you don't, you won't make it out of here alive. That's a promise." They shook hands. Rich smiled and slapped Bart on the back.

Beamer walked over to Rich, "Man, what was that about?"

"A misunderstanding."

Beamer replied, "Of course. Pip asked me to hand you these." He gave Rich two pills and a cup of water. Rich took them. "Rich pull up your pants. You have a flat ass. That must be an impediment in a fight." They went back to the conference table.

Suzy approach Bart in the corner. "What happened?"

"Pritchard was an ass, and I took him down."

"That was less than brilliant given where we are. Maybe you need medication too."

"I don't need medication! I can't see why you defend him.

You all are a bunch of enablers!"

"No, Bart, we are a family. We care about each other and support each other. You just don't get it, and probably never will."

Suzy walked off.

Sam's deputy broke people into teams and shifts. They would reconvene as a whole group at 7:30 A.M.

Everyone realized Forensic Specialists, LLP was the glue to the whole thing. Each of staff from Forensic Specialists, LLP, when called on, had been professional and concise. A full picture had emerged of what had occurred in the last few weeks. Sabat was the central character.

Sam took over and said, "Okay, before we break, let's try something. I want each of you to think out of the box. We will go around the table one more time."

When it was Frank's turn, "I want to be on the airplane passenger lists team. People with first names that begin with D and last names with P are leads on flights to Mexico."

"Done." Three people came over to Frank, and the four of them left the room.

Johnny was sitting next to Frank's seat. "We need to check out squirrel droppings at the Donna Dawson crime scene. If there is a little acrylic nail in the shit, like half size, it's Sabat's. Quantico has one nail we can compare any new one to."

Mouths dropped open on that one.

Kit said, "Dew Point Graphics is a link to financial transfers of Landmark Therapies and Sabat's personal funds. Who set up that account?"

Rich said, "Sabat had help. We have video on a guy. We need to bring in TSA at Reagan and Dulles."

When they broke, Rich went up to Pip. "They want to solve this thing in slow mo."

"Why do you say that?"

"No one focused on where Sabat is and how to find her."

Chapter 65

When Margaret got back from Tysons Corner, she noticed a text message on the cell phone Don gave her. "Changed your flight. Tomorrow departure instead of Friday—same time. I am leaving tonight. I'll meet you when you deplane. It is almost over."

Margaret fell on the bed. She cried, hard and long. She fell asleep with her clothes on.

At FBI Headquarters at 10:00 A.M. Sam wanted to focus on where Sabat might be. He asked Pip to lead the discussion.

Sara with D.C. PD said, "If she still has her government-issued Blackberry, the GPS may be activated."

Sam looked at two guys and they flew out of the conference room.

Suzy said, "Maybe Sabat is driving home to North Carolina. Her father's house there was never sold or rented."

Sam looked at another two guys and they flew out of the conference room.

Pip had a thought. "Let's think about Sabat's motivations for a minute, not whether she is looking for a safe place to hide. Remember, we know she is fond of to-do lists and checking things off.

"Why did she kill her stepmother—if she did? Or was it an accident that caused Sabat to recalibrate what was 'acceptable' for her to do?

"She may have killed Donna Dawson because she knew

too much.

"She may have tried to murder George Jones because he knew something about her.

"We have video of her in the nursing home around the time her ex-in-laws died. Why? To reduce her ex-husband's monthly expenses?

"What's left? What does she need to finish?"

For a minute there was silence, then it was like a chorus, "George Jones!"

Bart and Rich got up and flew out the door. Sam designated their backup, and they left.

He came over to Pip and said, "You are a little genius, darlin'." He leaned over and kissed her cheek.

Chapter 66

Thursday was beautiful. It was unseasonably warm, in the fifties. Margaret looked at her watch. She was going to see George and take him lunch. Finding out where he was relatively easy. The reception desk at Alexandria Hospital told her when she called. She said she was his girlfriend, Donna Dawson. She knew she would need to be careful. She wanted to know what kind of shape George was in.

About 11:45 A.M. she pulled into the parking lot of the hospital. At the reception desk she signed in as Donna Dawson and asked to see George. She knew there was an element of risk. She had picked up chicken sandwiches, fries, and Diet Coke. An attendant took her to a day room and brought George to her. No one else was there. She guessed people tend to do their visiting at night and on weekends. Besides this was a weekday of a holiday week. No one made a comment about her using a dead woman's name to sign in.

George had a bandage on his head, and his head had been shaved, but otherwise he looked okay. He had on running shoes, khakis, and a gray V-neck sweater. He had a curious look on his face. The attendant left. She said, "Hi, George. Do you remember me? I am Donna Dawson." George didn't say anything. He kept looking at her and gobbling down the food. His expression was a searching one.

Margaret kept trying to get him to say something. Finally, he sat back when he finished, smiled, and said, "Where's the dessert, Maggie? The chocolate-covered strawberries?"

Margaret's jaw dropped, but she recovered quickly. She had noticed a balcony off the day room. "Let's go out and gets some fresh air, George." They went on to the balcony and over to the low stonewall. They sat on it. Margaret kissed George on the lips. He smiled. He got up and pushed her over the wall head first. She screamed as she fell the four stories to the pavement.

At the same moment Bart and Rich had exited their SUV. They saw Margaret hit the pavement. Bart called 911.

They bent over Margaret. Her brown wig had fallen off. Her hair was jagged. It looked like it had been cut by a toddler with safe-for-toddlers' scissors. Blood was soaking the pavement around her head. Her eyes looked surprised. She was alive. She did not speak.

Epilogue

Spring came early in North Carolina. David Windson had brought Margaret, who was a quadriplegic who could not speak, to their childhood home to live. She had twenty-four-hour-a-day care. All charges against her were suspended, pending her recovery. No one anticipated that. No one knew if Margaret could talk and had chosen not to. No one knew if she could comprehend what was said in her presence. Without success, therapists had tried to get her to blink one for yes, and blink two for no. Her eyes were alert and full of expression—surprise, contentment, and distress. Her home-health aides became adept at keeping Margaret content.

The town embraced Margaret and her brother. David never had to cook. Someone always brought him a casserole or leftovers to heat up in the microwave. The "someone" was often a widowed, single, or divorced woman. David liked the attention, the lack of pressure. He taught at a medical school nearby. His course load was light. He started writing an autobiography. He thought if he put everything on paper, he would finally be free of his guilt. He held himself responsible for how Margaret turned out. Now he was doing what his dad told him he should do, "take care of Maggie."

The home-health aides worked eight-hour shifts. They were bored caring for Margaret. Their shifts passed slowly. One day things picked up—a new mailman materialized, Drew Parsons. He was very good looking, very friendly, brought doughnuts, and was willing to sit on the porch and chat. All the home-health aides began to vie for the day shift. The evening and night aides were jealous.

On a sunny day Drew showed up early. Margaret was on the porch with her respirator. Her eyes danced as she saw him bounce up the steps. She had not seen him on his previous visits because she was kept inside. Sally, the aide, came out the screen door.

Drew smiled at her. "Sally, I have some extra time today. Why don't you have some lunch at the café? I'll sit with Margaret."

"God bless you, Drew! You sure you don't mind? I will only take an hour."

"Take your time. Get out of here. Go have some fun."

When Sally was gone, Drew pulled a rocker up next to Margaret's hospital bed.

"I waited a long time for you at the airport, wondering what had happened. I thought the FBI had nabbed you. I have missed you, Margaret. I had our lives all planned. I'll tell you one thing, I never thought for one minute you changed your mind. All I wanted to do was give you a new start, without hurt, guilt, or the need to deceive or manipulate others.

"You know how you said I anticipated your needs? I have this one last time." He stood up and kissed her gently on her lips. Her eyes sparkled. He turned off the respirator. Her eyes showed surprise. He sat back down and held her hand till it started to cool. Then he closed her eyes with his hand, wiped her tears, and kissed her again. He turned the respirator back on. He picked up his mailbag and left.

CPSIA information can be obtained at www.ICGtesting.com
Printed in the USA
BVOW041206300512

291336BV00001B/1/P